Loving Neil

Loving Neil

Ronald Bagliere

For those who care for the people who've had their beautiful minds stolen from them.

Acknowledgments

This book is devoted to those who care for loved ones with dementia, especially spouses, and the difficult and often heart-wrenching decisions that they are often confronted with. In writing this novel, I would like to acknowledge some of the people who have given their precious time in providing insightful critiques and encouragement. They have been an invaluable source to the writer in the development of this novel. First and foremost – to the Syracuse Writer's Roundtable for their comments and suggestions; to the Central New York chapter of the Romance Writers of America for their timely critiques and informative workshops. Special thanks to Martin Meiss and Carolyn Ostrander who have been there from the beginning, and to my wife Linda for putting up with me for the last four years!

1

December 5, 1979 -

A blast of frigid air ripped through the parking lot whipping Janet's long, dark hair. She gripped the front of her coat, pulled it tight around her, and ran for the entry door of the banquet hall. Shaking her head to sluff the snow out of her hair, she opened the door and stepped inside to the warmth of the lobby. There, she removed her gloves, shoved them in her pockets, and made her way through the lounge to the reception hall.

She was an hour late and most of the one hundred or so guests for her brother's wedding were already there. Her gaze swept over the sea of white linen-covered tables and searched for her father. When she saw him, she took a deep breath and headed in his direction.

"Where've you been?" he said, getting up to greet her. He pulled her into a practiced hug as if they saw each other every day. But the fact was, he hadn't seen her in over six months.

"Traffic," she said. She flashed a smile toward his wife, Christine, and said, "Sorry I missed you at church. Love the gown." She took in Christine's long, black, strapless formal and the necklace of gold winking back at her, wondering how much they set her father back.

"Thanks. How've you been?" Christine replied.

"Not bad. Nice place."

"Nothing but the best for your brother," Christine said, flashing a pretentious smile at her husband. When Janet saw her father frown, she wondered what was going on between the two of them.

Janet's father said, "This is John and Sarah Barrett, friends of Christine's. They're loaning their beachfront house to Craig for his honeymoon. Isn't that nice of them?"

"Yes, very," Janet said.

"So, you're Craig's sister! The picture on your father's mantel doesn't do you justice," Sarah said.

Janet took the compliment in stride, trying to figure out just what picture that might be.

"My daughter here is a freelance photographer for one of those nature magazines out west," Janet's father said. "Is that what they call them these days?"

"Close enough, Dad."

"All very exciting, I'm sure," Christine said.

"Ah, there's my boy," Janet's father said, cutting in. His graveled voice stormed across the room. "Hey, Craig, come over here and tell your sister about that new job of yours." To Janet, he winked and said, "He hooked himself up with a firm down in West Palm Beach."

Craig looked up from talking with the band and started for them. "Hey, Janny," he said, giving her a brotherly hug. "Damned weather. Sorry we missed you at the church. How was the flight?"

"It was." Janet said eying her brother affectionately. She had long gotten over her envy of her father's favoritism toward her brother. It wasn't Craig's fault her father had always favored him over her. Craig was his shining star. A high school football legend and M.I.T. graduate, Craig had carved a place out in his father's heart long before she arrived on the scene and it was a place she could never fill.

2

At six-foot three, his sleek, muscular frame towered over her. "Yeah, I know, shitty," Craig said. "But you're here and that's all that counts."

Janet pulled away from him, straightened his tie, and patted the lapel of his tux. Even though he was eight years older than her, she'd always thought of him as a little brother who needed looking after. "So, Dad tells me you have a new job."

"Yeah, and I'm gonna need it 'cause Belinda has lots of plans."

"I bet," Janet said, knowing Belinda came from a large family.

"Say look, I gotta get back to her. Catch ya later?"

"Of course," Janet replied and gave him the thumbs-up.

The snow continued to fall throughout dinner, and with each glance out the window, Janet grew more wary of the drive back to her hotel. She nibbled at her dessert as the chatter flowed around the table, much of it about people she didn't know–high society friends of Christine's and their various exploits.

As she pulled her black sweater cape off the back of her chair and wrapped it around her shoulders, her father leaned toward her, and said, "So, how's things with June's estate?"

"It's in probate. Shouldn't be much longer, a couple more months maybe," Janet said.

"Any idea what you're going to do with another house and a rental cottage?"

"I haven't thought about it, to tell you the truth."

Her father finished the last of his cake and wiped his mouth with a napkin. "Well, you'd better start. The sooner you get them on the market, the better."

Janet frowned. "I'm not sure I want to sell."

"Well, what are you gonna do with all that property?" her father asked, eying her pointedly.

Janet didn't want to talk about it. It had only been five months since her beloved aunt passed away, and she missed her terribly. "Dad, can we change the subject please?"

"Yeah, sure." He was quiet a moment then nodded toward the window. "Wow, it's coming down pretty hard out there. You're welcome to crash at our place."

"Thanks, but no."

Now it was his turn to frown. "What is it with you, Janny? Do you hate Christine that much?"

Janet set her fork down. "I don't hate her, Dad. I just don't like everything I do being judged."

"Judged?"

"Yes." Janet sighed. "I'm sorry, but it's the way she makes me feel."

"I see." He turned and started for the bar.

Janet rose, collected her purse, and followed him. When she caught up next to him, she said, "Dad, I love you, you know that, right?"

Her father shot her a tight smile. "Right. Don't worry about it, Skeeter, it's okay." He glanced toward the windows. "You'd better get a move on. Don't forget to say goodbye to your brother."

Why does it always end like this? Though, in truth, she knew the reason. It was her always slapping away his helping hand. But then, it was a little late for his helping hand. Where was he when she needed him? "Yeah, right. I'll call you later. Maybe we can do something tomorrow."

"Sure," he said. "Sounds like a plan."

Janet looked off, biting back the urge to say, forget it, then reached up and pecked him on the cheek. "I'm gonna go find Craig. Love you."

He studied her a moment, as if he were trying to decide whether she meant it, then nodded. "Me, too."

4

Twenty minutes later, Janet was driving down the snow packed highway trying to avoid the deep ruts that were running along the shoulder of the road. The car skated back and forth, drifting dangerously close to the snow packed shoulder of the road. She backed the wipers off as the exit ramp from I-80 neared. On it was a semi moving at a fair clip. As it merged onto County Route 82, she moved into the passing lane.

"Just what I need," she growled. Her heart raced as she braced her hands on the wheel. The truck sprayed slush at her windshield. The road suddenly disappeared. Thunk! The wheel jerked loose in her hands and the car dove, knifing into the darkness until it jolted to a halt.

Janet sat shaking for several minutes. Her throat burned, and the taste of bile swam in her mouth. She swallowed, forced it down, and gulped a deep breath. The sound of her heart thumped in her ears. Her head ached. *Am I Okay?* Gingerly, she moved her legs and then her arms. Nothing hurt. That was good. She pulled the key out of the ignition. Sat back. Tried to make sense of what had happened.

Truck–slush–windshield–can't see–steering wheel–ouch. Her wrist. It hurt. She rubbed it. The car? Shit! Was there a huge gash on the front end? A tire turned under like a broken ankle? She brought her hands to her head. Kneaded her aching neck.

She looked out the driver's side window. Snow was up to the rear-view mirror. Getting out that way was impossible. She crawled across to the passenger side and peered out, put her shoulder to the door and pushed it open.

Outside, the wind whipped across the median and icy grit slapped her face. She burrowed her head into the lapel of her coat and trudged through the knee-deep snow. *Think, Janet, think.* But the only thing that came to mind was to walk. But to where?

She ground her hands into her pockets and kicked at a chunk of hard packed snow. Tears collected in her eyes and slipped over her cheeks. "What am I gonna do? I'm so screwed," she muttered, plopping back against the rear of the car.

As she stood there, a pair of bright headlights came over the crest of the road. A moment later, a large pickup slowed down and pulled up behind her. The driver's side window slid down.

"You okay?" said a voice from inside.

She nodded as the door opened and a man got out. He was big, towering over her. In the dark of night, he looked like a monster out of a B-budget movie. She backed up keeping her distance.

He put up his hand. "It's okay. I'm here to help. You look like you're freezing. Why don't you get in my truck while I call a wrecker?"

"No, I'm okay, really."

He trudged closer and she saw a ruddy hard-bitten face. Mysterious, dark eyes stared back. A bushy mustache spilled out under a broad nose. A mop of short, curly hair tickled his ears. Add a beard and a red suit and she could easily imagine him being Santa Claus. But he wasn't Santa Claus, and he was there with her on a dark road in the middle of the night. There was nothing between them except the wind and her long distance running legs, which were one step away from being jelly.

"Alright," he said. "At least let me get you a blanket." He went back to his truck and brought her a thick woolen wrap reeking of smoke. He handed it to her with an outstretched hand. "So what happened?"

"I was run off the road by a semi," she said, pulling the blanket around her shoulders.

The man shook his head. "Damn cowboys!" He eyed her then the car, then back at her again. "You sure you're all right?"

"Yeah, I'm okay." She backed up a step and turned around, sizing up the damage to her car. It didn't look like there were any dents or creases. It was buried. *If I could just get it out, no one would ever have to know. But doing it will need his help. That means...* She chewed her lip. "You think we could pull it out of there?"

"The car?"

"Yeah."

"Not without chains."

"You wouldn't happen to have any would you?"

The man's brow wrinkled. "I do, but I don't know. You're buried in there pretty good. I think it's best to call a wrecker."

"'Cept it's a rental," Janet said.

He drummed his fingers on the hood of his truck. At last, he said, "We can try it, but I can't guarantee anything." He waded out into the snowy median and surveyed the car. After a once around, he came back. "I really think it's better to call a wrecker. I could end up doing more harm than good."

She looked up at the blackened sky and closed her eyes.

After a relenting sigh, she heard him say, "Okay, you go around and climb in while I see what I can do." He stepped over to the back of his truck as she got in her rental, and two minutes later, she heard him pawing around underneath her car. It seemed like he was under there forever before he finally knocked on her passenger side window.

She rolled it down.

"Okay," he said. "When you see me flash my lights, you give her the gas, alright? Don't stop until you feel the wheels grip the road."

She nodded and watched him trudge back through the snow. A moment later, the truck's lights flashed in her rear-view mir-

7

ror. She stepped on the pedal, pushing it to the floor. The car lurched backward as the tires spun, screaming into the night.

Suddenly, the tension between the two vehicles eased. The pickup's lights flashed, and shortly afterward he was at her window again. "We made a little headway, but I just don't have enough traction. One last time and if you're not out, we call a wrecker."

She nodded. *Please, please. Just once, give me a break.* The truck's headlights flashed, and her foot slammed on the accelerator. The car shimmied and moved back inch-by-inch. She gripped the wheel, as if doing so would make the car try harder. *Don't stop, please don't stop!* The acrid smell of burning rubber drifted through the open window as the rear of the car shifted and came to a grinding halt.

The man got out of his truck and trudged back to her window. "You're half way out," he said, "but that's as far as you're gonna get."

"Just one more time ... please?" she muttered.

He wiped his brow with the back of his hand. "Okay, one last time."

He grabbed his shovel, dug more snow out around her tires, and got back into his truck. The lights flashed, and a moment later Janet's rental car lurched back, breaking free of the deep snow. Relieved, she sighed and got out as the man pulled his tow chain free.

"I don't know how to thank you," she said.

"Forget it. I have a daughter your age. I'd hope someone would do the same for her if she were in your shoes." He bent down and started clearing her snow-packed wheel wells. "You live around here?"

"I'm heading into the city."

"Alright. When I'm through, I'll follow you in. Make sure you get where you're going."

"That's alright, I'll be fine." She dug into her purse. Pulled out a ten-dollar bill. "Here."

He looked up and frowned. "Put it away."

Great, now I've insulted him. "Are you sure?"

"Positive." He stood up and dusted the snow off his jeans.

"Thanks. I'm Janet."

He put his shovel in the back of his truck. "Neil, Neil Porter."

2

Salem, Oregon, May 23, 1980 -

The rolling fields of the Willamette Valley were awake with reds, yellows, and violets as Janet drove along County Route 22. In her knapsack on the back seat was a submission for the *Willamette Reporter*. Riding shotgun with her was her basset-beagle puppy, Barney. When she heard a whine, she glanced over to see him standing on his hind legs looking out the window. Turning his head back, he barked.

"You hungry, boy?" she said. "I feel like a bite myself."

A mile down the road, she pulled off into the parking lot of a small deli where she ordered a couple of burgers, hers with the works, his plain: no pickle, no cheese, and no bun. Twenty minutes later, she was in Salem's business district. The *Willamette Reporter* was a mile north of the city off River Road. She crawled along with traffic until she came to the old brick building. The public parking lot was across the street, but employees and consultants used the back entrance, so she turned down a narrow drive and parked in their private lot.

"Okay, Barney, let's go see Megan," she said, leashing him. The dog jumped out into the warm afternoon sun as she grabbed her bag from the backseat. Shutting the car door, she walked him to the service entrance where her good friend, Megan waited by the open door.

"Well, hullo, Barney," Megan said. She squatted and let the dog put his paws on her knees. "You're getting so big!"

"He's an eating machine," Janet said. "But I love him to pieces. Mick around?"

Megan nodded. "Yeah, and he's in a mood, so watch it."

"Why?"

"Who knows? Come in. And Happy Birthday! It is your birthday, right?"

Janet grinned. "Yes, and thanks for reminding me!"

Megan threw back a perky smile, led her to her desk, and picked up the phone while Janet glanced at pictures of Megan's son, Kyle, on the wall behind them.

After Megan hung up, Janet said, "How's the little guy?"

"He's great…" She bent down and rubbed Barney's ears, then pointed a thumb toward Mick's office. "The man's waiting. See if you can cheer him up."

"Right, and thanks for the warning," Janet said then headed across the broad layout room to a suite of offices in the far corner. Mick's was on the far right and his door was shut. A glass window beside it revealed Mick on the phone. His voice rattled the walls.

"I have a hole in my roof that needs fixing. You agreed to do it yesterday … No, listen … I don't give a damn about your fucking truck. I want it done by tomorrow—understand?" He slammed the phone down and, raking his hand through his blond hair, stood up.

Janet had known Mick for about five years. Though she had never been a target of one of his legendary tirades, she knew enough to stay out of his way. She watched him rifle through the stack of files on his desk and pull one out. He was in his usual attire: jeans and khaki shirt. No suit and tie for Mick. He was a roll-up-your-sleeves-and-dig-in type of guy. Suddenly, he got up and before she knew it, was opening the door.

Fixing her with his slate gray eyes, he grumbled, "I need a Coke and a cigarette. You want one?"

She shook her head. "I don't smoke."

"I know that," he said. "I meant the Coke."

"Oh. Yeah, sure."

"Go in. I'll be back in ten." He turned on his heel, muttering and stalked across the open layout room. Even from where Janet stood, she heard him cursing under his breath. Tentatively, she took a seat in front of his desk amid a sea of banker's boxes, empty soda cans, and a haze of smoke. On his desk was a stack of files. Beside them was a small, oval framed picture of his daughter, Vicky. She was tall like her father and shared his facial features; narrow jaw, thin nose, hairline lip, and brown hair.

Mick came back and nudged the door shut with his hip. A copy of the *Reporter* was tucked under his arm. A soda was in each hand and a cigarette dangled from his lip. He set the paper and their sodas down on his desk, butted his cigarette in an overflowing ashtray, and said, "How was the ride?"

"Not bad. Hit a little traffic near the city."

"As always." He grabbed the file she had seen him pull out earlier and leaned back in his chair. His scowl had retreated but his furrowed brow remained. "So, how's things?"

"Good." She studied his expression, wondering what was going on behind his measured gaze.

"You know, we're quite fond of your work here."

"Thanks. Glad you like it."

He pulled a letter out of the folder and held it out to her.

Janet's heart jumped. "What's this?" she said, having an ill feeling. She knew the drill all too well; 'we like your work, but funds are low. We're sorry, but blah, blah, blah.'

"An offer. The boys upstairs are looking to hire another full-time photographer and I think you'd be a perfect fit. So, how would you like a permanent gig?"

Janet widened her eyes as she looked down the page, trying to grasp what had happened. At last, she looked up, hardly knowing what to say. "This is ... um, unexpected. You really want me?"

Mick crossed his arms. "Umm ... yeah."

"I don't know what to say."

"You could say, yes," Mick said, lighting another cigarette. He took a drag, and added, "It's a good offer. Thirty-nine 'K' to start and I got you three weeks of vakay with full med."

Janet took a deep breath to calm her nerves and studied the letter again. At the bottom she saw a blank line waiting for her signature, but a voice deep inside her told her to wait.

"There a problem?" Mick said.

"No, it's just so sudden and I've always been on my own. Used to my own schedule, you know."

Mick nodded. "I can certainly understand. I thought the same thing when they came to me nine years back and stole me from the streets. But you know what; it was the best thing that ever happened to me. No more worrying about where my next gig was coming from, whether or not I was going to make the mortgage payment and all that. And besides, you know we're not all that rigid around here. You can come and go pretty much as you please most of the time except for Mondays, Wednesdays, and alternate Fridays when we need you here at the office."

Janet scanned down the page, fighting the urge to give a quick answer. Mick wasn't a patient man. He liked people who could make sharp, snap decisions. She looked up at him. The last thing she wanted to do was burn a bridge. Her heart thumped. Thirty-nine 'K' was a lot of money, and full medical coverage was a luxury she had never been able to afford, say nothing of a paid vacation. But what if she was laid off? Finally, she said, "I'd like to think about it, if it's okay."

"Sure, but don't take too long. The boys up there are an impatient bunch."

The next morning, Janet lay in bed staring at her alarm clock thinking about Mick's offer. She put her arm under her pillow and snuggled her body around it. If she took the job, she'd have some modicum of security, but what about Barney? She wasn't keen on leaving him home all day alone in a crate, even for two days a week. Being her own boss she could take him along where ever she went.

She looked down at the dog lying on the foot of her bed. As she wrestled with the decision, the phone on her nightstand rang. She rolled over and picked it up.

"Skeeter, Dad! I missed calling you yesterday. Sorry 'bout that."

She sat up and plumped the pillow under her back. "It's okay. I figured something came up."

"No, just old age interfering with memory. Well, are we admitting to thirty?"

She shrugged. "Sure, why not? So … how are you?"

"I'm fine. You get my card?"

"I did." She picked it off her nightstand. The picture on the front was of an old lady in a ridiculous hat. A black flimsy dress was hiked up to her knees. Inside, he had signed it just, 'Dad.'

"I thought it was a hoot."

"Right." She grinned. She would have preferred a little more sentiment. But that was her father–always skimming the surface when it came to the mushy stuff.

"So, you spend the day at the beach?"

"No. Worked."

"On your birthday?"

"Yep. Creditors don't care about birthdays."

"I hear ya there."

Janet took a deep breath, and biting her lip, said, "Guess what? You remember the newspaper I consult with?"

"The *Weekly* or something like that?"

"It's the *Reporter*. Anyway, they offered me a full-time job."

"Fantastic!" he said. "When do you start, and how much? It's a salaried position, right?"

"I haven't accepted it yet."

"What'd'ya mean?" She heard him sigh on the other end. "Janet, it's time to start living in the real world."

"I am living in the real world!"

"Freelancing is not living in the real world, sweetie. You need job security, not to mention health insurance and a retirement plan, especially now with your aunt having passed away."

Janet closed her eyes wondering why she'd brought it up. Tightening her grip on the receiver, she said, "I wasn't asking for an opinion, Dad! I was sharing."

"Well, this should be a slam dunk. But as usual you have to analyze everything to the 'Nth' degree. You know, by the time you make your mind up, this opportunity will be toast."

Janet's chest tightened as she gritted her teeth. "Why do you always have to do this?"

"Do what?"

"Never mind! I shouldn't have brought it up."

"I'm trying to help you."

"You're trying to run my life, Dad! Let's just drop it, okay?"

There was a long pause on the other end. Finally, he said, "Sure, whatever."

Her throat tightened. "So, have you heard from my brother yet?"

"Yeah. They're back," he said, brightening a bit. "Had a great time."

"It was nice seeing him. I wish I could get back east more often."

Her father was quiet again, then said, "So, why don't you? We have room."

"Unfortunately, my schedule is–"

"Yes, I know. Busy, busy."

"You could come out to me."

"You know, I don't like planes."

Janet looked up at the ceiling, gritting her teeth. "Yeah, right. Well, I don't want to keep you. Say Hi to Christine for me."

"Will do. Take care of yourself."

The phone went dead as Janet looked through the window stuffing yet another disappointment into her heart. *Well, what did you expect?*

Fifteen minutes later, a stream of hot water pelted her back as she leaned against the shower wall. She pushed her hair off her shoulders and allowed the water to run through it down her back. Reaching behind her, she turned the hot water up another notch, and replayed the conversation she had had with her father over in her head. Why couldn't he just listen for once? Why did he have run over her like a truck? Then again, he never listened to anyone, let alone her. The ironic thing was, the one time she really wanted him to stand up and say something; he didn't. He let her mother take her away from him without a single word.

Stepping out onto the tiled floor, she stared at the mist-streaked mirror throwing a distorted reflection back. Though she was used to her solitary life and her father's ambivalence, she felt lost. She grabbed a towel, bound her hair, and went to her closet to pull out a pair of jeans and a sweater. But when she slid the closet door back, her gaze was drawn to the top shelf where a large box sat. She stared at it a moment, then reached up and took it down.

Setting it on the bed, she pulled the lid off and looked inside. It had been a long time since she'd pawed through the past, digging up memories, and she wasn't quite sure why she was doing it other than there was a compelling need to feel attached to something, someone, anything. She lifted out the cellophane-wrapped magazine on top and ran her finger over it. Peeling the wrapping away, she leafed through it until she came to a shot of Boiler Bay. It had been taken at high tide, and it was her first published photo.

She studied it for a moment then set it down. Soon after, she was going through faded photos of family taken at camp years ago. She smiled down at the photos of Craig and her eating s'mores by the campfire and the shots of her father at the grill flipping burgers. But the ones of her father and her standing on the dock looking out over Lake Erie at dusk were the ones that burrowed into her heart. Even now, she could feel his bony fingers on her shoulders. She closed her eyes, wondering how they had grown so far apart.

"I need to get out of here—get some air," she muttered as she set the photos back in the box. Looking down at Barney, who was sitting at her feet, she took a deep breath. "Come on, we're going for a ride!"

The fields of tall rangy grasses and hawthorn stretching along-side the two-lane highway were in full bloom. She glanced at them now and again during the fifty-minute drive to Lincoln City. There she would hook up with Route 101 that skirted the coastline and head for Boiler Bay.

The first forty miles passed quickly—the road straight and fairly level until it melted into the woods. There, it ran around winding curves with treacherous swales. She eased off the pedal as the ponderosa pine, hazelnut, and cypress marched past her window. The radio murmured. An hour later, she turned into the entrance of Fogarty State Park and parked in the tree lined deserted lot. Flipping the hood of her jacket over her head, she shut the car door, leashed Barney, and started down a winding trail to a broad underpass running under the highway.

On the other side, she let the dog loose to run through the knots of windswept grasses lashing the sculpted, crescent dunes. Above her, gulls floated in the gray sky. A wafting scent of fish wrinkled her nose as she trudged out onto the hard-packed sand. Thirty yards ahead, the ocean pounded the beach, and its surging froth baited the barking dog. Janet watched the back and forth of the rushing water thinking of the job offer as Barney barked at the waves. As she watched him run back and forth, her father's face flashed before her. Why couldn't he let her talk instead of trying to fix her all the time?

She shook her head, and continuing down the beach, saw a black form lying on the wet sand some ways ahead. She stared at it a moment before calling Barney to her. Leashing the dog, she moved forward cautiously until she saw it was a seal. As she approached the animal, she expected it to dart into the water. When it didn't, she short-lined Barney and circled around it. Lifting its head, it opened its mouth and moved its flipper. The dog pulled on his leash, straining to get a sniff.

"Stop Barney!" she commanded. To the seal, she said, "You all right, little guy?"

The seal slapped the gritty sand with its tail, and as it did so, she saw a fresh gash on its flipper. It wasn't a deep wound, and it would more than likely heal. Still, a silent battle waged inside her, and though she knew the code of conduct around a wild animal, she couldn't help from wanting to put her arms around it.

The dog whined as she battled her nurturing instincts. "Barney, behave," she muttered as the seal closed its eyes and exhaled with a grunt. "Come, boy, we need to leave him be." But as she stepped away from the animal, she didn't like how she felt. She knew what it was like to be abandoned.

3

June 24, 1980 -

A warm, sunny day with just a whiff of cloud kissed the rolling hills as Janet neared Salem's city limits. Today, she would officially inherit her aunt's cottage in Fogarty along with the cozy little bungalow a couple miles north of Route 99. She cranked the window down and turned the radio up, pondering why her aunt had never told her that her father's name was on the cottage deed. Hopefully, there would be no more surprises. Barney stood on the passenger seat beside her with his nose wedged into the open window.

"Enjoying the sights little man?" she said. The dog looked back at her, barked, and returned his attention to the passing buildings. Barb-b-q was in the air, and it roused a rumble in Janet's empty stomach as she slowed for the exit to Northgate. A couple of miles later, she pulled into a sweeping horseshoe driveway and parked behind a line of cars.

Janet opened the car door, and Barney jumped out as Megan pushed through a gated opening of a tall wooden fence. Megan's son, Kyle, was in the woman's arms.

"There's my Barney!" Megan said. She bent over and let Kyle run his chubby little fingers through the dog's fur.

"You didn't tell me you had company," Janet said.

"You didn't ask. Just family–no big deal."

Janet sighed. "You're too much. You sure Barney's not an imposition?"

"Not at all," Megan said, waving her hand. "Come on back. I'll introduce you around."

"I'd love to, but I really need to get into town," Janet said.

"When's your meeting?" Megan replied.

Janet looked at her watch. "One-thirty."

Megan furrowed her brow. "You have oodles of time!"

"But there's parking and–"

"You can take fifteen minutes," Megan insisted. "Have you eaten?"

"No ... I mean, yes. Had a bite at Joey's on the way in."

Megan eyed her dubiously. "Liar!"

"Really, I did," Janet insisted.

"I.don't believe you," Megan said. She gave her a look, Mick called, *tank mode*. "I'll have Brad throw a burger on for you."

"You're not taking, no, for an answer, are you?" Janet said, following Megan through the gate to a spacious back yard rimmed with tulips and daffodils. A kiddie pool huddled up next to a large deck. People milled about in small groups of three and fours, chatting amongst themselves.

Megan dragged her over to a middle-aged couple standing beside a picnic table. "This is Brad's mom and dad, Tom and Theresa."

Janet smiled, shook hands, exchanged greetings as Kyle squirmed in Megan's arms. Megan put him down and waved at her husband who was tending grill on the deck. "Hey Hon, throw a burger on for Jan?"

He looked up, smiled, and opened the cooler lid beside his feet.

To Brad's parents, Megan said, "Janet freelances for the *Reporter*."

"Are you a writer?" Theresa asked.

"She's a photo journalist," Megan replied, then reached out and tagged one of the little boys running around them chasing Barney. "Jimmy, slow down."

The red headed child came to a halt and looked up. Barney raced ahead toward the other children playing by the kiddie pool. Megan bent down next to the boy. "We need to be careful, honey." She tousled his hair. "Can you do me a favor? Bring a soda for our guest?" After Jimmy flew off, Megan turned to Brad. "You see my father?"

"Went inside a little while back," Brad said, nodding toward the sliding glass door. "Think he's watching the ball game."

Megan frowned. "He better not be!" She stalked up the stairs onto the deck, slid the screen door back, and went inside. A moment later, she returned. "He'll be right out."

"Meg, it's okay," Janet protested then froze as a tall burly man in jeans stepped outside behind Megan. He ran his thick fingers through his red hair and stared at her.

As Janet stood in shocked silence, he said, "I'll be. Janet, right?"

"Yeah ... You're Megan's father?" Janet uttered, dumbfounded. She glanced at Megan. Saw the surprise in her friend's eyes then looked back at him.

Megan pulled her jaw up from the ground. "You two know each other?"

Her father put his arm around his daughter's shoulder and pulled her tight to him. "That we do, pumpkin." To Janet, he said, "She's my baby."

Megan shook her head. "How?"

He laughed. "Met on a stretch of nasty highway." He put out his hand to Janet. "So, this is where you live when you're not traipsing around back east."

"Actually, I'm sixty miles southwest," Janet said, still in awe of meeting him again.

"That's a bit of a commute."

Megan cut in. "She's a freelancer. Sort of like a sub-contractor. She does a lot of pieces for the *Reporter*."

"She keeps me in the loop," Janet added.

"Doesn't surprise me. Megan's quite the organizer.

Rather insistent, too, if you haven't noticed."

Janet grinned. "Oh, I've noticed. She tells me she's trying to get you out west."

"Yeah. It's nice out here, but I don't know. I'm afraid she'd be running my life before long. Telling me where to go and when." Megan frowned and swatted his arm. He rubbed it. "See what I mean?"

"You never had it so good," Megan replied. Just then, Kyle cried out. "Excuse me, while I go see what he wants."

After Megan left, the two of them stood in their own thoughts. Janet fidgeted. *Okay, this is uncomfortable? Should I say something? But what, I see you've lost some weight? That's stupid! I hate meetings like these.*

"So," Neil said, clearing his throat, "Megan told me you're inheriting some property."

"Yeah, I'm turning right into another Donald Trump," Janet quipped, as his name finally popped into her head. The boy came back with her soda. After he scooted off, Janet said, "So, what'd'ya do?"

He smiled. "Draw pretty pictures. I'm an architect."

"I thought about doing that when I was in high school. I guess I liked photography better," Janet said, sipping her Coke.

"Good decision."

"You don't like it?"

He shrugged. "Oh, I enjoy it well enough."

They observed the children playing on the swing set for a couple of minutes. Janet said, "I should let you get back to your ball game."

"Oh, don't worry about it. I should be out here anyways."

"And I should be getting back on the road. Have to see the lawyers. Can you let Megan know I had to go?"

He nodded and walked her to the gate. "You know, I'm going to catch hell letting you sneak out of here like this."

"Just tell her I tricked you."

"Right," he said with a smirk. "Well, it was great seeing you again. And good luck."

Janet forced a smile. "Same here–seeing you that is." She didn't know what else to say, so she went over and said good-bye to Barney, then pulled the gate shut behind her. As she headed for her car, she wondered what the chances of meeting him again were? The odds against it were ... well, she didn't know what they were.

After the reassignment of June's house was complete with the exception of transferring tax documents, Janet picked up Barney and headed for home. When she got there, she found her father sitting on the chase-lounge on her porch with his carryon bag beside him. Astonished, she blinked, then suddenly wondered what was wrong. Last she knew her father wasn't interested in coming out west. That meant what? She got out of her car with Barney following behind and braced herself for bad news.

"Hey Skeeter," her father said rolling his newspaper up. He tucked it under his arm and stood. "I see you got yourself a pooch."

Janet took a deep breath and tried to control her pounding heart. "Dad, what're you doing here?"

"Thought I'd surprise you."

Janet had a hard time swallowing his surprising her, but she was glad to see him all the same. "You drive all the way out?" she said, not believing it for a moment as they came together with a quick hug.

"No, I flew."

"You don't like planes, remember? What's going on?" Janet said, and eyed him suspiciously while Barney raced around them barking. "Barney, down," she commanded.

Her father pulled back, offering a tight smile. "No, I don't and nothing's going on."

Janet shook her head, but she wasn't in the mood for an argument. Instead, she opened the door and let him in, then went back to the car to retrieve her satchel. When she returned, her father looked up from studying a photo of her mother.

"You've added a few more pictures since I was last here," he said, averting his gaze to a piece hanging over the mantle. It was a recent shot she had taken of Mount Shasta.

Janet set her satchel down on the dining room table. "Yeah; that one caught my eye." She stepped into the kitchen and went to the fridge. "You want something to drink? I have a bottle of Merlot that's chilled and ready."

"Maybe later."

"So when did you get in?" she said, uncorking the bottle and pouring herself a glass.

"'Bout three hours ago," he replied as he came around the corner. "So, how have you been?"

"Busy ... Barney, you hungry?"

The dog barked and licked his chops as she went to the cabinet to pull his kibble out. After filling his bowl, she drew back the vertical blinds from the sliding glass door that led to her backyard deck. As she did so, she felt her father's gaze on her. At last, he said, "So, how'd things go with the lawyers?"

Janet sipped her wine. "Just finished up the last of it, 'cept the taxes. How come you never told me you were on the deed?"

"Never thought about 'til they called."

"Why were you on it anyways?" Janet said.

Her father shrugged. "Your aunt needed a co-signer, and I thought it was a good investment at the time. I assume they got everything they needed from me?"

"Yeah, they did, thanks," she said, and couldn't help wondering if his being out here with her had anything to do with it.

"You're welcome. So, still planning to keep 'em? They'd fetch a fair dollar on the market."

"Yeah, I know. But I don't want to throw Tom out."

"He's her tenant in the cottage, right?"

"Yeah, and I'd really rather not talk about it right now if that's okay."

"Fair enough."

"Well," Janet said, leaning back against the counter, "how long do I have you for?"

Her father looked away. "A week. Say look, I'm a bit lagged. Mind if I lay down awhile?"

"Oh, not at all. You know where the guest room is. I'll put some fresh towels out for you."

He went and snatched up his briefcase and carry-on bag. "Wake me in couple hours, would you?" he said, and didn't wait for an answer. Then again, she didn't expect him to.

The next morning, Janet woke early and put a pot of coffee on. As she waited for it to brew, she sat perusing the morning paper at the kitchen table. She liked this time of the day, when it was quiet except for all the little creaks and noises of the house.

Her father shuffled into the room part way through her second cup of coffee. She looked up from working her puzzle and saw him wearing the blue, terry cloth robe she'd bought him a couple of years back for Christmas.

"Morning," she said, setting her pencil down.

He nodded. "That decaf?"

"Yep." She watched him pull a mug down from the cupboard then pretended to go back to her puzzle. But from the corner of her eye she saw his furtive glances. At length, he sat across from her, coffee in hand, his hair in an uproar. "Want some?" she said, offering him the sports section.

He yawned and took it as she jotted down the answer to 67 across. "So, should I take the day off?"

He leafed through the section and looked up, "Nah. I have a few things I need to take care of. Tomorrow maybe?"

She shrugged.

He got up, walked to the window and looked out over the back yard. "She was a good woman, your aunt."

Janet set her puzzle down, wondering where that came from. "Dad, you barely saw her the last twenty years."

He sucked down a gulp of coffee. "We wrote each other occasionally."

"Really?" Janet said, pointedly.

He looked at her and hardened his long face. "You have a problem with that?"

Janet picked her puzzle back up. "Doesn't matter what I think."

He knotted his brow and turned his gaze out through the window. He was quiet for several minutes and the only sound in the room was the ticking of the wall clock. Finally, he said, "Janet?"

"What?"

"I'm sorry. I should've been there for you when you were growing up."

Janet sat back. *Where's this going?* "What's wrong, Dad?"

He sighed. "There's something I don't know what to do about."

"What?" Janet said getting up from the table. She tapped him on the shoulder. "Care to turn around and talk to me?"

He shook his head and set his coffee cup down. "I don't know where to begin."

Janet pulled him around to face her. When she saw his rigid jaw, her heart thumped. She had never seen him like this before, and it scared her. "Dad, talk to me. Is Craig all right?"

He nodded. "It's not him. It's Christine. She's left me."

"What happened?"

He coughed and looked away. "Who knows? I'll be searching for apartments when I get back. For the time being, I just need time to think and I didn't want to barge in on your brother so soon after he got married."

Janet ignored the fact that she was second choice and reached out to him. "I'm so sorry, Dad. I love you. Take as much time as you want."

Her father drew a deep breath, nodded, and for the first time in a long, long while hugged her like he meant it."

4

August 14, 1980 – three months later -

Janet took a deep breath and pulled into the long, narrow drive curling around June's house. It had been a month since she had last stepped inside the cozy little bungalow nestled within a copse of hazelnut and ash. She opened the car door, letting Barney out and went up the porch stair with a box of cleaning supplies. As she pulled back the screen door, the memory of finding her aunt on the floor came roaring back. She took a deep breath, forcing the memory away and unlocked the front door. Once inside, she set the box down and pulled the drapes back to let the warmth of the summer sun flood the dark musty room before heading to the kitchen.

As she entered in, a vision of her Aunt rolling out dough for one of her famous strawberry-rhubarb pies flashed before her. Aunt June was a round woman with an ever-present smile that went along with the old, tattered apron that stretched around a generous body.

A smile tugged at Janet's lips as she panned the dirty dishes, pots, and pans that were spilled across the white Formica countertops. The room was just as her aunt left it. Mixing bowls and utensils were still stacked in a porcelain sink. An open cookbook and a pile of papers lay on an old wooden table.

Janet rolled her sleeves up, turned the small radio on to a local station and went back to get the box of supplies. An hour later, she was wrist deep in a sink of dishwater finishing off the last round of pots and pans. Rinsing a baking sheet, she set it in the dish drainer and pulled the sink plug.

"I need a glass of something cold. How about you, Barney? You thirsty?" The dog got up from where he was lying by the bay window and wagged his tail. Janet grabbed a soup bowl, filled it with water, and after setting it down for him, grabbed a can of soda from June's refrigerator. As she pulled back the tab on the can and sat, an envelope on the cluttered kitchen table caught her eye. She pulled it out and opened it. Inside was a letter to her aunt from her father.

June

Thanks for keeping me posted on Janet. It's nice to know she's doing well. She called me a while back wanting me to come out, but I couldn't. Things are not good back here. Christine has decided she's not happy. I have no idea why. I thought we were doing great.

I know you're right about Janet, and I wish I could've been the father she deserved. But it's a little late for that I'm afraid. Every time I try to do something, she shuts me down—not that I blame her. If I could only tell her what happened between her mother and me. It wasn't her fault...

Janet peered out the kitchen window at the hawthorn bush mystified and uncertain of her feelings about the letter in her hand. How many more secrets were her father and aunt holding back from her? She finished her soda, wondering if she'd ever find out.

By the time four o'clock came around, she was bushed. She packed up a few items and threw them in the back of her car as Barney scooted into the front seat. Although she was tired, she felt a need to walk along the shores of Fogarty. It was only an hour away, and she'd be home well before bedtime. She locked up June's house and before she knew it was cruising down the main road through Lincoln City.

Fifteen minutes later, she pulled into Fogarty's entrance and found a spot close to the underpass leading to the beach. When she opened the door, Barney bounded out and danced before her. "Okay, no leash today. But you be good," she said shutting the door behind him.

With journal in hand, she made her way through the underpass and meandered out onto the beach toward her spot in the bluffs. As she walked, a stiff gritty wind raked her sleeves and played with her hair. Up ahead, Barney splashed through the frothy water, barking at the floating birds off shore. She laughed, loving how her little dog found so much fun in the simple things. Bending over, she picked up a stick and tossed it into the surf, sending him into a mad scramble.

In the crook of the curling bluff ahead was an outcropping of sandstone that she claimed as her own. Its smooth sloped face rose up over the beach, and notched within its face was a small indenture. A grotto, and from it, a view of the entire coastline could be seen in either direction. She headed for it. Climbed to her spot and sat in the sheltered notch.

With her knees pulled up under her chin, she thought of her father. All her life he had been distant. Now he was reaching out. Did it have to do with his divorce? The secrets he held from her? Did the prospect of being alone drive him to her? He had been alone before. Did getting older focus one's priorities?

Barney climbed up on the rock and sat beside her. She pulled him close. The dog rolled his deep brown eyes upward and then pressed himself against her. "You're a good dog, you know that?" she said, and pulled out her journal to write.

After a light dinner in Depoe Bay, Janet headed back home. There was a submittal due for the 'Oregon Trails' in three weeks. The photos had already been shot, but there was developing and editing to do. She already had an idea on how she'd crop the shots. And then there was another shoot for a new account in Newport–"Lives of the California Seals". And ... and another one, what was it?

Suddenly her heart flipped. She slapped her hand down on the steering wheel. *Oh no, the Reporter submittal! I told Mick I'd have it for him a month ago. I can't believe it. He's gonna be so pissed.* She pushed the accelerator down, tipping the needle towards seventy-five.

The changing landscape swept by with deceptive speed. The needle drifted toward eighty. Suddenly, a loud pop! The steering wheel jolted out of her hands. The car slashed across the road. Launched into the air. Her body froze. The car twirled, hung in mid air–her breath caught with it. Then, all at once the ground came up with a crushing thud.

Her neck hurt. She blinked and looked down, except down was up. "Barney," she cried as a tapping sound pattered nearby. She struggled with the seatbelt. Saw the dog lying on his side on the roof of the car below her. Smoke was creeping into the vehicle as a sudden jolt shot up her leg. She winced and her eyes rolled back as she fought to stay conscious.

In the thick, gray miasma, she heard voices. One, very close, hollered, "Hang on, help's coming!"

"There's a dog in there too!"

She opened her mouth, gasping, and in the swirling dark cloud above, saw her father on the dock fishing. The way they used to do when she was little before things fell apart. He was leaning back, sipping a beer–smiling. She was sitting on the edge, her feet dangling in the water. A little Zebco 202 rod and reel was in her hand. It was just the two of them.

Daddy, her mind cried out. *I love you.*

Janet winced, and with an effort, opened her eyes then shut them against the piercing light shooting down from above. Her head felt as if it might explode as the echo of nearby voices clanged in her brain.

"She's regaining conscience. Pulse 54, BP 62 over 44."

I'm cold. She shivered. The sensation of spinning in mid-air sent a wave of nausea through her. An odd noise–thop, thop, thop–thumped in her ears. *Where am I?* She opened her eyes; saw a dark shadow bent over her.

Licking her lips, she tasted the acrid remnant of smoke. *It hurts.* She glanced down at a blurred sea of white. Saw something around her leg.

A shadow moved over her face. Something tightened around her nose and mouth. A face veered into focus. A man. Dark eyes. The world spun again. Shapes stretched and contorted. Visions of fire flashed before her with detached arms pulling her through the flames.

Janet awoke and blinked at the world coming into focus. A bright light blanketed her. *Where am I? Ouch.* She drew breath, coughed, and tasted smoke. *Ugh! My throat! What's that sound?* She turned her head, saw a rack of monitors and watched the little bright light running continuously from left to right, making up and down movements.

A soft warm hand settled on her arm. She rolled her head and looked up at a pair of soft brown eyes. "Well hello there," a woman said, fiddling with something over Janet's head. "My name's Gina, and you're in Salem Memorial. You gave us quite a scare."

Janet coughed and swallowed. "My mouth feels like an ash tray."

"Don't try to talk. You inhaled a lot of smoke," Gina said and stepped back out of focus only to reappear on the other side of Janet. She hit a button on one of the monitors, and a long strip of paper spewed out. After she tore it off, she folded it and put it in her pocket. "Are you in pain? Just nod if you are."

Janet moved her head up and down as she tried to get her bearings, and as she did so, realized there was a wide bandage above her brow. Gina turned and pushed a button on a device sitting in the monitor rack and adjusted the knob on the IV. When she finished, she picked up what looked like a small foam paintbrush, dipped the end of it in a glass of water, and put it to Janet's lips. "Here, suck on this."

Janet put her fingers to her face and felt the spongy gauze dressing. With an effort, she whispered, "What happened to me?"

"You were in an accident," the woman said as Janet sucked on the foam tipped stick. "Now, you need to save your voice or you'll hurt your vocal chords. I'm going to check your wounds now. It might hurt."

Janet watched as Gina pulled back the bandage around her head then she looked down her body at a bruised and misshapen leg. It was swollen to grotesque proportions and was suspended in a sling. She gasped, and the room slowly started to spin again, pulling her up with it. Suddenly, faces of people flashed before her. Jimmy Coates, her high school prom date; a girl named, Amanda, who bullied her incessantly throughout middle school; her mother folding laundry in the back room of their house. Janet saw the open door behind her mother leading into darkness. Her heart thumped as a dull ache radiated through her, growing in strength with every passing moment. She shuddered then fell mercifully into the darkness of sleep.

"Hey, there young 'un," said Tom, his weather-beaten face staring down at her. "Take it easy. You're all right." Warm, calloused fingers wrapped around her fingers as she sucked a big breath and winced. "You in pain?

She looked at the old man who was her aunt June's dear friend, and was now her tenant, and nodded. It was good to see a friendly face.

"Hold on then, I'll get the nurse."

As his hand pulled away, she grabbed it and whispered, "Don't go."

Tom patted her hand. "I'm not going no where's, don't you worry 'bout that, but you need something to ease your hurting right now." He slipped his hand out of her grasp and scurried off.

Janet squeezed her eyes shut as another crushing wave rolled up her leg, seizing her breath. Her body stiffened, and she cried out as Tom's voice drifted into the room. "Nurse is on her way," he said, his words close to her ear.

She bit down on her lip and opened her eyes.

"I know, I know," he whispered, clutching her hand. "Hang in there, she'll be right here."

Janet drew a deep breath as the sound of footsteps came beside her. "Janet, you in pain?"

She shifted her gaze to a short, wiry woman standing beside Tom. The woman reached up as Tom backed away, checked the I.V., pushed a button on one of the machines beside Janet's bed and showed her a small remote.

"This is a self dispensing pain reliever. See this button here?" She pointed to a little blue button on the remote. "Push it whenever the pain gets too much for you, okay?"

She put the device in Janet's hand, and watched as Janet focused on the button and pressed it.

"Good. You'll start feeling better in a couple of minutes." To Tom, she said, "They're coming around with breakfast in half an hour. Would you like a plate brought up for you?"

Tom shook his head. "I'm good. There a coffee machine up here anywhere?"

"There's a kitchen off the nurse's station down the hall on the left," she said, grabbing a clipboard hanging off a hook. As Janet watched her flip the pages over, she felt the drugs kick in.

After the nurse left, Tom returned to Janet's bedside. "How ya feeling now young 'un?"

As the pain began to recede, she smiled and whispered, "Much better. How did you know I was here?"

"Apparently, you're pretty fond of me. Had me as a contact in case of emergency," Tom said. "I rung your father up. He's catching the first flight out."

Janet closed her eyes. Saw her dad in her mind's eye. Remembered the time she fell out of the old willow tree and broke her wrist. It had happened in the wooded lot behind their house. She was six or was it seven? It was so long ago. She could still feel his arms around her—feel the soft cottony texture of his flannel shirt on her face.

Suddenly, Barney flashed into her thoughts.

"What?" Tom asked.

"Barney," she answered.

Tom winked. "The little feller's staying with ole Tom here."

"Thank you. Is he all right?" Janet said.

"Got a few scraps, but he's up and bouncing around."

Janet eyed the I.V. tube. "Say, this is really good stuff."

"Only the best," Tom said, pulling a chair beside her. "You know, I've seen way too much of the insides of this here place."

"Me too," she whispered, licking dry and parched lips and trying to stay focused. "So, when's my father due?"

Tom looked at his watch. "Somewhere around this time tomorrow, I expect."

Janet awoke the next morning, turned her head and found her father sitting in a chair next to her window reading the paper. *He's here.* She watched him, drinking in his face as his eyes shifted back and forth across the page. "Hi, Dad."

He dropped the paper in his lap and beamed a broad smile. "Hey sweetie!"

"How long have you been sitting here?"

"'Bout an hour." He leaned over and kissed her cheek. "Your brother sends his love. He would have come, but I told him to stay put unless ... well, you know."

That's my dad–Mr. Practical, Janet thought. "You look tired."

He shrugged. "Just a little jet lag. Nothing some sleep can't cure."

"For someone who doesn't like flying, you're doing an awful lot of it lately."

"Yeah, I know," he said putting his hand to her face.

She smiled then peered down her body at her misshapen leg. It was a hideous sight. "Pretty ugly, huh?"

Her father nodded. "Looks worse than it is. You'll heal up quick and be up and around in no time."

Right, Janet thought. "I'm guessing my car won't be though."

Her father shook his head. "Ah ... no. Here, have a drink." He reached beside him and picked up a small Styrofoam cup.

She drank a sip and gave it back to him. "Do they know what caused the accident? I can't remember anything."

"They're still investigating, but they think it might have been a blown tire."

Janet nodded and looked up into his careworn and jet lagged face. What she wanted to do was wrap her arms around him and tell him how much she missed him, but she was afraid to risk the fragile moment they were sharing. Finally, she said, "Doesn't matter. You're here and that's all that counts."

September 1, 1980 -

Janet hobbled through the front door of her house with her father tagging along behind. The scars over her right eye were fading and the patch of hair that had been cut away was coming back. As for the surgery to repair her broken leg, that had gone terrifically, and with a steady regimen of PT, she expected to be walking on her own without crutches within the next couple of weeks. Her father set her bags down on the couch and helped her sit.

The house was spotless. Her father was obsessive when it came to cleanliness. He went to the kitchen and a few minutes later returned with a glass of iced tea. "Tom'll be here shortly with Barney. I told him to hold onto him until you were back home, seeing how I was back and forth to the hospital."

She relaxed in her chair as he turned the TV on and went about putting things away. An hour later, the doorbell rang. She shot a perplexed look at the door.

Her father said, "You expecting anyone?"

Janet shrugged. "Not really."

He went and opened the door. On the other side, Janet heard Megan's cheery voice.

"What're you doing here?" Janet said, shifting around in her chair.

"I came to welcome you back," Megan replied, coming in with a bouquet of daisies. She handed them to Janet's father and nodded back toward the front door. "And I brought someone with me."

"Mick! You guys!" Janet said as Megan dropped her purse on the couch. She came over and bent down to give Janet a hug.

Mick said, "We wanted to give you a warm welcome home."

"Brad would've been here too, but Kyle got an ear infection. Nothing major," Megan said. She looked around. "Where's Barney?"

"He's with Janet's tenant," Janet's father said. He put his hand out to Mick. "I'm Will, Janet's father."

"Mick Danzer. I hear you're from back east."

"Yeah, Ohio Valley," Will said. He lifted the flowers in his hand, and appraised them. "Why don't I get these in a vase and let you guys have a moment together."

As Will walked down the hallway, Megan said, "So, how's it going between you two? Looks like you're getting along."

Janet smiled. "We're doing good."

Mick reached into his jacket pocket, pulled an envelope out, and handed it to her. "What's this?" Janet said, looking at him.

"A little something to tithe you over," Mick replied.

"We took a collection," Megan added.

Janet shook her head. "You shouldn't have."

"Don't worry about what we should or shouldn't have done," Megan scolded.

Mick said. "Take it. There's a check in there, too. Call it an advance on your next shoot."

Janet fought to stem the tide of emotions roiling inside her. She folded the envelope and tucked it in her purse.

"Hey, Mick," Megan said. "Mind stepping out for a minute?" When he looked at her puzzled, Megan added, "Girl talk."

After Mick took the hint and left, Megan kneeled beside Janet's chair and said, "So, how are things, really?"

Janet shrugged. "I'm exhausted, but I'm good."

"You need any help?"

"No, my dad's here, so I'm fine."

When Megan grew quiet, Janet could see there was something on her mind. Finally, Megan said, "My father has finally decided to move out west."

"That's great!" Janet said, as she wondered what all the trepidation was about.

"Yeah, I'm really excited. Ummm ... I don't know how to ask this, and I don't want to sound like a ... well, you know, a –"

"What is it, Meg?" Janet said, bracing herself.

"I heard you talking about your aunt's house a while back, about how you didn't know what to do about it, and I was thinking maybe ... maybe you might be interested in renting it."

"To your father, I suppose?" Janet said, eyeing her dubiously.

"Well, yeah, it sort of crossed my mind," Megan replied, nibbling her lip.

Janet took a deep breath and forced a grin. "Sort'a?"

Megan giggled nervously. "Well, the way I see it, it's the perfect solution for both of you."

Janet shook her head. She didn't want to expand her role as a landlord. Yet, Megan was her friend, and her father had helped her out of a tight spot on the snowy highway. She sighed. "When's he coming out?"

"In the spring, but he could fly out earlier."

Janet pursed her lips. "Let me think about it."

5

May 23, 1981 –

Janet stepped onto the crowded outdoor deck of Sal's Bistro and sat at a linen-topped table. It was her birthday and this year her father made a point of coming out to celebrate it with her. As he joined her, she unfolded her napkin and took in the Locust and Dogwood dotting the grounds.

Although it was nine months since her accident, she still felt conscious of the brace under her skirt. She stretched her leg and inhaled the fragrant scents of the flowering lilies bordering the deck. Beside her, her father sat reading his menu and sipping ice water. *I wonder what's on his mind,* she thought. *He's been acting really nervous since he came out last week.*

At length, he put his menu down. "I think I'll have the grilled halibut. What about you?"

She studied the knitted brow on his sculpted face and noticed the shaving nick on his chin. She offered him a smile and pointed to his face. "You cut yourself."

"Yeah, sometimes I go a little faster than I should with the old razor."

"I love you, Dad."

He put his fingers to her cheek, looked into her eyes. "Thank you. I love you, too." He paused then and she saw him take a deep breath. Finally, he went on. "I ... I've been thinking. Craig's in Florida and married. Seeing how there's nothing back east for me anymore, I was thinking of ... picking up stakes and moving?"

She nodded and forced a smile, "I'm sure he'd love having you close."

Her father gazed at her for some time with an enigmatic expression, then said, "I was thinking of coming west."

Her heart leapt. "Are you serious?"

He paused, as if giving the idea one last thought. "Yeah, that is if you'd want me underfoot."

"Dad, you wouldn't be in the way," she said reaching out and folding her hand over his arm.

He gave her one of his classic thin-lipped smiles. "You're all right with it then?"

"Absolutely," she replied. "When can you come?"

"I was thinking right after my lease runs out in July."

June 30, 1981 -

Janet scrubbed the last stain away from June's kitchen sink while Tom worked on the upstairs bedrooms. She hadn't asked him to come help, but he insisted, and she was glad of it. As she wiped her brow with the back of her hand, she re-assessed the decision she'd made months ago about renting the house to Neil.

He's Megan's father, so that should count for something, and he is older. Suddenly, her brow went up. *Oh, crap, you idiot! He smokes! I can't believe I didn't think of it 'til now. What do I say if he likes it, no thanks?* She shook her head as the wall clock rang out the half hour. She looked up at it. *Shit, it's eleven thirty. They'll be here any minute!*

After rinsing the sink, she ran through the empty house to the downstairs bathroom. Pushing the door open, she flipped the light switch, shut the door, and faced the mirror. Sweat and grit spattered her white painter's shirt and her hair was all over her face. "Damn it, I look like hell."

Grabbing a washcloth, she turned the water on. As she scrubbed her face, a knock came to the front door. *Shit!* Cracking the door open, she yelled up to Tom, "Can you get that? I think it's them."

Tom's graveled voice trickled down from upstairs. "On my way." A moment later she heard the stairs creak under his footsteps. Through the bathroom door, she heard voices. "Come on in. How was the drive?"

"Not bad," said a deep voice that was unmistakably Neil's.

"Where's Jan?" Megan asked.

"Be right out," Janet replied peering through the crack of the partially open door. She blinked when she saw Neil. He had shaved his beard and mustache and looked like he'd lost another ten pounds since she last saw him.

"Take your time," Megan called back. "We're in no hurry."

Janet pulled a scrunchy out, put her hair in a ponytail, then opened the door and walked out to greet them.

Neil, who had his back turned toward her, turned and shot Janet a broad smile. "What a cozy little place you have."

Janet shrugged as he panned the room with a discerning gaze. "It needs a lot of work," she said, apologetically.

"Oh, I don't know about that," Neil replied.

Megan turned to Janet. "That's my dad, always looking on the bright side."

Neil eyed his daughter affectionately. "What's wrong with that?" To Janet, he added, "I look at old houses like blind dates."

Tom broke out laughing. "Never heard it put that way!"

"Me neither." Janet chuckled. *Strange choice of words.* Can I get you guys something to drink? There's soda in the fridge."

Megan's glance darted around. "Sure … where's Barney?"

"Home, watching the house."

"You trust him alone. Brave girl!"

Janet grinned. "He's in his crate, but actually, he's very good most of the time," she replied, leading them out to the kitchen. Over her shoulder, she continued, "Please excuse the walls. God knows they could use a coat of paint."

"Painting's not a problem," Neil said, and a soda sounds great."

They stood around the kitchen sipping drinks for the next ten minutes, talking about the weather, until Neil said, "Do you know when your aunt added this kitchen?"

Janet felt her brow go up. "Added?"

"Yeah." He pointed to a ridge in the floor tile. "See how the floor dips there and slopes away toward the dining room?"

Janet frowned. *Huh, why haven't I noticed that before?*

"That's the old house over there," Neil continued. "And from here back to the bay window is the addition. You can also tell by the faint line in the ceiling, there and there. It's where the wallboard meets up with the old plaster. Whoever did the finish work was pretty good."

Tom beamed from where he stood in the corner of the room.

"Oh," Janet said. Her gaze went back to the floor. "The dip there, is that bad?"

Neil shook his head. "Nah. Old houses have their own per-sonalities. Just like old men ... belligerent." He winked at Tom.

Janet cleared her throat. "Okay, where to?"

Neil's eye caught sight of a narrow door at the end of the room. "Where's that lead?"

"The basement."

"Really?" He headed for the door. "You know people didn't dig many basements out here."

Janet never thought about it, but now that he'd mentioned it, he was right. "You don't mind if I wait here? I'm not a fan of spiders."

Neil opened the door. "No problem at all."

As he went downstairs, Janet heard the old wooden treads complain under his feet. "I think there's a switch somewhere at the bottom," she said, edging toward the door.

A soft yellow glow from a light bulb pushed the darkness away and Janet heard Neil knocking around below. Suddenly, he was back at the bottom of the stairs looking up. "I think you ought to come down and take a peek at something."

Oh no, Janet thought. *I'm not going down there.* She glanced at Tom. "Can you see what he wants?"

Tom set his soda down and patted her shoulder as he passed.

Ten minutes later, she heard Tom and Neil coming up the basement stairs. "Those porcelain isolators are a fire hazard," Neil said. "They need to be ripped out and new 14/2 wiring run through conduit."

"You're damned right," Tom said.

Janet blinked. *Fire hazard?*

"How much you think to rewire it?" Tom said, stepping into the kitchen through the open basement door.

Neil followed and shut the door behind them. "Depends on how right you want to do it. At a minimum, I'd say a thousand, maybe a bit more."

"I guess that ends the tour," Janet muttered, closing her eyes. *How am I going to come up with that, being out of work and owing everyone on the planet?* She felt as if she'd been punched in the stomach.

Megan's face darkened and she let out an audible sigh. Neil glanced at his daughter and looked back at Janet in confusion. "What's the problem?" he said.

Janet stared at him; incredulous he could ask such a dumb question. "Isn't it obvious?"

Neil shrugged. "No."

"I can't rent this out," she answered. She looked at the ceiling.

"Sure you can," Neil replied. "I'd rent it." He thumped the bay window casing next to him. "Foundation's in good shape. Plumbing, too. There's a well, right?"

"Yeah," Janet said. "Pump's a bit cranky at times. But–"

"But what?" Neil argued.

They were all quiet a minute, until Janet said, "You're serious: you'd still rent this, even with the bad wiring?"

Neil cocked his head and eyed his daughter. "Sure. It's been standing this long. I'll make you a deal. I'll get her straightened out for two month's free rent."

Janet swallowed hard as the offer hung in the air. "I, I don't know."

"What's to know?" Megan said, brightening.

Tom piped up, "You gonna do the work yourself?"

Neil laughed. "Oh, no. Electricity and I don't get along. I'll find someone to take care of it."

This is going way too fast. Slow down, Janet thought. "Well, I guess I ought to show you the rest of the place."

Megan grinned, and Janet knew what that meant.

Janet rolled the car window down as she drove along Highway 22 listening to the Beatles, 'Hey Jude.' The crisp autumn breeze carrying the resinous scent of pine tossed her hair. *Well, I'm a landlord again, that is if I want it,* she thought, and considered the strange turn of events that kept bringing Neil into her life. If she were religious, she'd have called it God Sent, Karma, or Destiny. She grinned as she drummed her fingers on the wheel. It was just chance, yet still–

She put her foot to the pedal, and a half hour later Salem's familiar skyline crept into view with its modern office buildings under dark threatening clouds. Tiny raindrops pelted her windshield. By the time she pulled into her driveway, it was a downpour. She rushed to the house, covering her head with a newspaper. When she opened the door, a wet tongue and wagging tail greeted her.

"Hi Baby, how did you get out of your crate?" she said, bending down to pick her mail up. When she realized she had not latched the door to his crate, she took a deep breath and braced herself. "Okay, mommy screwed up. Now, let's get you outside while I look around and see what you've been up to?" She let him out, then pulled the door shut behind her and glanced around, hunting for telltale signs of mischief.

After finding there were no accidents, Janet kicked her shoes off and scooted to the bathroom. Her body cried for a hot shower, so she ran the water and skipped into the bedroom to peel her work clothes off. She threw a robe on and let Barney back in, then inserted a tape of Van Morrison into her cassette player. Suddenly, she found herself dancing around the room.

For the first time since her aunt died, she breathed easier. Her father was moving out west and the dilemma with the house could be over. The only thing that remained was ramping up her starving practice again. Whether or not she should've taken the job Mick had offered her was a moot point now, yet she couldn't help but wish she had.

Twenty minutes later, she was showered and in the kitchen. As Barney dug into his chow, she set the teakettle on the stove and filched a couple of Oreos from the cookie jar. She was about to sit down and go through the pile of mail when the phone rang.

"Hello?"

"Skeeter. Dad."

She leaned back in her chair. "Hey, I was just thinking of you."

"Yeah? Didn't do it!"

"Do what?" she replied.

He laughed on the other end. "Whatever you think I did. Anyway, ya hear about Belinda?"

"No, what?" she said.

"She's pregnant. You're gonna be an aunt again."

"That's fantastic!"

"Yeah. I'm flying down to see them next week if I can find a decent flight," he replied.

"I'm sure he'll love that." She grinned. "You're becoming a real jet-setter."

"Don't remind me."

"Oh, and I've got some news of my own. I might have found a tenant for June's house."

"Really?" Her father said, his tone becoming cautious. "You sure about adding another tenant? Tom is someone you know, but a stranger–they could leave a giant mess. You have a lease, right?"

Oh no, here we go again. But I'm not gonna let this get into an argument. Taking a deep breath, she fought off the urge to snipe back. "Of course there'll be a lease."

"That's good. By the way, what are you going to ask for rent?"

"Four-seventy-five plus utilities. He says he can do some work on the place, too."

"You mean painting?"

"That and other things," Janet said, nibbling her lip.

"Such as?"

"There's some electrical issues and I guess there's a sag in the porch beam or something like that."

"Skeeter, hire a contractor. Get someone experienced. Last thing you want is a do-it-yourselfer working on your house."

"He's an architect, Dad," she argued.

"And I'm a mechanical engineer," he replied. "Doesn't mean I can fit pipes together. Not saying he's not capable. Just make sure if you rent to him, he can do what he says he can, okay?"

Janet nodded. Her dad was trying to look out after her, and she couldn't fault him for it. "Will do."

"Say, I'm starved, and I have a crap load of paper work to get through. Call you later in the week?"

"I'm out of town on a shoot till Wednesday," Janet replied, "then over to the house the rest of the week. How 'bout I call you?"

"That works."

"Love you, Dad."

"Ditto, sweetie."

Janet hung up feeling anxious and it got worse when she saw an invoice from the lawyers office sitting on the table staring back at her.

6

From the front porch window, Janet and Barney watched Neil pull into the gravel drive. His long white truck was towing a trailer. The dog barked. She hushed him and made a last cursory glance around June's empty house. The front room was freshly painted. The last of June's items sat by the front door, waiting to be taken out. Tom was upstairs, whistling away as he put the final shine on the tub.

He came down and joined her and the dog. Outside, Neil was unhitching the trailer as Megan and Brad dug boxes out from the back of the truck. Tom handed Janet a stack of letters. "Found these upstairs. Thought you might want 'em."

"Oh, thanks." She glanced down at them and seeing her father's bold script, wondered what secrets they might hold. She tucked them in one of the boxes by the front door, made a mental note to look them over in the near future, and said, "At least Neil has a good day to move in on."

"Right. I'll take these boxes out to the car while you see 'em in." He gave her hand a squeeze and scooped up the last remnant of June's effects as Megan appeared at the door. Barney jumped as Tom let her in.

"Hey, you brat, you should've called me," Megan said, looking around. "I would've helped if I'd known you were working up to the last minute."

"Don't sweat it," Janet replied as Megan stood and put her arms around her.

"Looks bigger, somehow," Megan said. She drew back and gave the empty rooms an appraising gaze. "I know I've told you a thousand times, but I'm really grateful." Janet raised her hand to silence her, but Megan cut her off. "No, really. I was wrong to push my father on you so soon after..." She averted her gaze to the floor.

Janet tagged her on the arm with a friendly jab. "Come on," she said, "there's a small supermarket in Junction Valley that has the best pastries in town. We'll pick up some treats for the boys." She felt Barney's paw on her leg and looked down at shining brown eyes. "Yes, you too."

"So, are you coming to our company picnic this year?" Megan said, playing with the car radio.

Janet shrugged. "Maybe. Depends." She shot Megan a passing glance as she drove. "I have a couple of shoots next month." She eased up on the pedal. The road gently wound around a cluster of Douglas fir and straightened out in a long inviting track. Tall rambling bushes and scraggly pine ran along the shoulder of the road. Speed-trap Alley! At last, she said, "You must be excited having your father out here."

Megan nodded. "Oh, yes. I've been trying to talk him into coming out since my brother ditched him for Germany."

"You never told me you had a brother," Janet said.

"Really? I thought I did," Megan replied, her tone oddly cold and rigid. "He's in the Air Force."

"Really? I don't think I'd like being in the service."

"How's that?" Megan said.

"All the uprooting, leaving family behind and stuff. I couldn't do it."

Megan was quiet a moment. "Well, yeah, I guess. Except my brother, Trevor, couldn't have cared less. He lives in his own world. Everything's about him you know ... asshole! Sorry, but thinking about him pisses me off."

Janet was surprised at the icy hostility Megan had for her brother. She couldn't ever imagine feeling that way about Craig. *Hmmm ... I wonder what that's all about?*

The trees parted and the land opened up on both sides of them revealing careworn countrified homes that sat a hundred yards back off the road. In the distance, golden blankets of tall grasses pooled around silver silos.

Janet slowed down and turned right onto the road heading towards Valley Junction. The radio chattered, softly filling the inside of the car with Casey's Weekly Top 40. The number one song, *'Bad Girls'* rattled the speakers.

Megan tapped her palms on her knees to the beat and turned the radio up a notch. "Reminds me of the good ole days." When Janet turned and cocked her brow, Megan cuffed her on the arm. "Okay, Okay ... you're not much older than I am, you know."

Her gaze wandered out the passenger window a moment, then turned back. "Oh, did you know Mick has a girlfriend?"

"Really? That's interesting," Janet said. "She must be something else. Mick's picky."

"Oh, yeah. She's a real looker. From what I heard, she teaches up at the university–psychology or something like that."

"Oh, wow! He'll have fun with her," Janet quipped thinking of Mick's modus operandi. She could see him now trying to order the woman around. There was definitely going to be some bloodletting in the near future, and it was going to be Mick on the short end of it.

By five o'clock, most of Neil's stuff had been set up or stacked in piles on the enclosed porch. Janet carried in the last box and set it on the kitchen counter as he pulled the truck ahead and parked. A few moments later, he pushed through the front door, keys in hand. "That'll do 'er. I'm starved. Anyone know if there's a takeout joint around here?"

"There's a pizza shop down the road," Janet said. "I think they might deliver, not sure."

"Is the phone still hooked up?"

"Yes, 'til Monday. I guess you'll need a number," Janet said. "I think I have one in my address book."

"Great, and now for something cold," he said and went to the fridge and pulled out a beer.

An hour later they sat in the back room munching slices of pepperoni and sausage pizza. Megan and her father sat on the sofa, Brad and Janet on chairs they'd pulled in from the dining room. Tom had already left.

Janet set her Coke down and leaned back in her chair. "So, how was the trip out?"

Neil wiped his mouth with a napkin. "Wasn't too bad. Iowa and South Dakota were dicey. Hail, lot's of it, and heavy rain."

Brad gulped a swig of beer. "You think you've seen rain? Wait a bit. You'll see it here like you've never seen it before."

"But the mountains break it up," Megan said, peeling a piece of cheese off her slice and popping it into her mouth.

"Sometimes," Brad added with a snort.

Janet glanced around at Neil's utilitarian furniture, trying to get used to the new trappings in her aunt's house. "I remember my trip out with my mom. I'll never forget the endless fields of corn and alfalfa. They went on as far as I could see. Sometimes the skies were so blue, they hurt my eyes."

"I know what you mean," Megan said, setting her plate down. "When I came out, I felt the same way."

Neil licked his fingers and waved his hand toward the window. "Yeah, it's a wide open country back there, and plenty dangerous when the weather kicks up." He turned his gaze toward Brad. "In Iowa and the Dakotas, it's twister country, and there's nowhere to run to when they come roaring through."

Brad shrugged. "Guess you got a point there. We do get some nasty downpours though, some lasting for days."

"Days, Brad?" Megan said, rolling her eyes.

Brad stretched and stood. "You know what I mean." To Janet, he said, "This place is sweet. How far's the property run out back?"

"To the tree line over there," Janet said, pointing out the window to a long thin line of hazelnut and pine. "It's a fifteen minute walk depending on whether you cut through the meadow or take the footpath."

Brad surveyed the rolling landscape and aimed a finger at a stand of spindly sumac. "Is that a pond out there by those little trees?"

"A small one, yes," Janet answered. "It's pretty low this time of year, but we've had a wet summer. It's not much to look at."

"Mind if I check it out?"

"No, go ahead."

Brad glanced at Megan. "You wanna come?"

"Sure, why not?" Megan answered then looked at her father. "What about you, Dad?"

"Oh, I'll see it soon enough," he replied. He looked at Janet and nodded toward the door. "Why don't you go with 'em?"

"Oh, no, I'll pass," Janet said, spying the stars that were beginning to prick the sky. In the distance, the harvest moon was making an appearance within the fading blue above.

After Brad and Megan went out, Neil knocked the pizza box down and stuffed it in the trash. "Umm ... so how does trash work? Someone pick it up or do I take it to the dump?"

"No, it's collected Thursday mornings. Is there anything else you'd like to know before I leave?"

He downed the last of his beer and started digging a fingernail at the corner of the bottle's label. "I think that about covers it. Hey, I want to thank you for all you've done. Tom, too. Helping me move in wasn't part of the deal." He paused. "Life's strange isn't it? Who'd'a thought we'd end up here?"

"It is a bit odd," Janet agreed, wondering what he was thinking.

He raked his fingers though his hair. "Oh, the lease. You have it?"

"Yes, out in the car. Be right back."

"Hold on, I'll walk you out. By the way, here's your last month's deposit check." He reached into his shirt pocket and pulled it out along with a business card. "My number at work," he said. "Just in case you need to getta hold of me during office hours."

"I doubt I will, but you never know," Janet said, tucking it away in her jeans pocket along with the check.

The following week was hectic and Janet was glad Friday had finally rolled around. Between Neil's moving into her aunt's house and finishing off an assignment for Mick, she had been running ragged. She opened the fridge and took out the package of ground beef. As she pulled the wrapping off, she looked up at the clock. It was only four. "Screw it, I've earned a meal out." She wrapped the hamburger back up and shoved it in the meat tender and coerced Barney into his crate. "Sorry puppy. But mommy will bring you home a treat, promise."

She grabbed her purse and opened the door to the garage.

Inside, sat her brand new shiny red Mazda gleaming under the glare of a fluorescent ceiling light. She slipped into the leather-scented interior and thirty minutes later, pulled into the graveled lot of Jake's and parked.

Jake's Steakhouse Tavern was a sprawling timber-framed building with a wrap-around porch. The joint was busy tonight, and the scent of barbeque made her mouth water. She walked to the front door and once inside, waded through the crowd up to the bar.

First things first. She ordered a Jake-a-ria–sans the shot of rum. It was her favorite, created by Jake himself, and a popular choice of the locals. Made with a shot of red wine, brandy, club soda, orange juice and topped with a splash of Jamaican rum, a Jake-a-ria provided a hell of a kick if you had too many.

"Janet?"

She jerked her head around and found Neil behind her. "Oh, hi. I see you discovered Jake's."

He pointed to a small round bar table with two tall chairs. "Wanna join me?"

"Ummm," she said, trying to buy some time to decide if she wanted to decline. She furtively scanned the crowd, looking for someone she might know and finding no one, shrugged. "Sure, why not?"

"How's the leg?"

"Getting back to normal," she said.

He craned his head over the crowd as if looking for someone. "You eat yet?"

"No. Just got here."

"Great. I hate eating alone." He cleared his throat. "I'll get us a menu."

"Ahhh, well ... umm."

Neil's brow wrinkled and she could feel his embarrassment. "Oh, I'm sorry. What was I thinking? You're probably meeting someone."

Janet felt like a jerk. She shook her head. "No, no one. I, I just, well, sure why not?"

"You're certain?" Neil said. The way he said it let her know he didn't want to be a charity case.

"Absolutely," she replied, and went over and sat.

An hour later, they were buried in conversation–Neil peppering her about photography. "So, it keeps you pretty busy, huh?"

Janet nodded. "Busy enough, before the accident that is."

"Right."

Janet dragged a French fry through a pool of catsup on her plate. "I'm curious. Why the interest?"

He took a swallow of beer. Gave her a discerning gaze. "Actually, I was thinking of calling you in a couple of weeks. The firm I work for is thinking about upgrading their portfolio. You know, marketing stuff. Ever do a photo-shoot of a building?"

"Not really."

"Would you consider it? I mean if it were offered?"

Hmmm, Janet thought. *Interesting.* She sat with that thought as Neil told her about the proposition. At first, she wondered if he was throwing her a bone. But the more he talked, the more she realized the offer was legit. Finally, she said, "I suppose I could look into the mechanics of it."

He cocked an eyebrow. "Mechanics?"

She shook her head. "I love how everyone thinks you just point, click, and shoot. There's more to it than that."

"Oh, I believe you. Mind educating me?" he said.

"Well ... lighting for one thing. If we're outside, there's reflective glare from windows and metals that needs to be accounted for besides all the other stuff I normally look at. And if we're inside there's a whole other set of rules. Not to mention composition."

He gave her a boyish grin. "I guess that's why you're the expert and I'm just a dumb old architect."

She laughed, and since he left the door wide open, she gave him a sidelong glance and said, "Don't be too hard on yourself. That's what 'I'm' here for!"

Janet thought about the offer Neil had made over the next couple of weeks. Although the shoot he had in mind for her wouldn't happen until mid-September she was hesitant. A photo-shoot of a building was an unfamiliar subject to her. Being a perfectionist didn't help, either. She worked in mediums she felt comfortable and confident in.

She opened a book she bought from a local bookstore and poured through the plates, learning the trade lingo, understanding what architects looked for in photo spreads.

Sipping her iced tea, pencil in hand hovering over her notes, she determined wide-angle lenses shot most of the photos in the book. This made sense. She guessed a 24mm for exterior shots and 20mm for interiors. More than a few had used polarizing filters. The film: definitely an ISO 200 and a few using ISO 100.

Well, I have the equipment. She scribbled a few notes, took some educated measurements for distance and preferred angles then sat back. *I can do this; the question is do I want to? And, will it be worth it?* She glanced at the phone, debating. *It's late, going on ten. But he said, 'call any time.'* She tapped a fingernail on the table and got up, dialed the first five numbers, stopped and hung up. A minute later, her gaze went back to the open book on the table. *Oh, hell!* She picked the phone up and dialed again.

7

September 10, 1981 -

Janet pulled into the parking lot of the Wilson office building; a two-story red brick structure with a band of tinted green windows around it. A bright, clear sky soared overhead. She got out of her car and studied the building's broad cream-colored, stone entrance. Flanking its north side was a glass-enclosed stairway with a terrace beside it that was sprinkled with tables. People were out eating their lunches on them.

Neil, you were supposed to meet me here at noon. It's quarter after. I'm here, where are you? Janet thought. She went around her car and popped the trunk. As she rummaged through her camera case, taking inventory, Neil pulled up and parked beside her.

"You found it," he said, shutting his door and coming around behind the back of his truck.

"Yeah, it wasn't too hard. I live here, remember?"

He smiled. "Keep forgetting I'm the out-of-towner." He took her tripod and helped her with the rest of her gear.

"So, where do you want me to start?" she said, pulling her light meter out.

"I was thinking a few shots of the entrance then working your way around to the rear. But first, let me introduce you to the owner."

They walked across the lot, Neil pointing out the finer points of the architecture to her. *It's okay I guess, if you like working in a fish bowl all day,* Janet thought. "So, is there a special name for this kind of architecture?"

"Modernist."

"Right." She followed him around front and into the lobby. A dark green marble floor clicked under her heels. A muted wall, accented with abstract prints, fanned out behind the reception desk. Above her was a gossamer thin metal artwork that spiraled down from the ceiling.

Neil gave their names to the receptionist, and a moment later, a man strode into the lobby. Tall, fit, tanned with a drift of silver hair brushing the top of his ears, he reminded Janet of a typical politician. He put his hand out to Neil.

"Janet, this is Mr. Wilson," Neil said, shaking hands with him.

"Call me, John," the man replied, offering a broad wolf-like smile to Janet.

"Janet's going to be shooting the building for us today," Neil announced.

"Great. We're very proud of it," Mr. Wilson said, giving Janet a measured glance. "Can I interest you two in joining me for a bite before you get started. There's an exceptional Thai restaurant down the street that delivers."

"No thank-you," Janet said.

Mr. Wilson frowned subtly, then smiled. "Alright then, I'll let you two get to work," he said. As his hazel eyes gave Janet one last perusal, Neil frowned.

You just keep on looking mister, cause that's all you're gonna get! To Neil, she said, "Shall we?"

That night, in her dark room, Janet opened the last film cartridge and threaded the roll inside into the reel of her developer. A dozen shots hung on the line above her worthy of enlarging. She pulled her hair back, knotting it loosely and loaded the first shot into the enlarger. After snapping it down and calibrating, she made the exposure. Behind her, a print hung next to three plastic tubs in a triple bowl sink. She hurried over and ran it through the developers and washes and watched the emerging image taking shape.

She frowned. *I better get something better than this or I can kiss this gig good-bye.* The phone rang on the wall beside her. She glanced over at the clock. *Almost nine-thirty–who the hell?* She hung the enlargement up and stripped off her gloves.

"Hello?"

"Janet, it's me, Megan. My father just told me you're working for him! How great is that?"

Janet smiled. "I'm not working for him; I'm working for his firm, just like I work with the *Reporter*."

"Details! You are so anal sometimes. So, how was it?"

"Okay, I guess. Different from what I'm used to ... So, how's Mick?" Janet said, hoping word hadn't gotten around about her taking on this new venue. It was, what many of her peers would call, 'pedestrian photography'.

"Mick is Mick. Oh, by the way, he's getting pretty nervous about next Sunday's *Reporter*."

"He'll get it," Janet said.

"'Kay, I'll let him know. When you thinking on coming in?"

"Probably next Friday," Janet replied.

"You like giving him indigestion, don't ya?" Megan clucked, and Janet detected a smile on the other end. Megan liked twitting Mick. Suddenly, Megan said, "Say, why don't you stop by when you come? We're having a party for Brad on Saturday. It's his birthday."

"I don't know, Meg. I'm pretty busy. You know my dad's moving out west and everything."

"Come on. It'll be fun."

"What about Barney? What am I gonna do with him?"

"Bring him."

Janet sighed. "I just don't think so, Meg."

"Why?"

"Meg, please."

"This have anything to do with finances? Cause if it does, my father's coming. You could ride with him."

Janet rolled her eyes. "I don't think he'd appreciate me being pushed on him."

"You wouldn't be pushing yourself on him. Think about it … for me?"

"I'll keep it in mind," Janet said, well aware Megan was relentless when she wanted something. "Say, I'm developing right now. I'll call you tomorrow."

Janet licked the flap of the large, manila envelope holding her '*Reporter*' submittal and set it on the table. She'd finished it two days ahead of time. Another late night, but it would be the last for a while. It felt good to be back at work, doing something she loved.

Breakfast crackled and spit in the frying pan. She grabbed the spatula, flipped her eggs, and sucked a gulp of coffee. As she stood watching things cook, the phone rang. She looked up at the clock. It was a little after nine.

"Hello?"

"Janet, Neil here."

"Oh, hi." *Uh, oh, something wrong at the house?* "What's up?"

"Well, I heard you were traveling into town this Friday and were invited to my son-in-law's birthday party. I was wondering if I could catch a ride with you. My truck's been acting up lately. Think it's the tranny."

Megan! "I see a little birdie has been whispering in your ear," she said, turning the burner off. She cradled the phone between her ear and shoulder and pushed the eggs onto her plate.

"Well, yes. You're not upset, are you?"

"No." *Great, now what do I say?*

"I don't bite."

She popped a slice of bread into the toaster, looked at Barney and smiled. "I'm not worried, but you should be. I'll be bringing Barney and he gets a little jealous of folks taking his front seat."

"I'll take my chances."

Hmmm... She dashed salt and pepper on her eggs. *It might be a chance to talk more business.* "I have to go into the city, and I'm not sure how long it'll take."

"Not a problem."

"Okay," she said. "Would you like me to drop you off first?"

"Naw, I can wait."

"Eleven, then?" she offered.

"Eleven it is," he said. "Shall I come to you?"

Janet shrugged. "Yeah, that probably makes sense."

"Great. I'll pick some coffee up on the way. How do you take it?"

She grinned. "Just cream. And thanks. You have a good day now."

"You too."

After he hung up, she wondered if she'd made a mistake. But the idea of having someone ride shotgun felt good.

Neil sat with Barney on his lap as Janet pulled out onto Route 22 and melded into the traffic. From the corner of her eye, she saw the dog pushing his nose into Neil's open lapel and whipping his tail back and forth. "Barney, stop."

"He's alright. He's just being a dog," Neil said.

"Yeah, I know, but I don't like encouraging bad habits."

Neil laughed. "I'm afraid he's way past that ... aren't you boy?" He ran his thick fingers through Barney's fur. "I had a dog ... once ... when I was a kid. Little Lab mix; tough as nails. Wouldn't back down from nothing. Anybody came at me, they faced a mouthful of teeth."

"I don't think that would be my kind of dog."

"He wasn't mean or anything. He was just protective. Anyway, we got him at the pound. I can still remember the day we picked him out. I was looking for a German Shepherd until I saw this little guy looking at me like I was his last chance."

Janet nodded. "You were being adopted and didn't know it."

"Yep. He was a great dog. The best. I still think of him sometimes. Keep wondering what happened to him."

"You don't know?"

Neil rubbed Barney behind the ear. "Nope. Disappeared one day. Never saw him again."

"Our dog was a collie," Janet said. "Car chasers, if you know what I mean."

"Gotcha," Neil said. "Hey, what'd'ya say about stopping for a bite? My treat."

Janet reached over, gave Barney a scratch behind the ear. "Thanks, but–"

"But nothing," Neil said firmly. "You're doing the driving, so I'm doing the buying, no arguments."

Janet parked in the *Reporter's* lot and left Neil and Barney to occupy themselves in a grassy lot that backed up to the property. When she walked through the back door, she saw Mick in the layout room, soda in hand. Beside him, a cigarette burned in an overflowing ashtray. No one else was around, a rare thing on a Friday afternoon before a Sunday printing.

Mick looked up as she slid next to him. "Hey."

"Hi. Where's everybody?"

"Out for a late lunch. Got a long night ahead of us." He reached for the manila envelope in her hand. "That for me?"

She handed it to him and peered over at a pod of empty desks. "Megan with 'em?"

"Yep, they went to that Pan-Am restaurant down the street." He motioned her to sit as his fingers worked the metal clasps and tape off the envelope.

Janet frowned. She was hoping to see Megan and chat about what to get Brad besides the card she'd already bought. "I'm good standing. Been sitting for the last hour, and sorry this took so long."

He waved a hand and pulled the proofs onto the long metal table. Janet heard him ticking off the keepers under his breath. "Not bad," he muttered. He sorted them into piles and looking up, added, "Don't worry, you'll get up to speed."

Up to speed? Janet forced a nervous smile. Mick had never given her work an up-to-speed review. "Little rusty."

He slipped the short pile of proofs in an envelope, put them aside and picked up his cigarette. "It happens, just like I keep lighting up these damned cancer sticks. Shit," he said, noticing the butt had burned down on one side almost to the filter. "You know, sometimes I feel like one of these, just burning away down to nothing."

Janet braced herself. She knew Mick had something on his mind that he had to say but didn't want to. He bent his gaze toward her and cleared his throat. "I don't know how to tell you this, other than just coming right out with it. I gotta cut your freelance work back. Sorry."

Janet felt the air go out of the room. "Of course."

"It's not my idea. You're a great photographer, but it is what it is."

But what you're really thinking is: I should've taken the job, isn't it, Mick?

He pulled another cigarette out and lit it. "Look, there's a new rag down on Main Street focused on ecology-based vacations like whale watching and shit. I heard they're shopping."

Janet sucked a breath and straightened her back. She had been freelancing for the *Reporter* since college. To think it might be coming to an end seemed surreal. She held out her hand. "Well, it's been a ride."

He took a drag, tilted his head up, and blew a ring of smoke toward the ceiling. "Yes it has. It's not like it's the end, you know," he said shaking her hand. "Soon as things loosen up, you'll be back."

"Yeah." *But we both know differently,* Janet thought. "I'll check 'em out. Well, umm ... I guess it's, don't call me, I'll call you now, huh?"

"'Fraid so."

Two hours later, Janet sat munching fish sticks at Megan's dining room table. Her thoughts were far away from the lively banter of Neil and his son-in-law across from her. Kyle sat in his high chair, his little round face smeared with tomato sauce. Active and curious hands clutched a sliver of bread.

Janet wondered where she was going to pick up another contract as she gazed through the sliding glass door and over the white-picket fence hemming in the back yard. In the adjoining lot, she heard squealing voices and saw a white soccer ball loop up into the air.

"Penny for your thoughts," Neil said.

She blinked and turned back. "Oh, just thinking." Standing, she took her plate to the sink and ran water to wash dishes. As she waited for the sink to fill, she watched Neil make funny faces at his grandson.

When Brad took Kyle into the other room for a diaper changing, Neil got up and started clearing the table. After stacking dirty dishes on the counter beside her, he took up a dishtowel and started wiping. They worked quietly side by side until he said, "There's an ice-cream parlor a couple blocks down the street. Interested?"

"You mean now?"

"No, later, after Brad and I put Kyle to bed."

She eyed him thoughtfully, saw the little kid in his expression and remembered her mother's saying; ice cream is the ultimate band-aid.

Neil opened the cabinet door and set the glass he had just wiped on the shelf. "Somehow, I get the feeling you're having a bad day."

She shrugged and pulled the stack of plates beside her into the dishwater. "Just feeling quiet."

He nodded. "My Meg thinks I'm lonely when I'm quiet. Says I need to get around people. I tell her people can't make you happy, you have to decide that for yourself."

"Right," Janet said rinsing a plate. "So what makes you happy?"

A twinkle came to his eye as he took the dish from her. "Make a deal with ya. I'll tell you over a cone."

Janet swatted his arm. "That's just wrong!"

Neil laughed and put the plate away. "I see there's one thing Meg hasn't told you."

"That being?"

"I cheat when I'm behind."

An hour later, the two of them walked leisurely down the winding lane where the streetlights were just flickering to life. Barney tugged at his leash with each new smell he detected. Tiny stars pricked a darkening sky in the throes of giving way to the oncoming night. Janet said, "So, now that I've agreed to this ice cream, what makes you happy?"

Neil was quiet a moment then said, "Seeing my daughter grow into a beautiful woman; being with my grandson. I missed them when I was back east, but I didn't know how much until I came out here. I was too busy mourning my wife."

Janet spied him. She knew his wife had died in a car accident a few years back.

He shot her a half-smile. "So, now that I've answered your question, what makes you happy?"

Janet looked away, unwilling to meet his probing gaze. *Me, and my big mouth!* "I know you're not going to believe me, but I honestly don't know."

He frowned. "Now you're cheating."

"No, really, I mean it."

He quietly assessed her. "Okay, fair enough. Now that I think of it, not many of us know what makes us happy anymore."

"Sort of sad, isn't it?" she said as they came up to the ice-cream stand.

"Yeah, it is." He pulled a twenty out of his wallet and eyed her defiantly as she went for her purse.

They sat on a wooden bench beside the parlor under the soft yellow glow of a streetlight. The stand hummed with the chatter of adults and teens. Someone in line had a radio tuned to a rock station. Neil looked around at the patrons moving in and out of line and plowed into his cone. When he pulled back, Janet giggled.

"What's so funny?" he said, wiping his mouth.

"You attack that thing like it's gonna run away. Ice cream should be eaten slowly ... savored."

"Except when you're old," he said with a grin.

"Oh, please!"

He grunted. "Hey, I'm a grandfather now so that gives me the right."

"Really?" She eyed him as he shot her a cock-eyed look. "I think age is all in the head. If you think you're old; you are." She crossed her legs.

"Maybe." He paused and after a minute sat back. "If you asked most of these people here if they were happy right now, I bet they'd say they were, and for no other reason than they wouldn't want to be seen as gloom and doom."

"Good point. So do you fall into that category?"

He nodded and took another bite of his cone. "Sometimes. I mean, there are times when I feel good, like when I'm around family or when I'm busy doing something I enjoy. But being happy all the time ... I think that's impossible. If you were, you'd get pretty boring after a while."

"My thought, too. I wonder if people in church ever consider the down side of heaven. I mean, it's supposed to be no more tears and all that stuff."

He shrugged. "Never considered that before. Hmmm, there's more to you than meets the eye young lady."

"Young lady?" she said, and bit into her cone. Barney pressed his jaw onto her knee, letting her know he was waiting for a treat. She gave him a scratch behind the ear.

Neil said, "Well, you are to me."

"Uh-huh. But I think it has more to do with me being a woman than age. You know, women mature quicker than men."

"Yes, I've heard that."

"Well, it's true ... old man!" She stuck her tongue out at him and smiled.

"Ouch!" he said.

At that, she licked her finger and drew a '1' in the air. He shook his head and they both laughed. She said, "Shall we start back?"

He got up and took their napkins to the trash. When he returned, he had an odd look on his face as if he wanted to tell her something but didn't know how to go about it. They stood looking up at the sky, occasionally exchanging glances.

Clearing his throat, he pointed upward and said, "See that cluster of stars shaped like a 'W'? That's Cassiopeia. And the star to the right over there is Polaris."

Okay, where did that come from? Janet thought. "Yes, I know." She was about to point out Leo Minor but held back. "I see you're an astronomy buff."

He smiled. "Not really. Just dabble in it from time to time. You probably know more than I do. I better shut up before I make a fool of myself." He eyed her again. "This was fun."

"Yes, it was." She waited for him to make the first move back to the house. When he did, she added, "I was thinking about sitting out on the back deck. Would you like to join me? We could go over the next photo-shoot."

"Sounds like a plan," he said, and flashed a broad grin. "I think Meg has a bottle of wine floating around somewhere. We could keep our bones warm with it."

Janet cocked her brow. "Ice cream and wine?"

"But of course!" he said with a poorly rendered French accent.

"That was awful," she replied, and they both laughed.

As darkness crept in over Megan's back yard, they sipped wine and watched the lights in the upper windows of the houses around them turn on and off. The murmur of the TV trickled out from the den where Brad watched a game. Janet peered up at the sky. The raw beauty and incomprehensible ancientness of it always took her breath away.

Neil broke into her thoughts. "When I was a kid, we had a hammock out in the back yard. I used to climb into it at night and watch for shooting stars. My grandfather told me they were Orion's arrows."

Janet smiled. "Did you know early man used to believe each star represented a campfire of their ancestors?"

"No, I didn't. That's a neat thought."

"Yeah, it is," she muttered as Barney curled into a ball at her feet. Breathing in the night air, heavy with the perfume of stargazer lilies, she added, "Do you believe in a higher power?"

"You mean, God?"

"Yeah."

He sipped his wine and was quiet a moment. "Not in the traditional sense."

"Me neither," she agreed. "So, what do you believe?"

He chuckled quietly. "You really want to know?" When she nodded, he sat back. "A friend of mine, long ago, once told me he believed that Creation is becoming aware of its existence. He said to me ... 'Since all life comes from star-stuff, and man is asking questions about where the universe came from, then it stands to reason that humanity is the universe asking questions. It's becoming aware of itself, and it wants answers.' That, in a nut-shell, makes me believe there's something beyond our wildest imagination out there."

"That's a mind bender," she said, intrigued with the idea. "Sort of like a child asking questions of its parents."

"Exactly." He stretched his legs out in front of him. "So, what do you believe?"

"I don't know. I want to believe in something, but I don't know where to look," she replied, sinking into the warmth of her jacket. "I just know I don't want to go through life the way I was before the accident ... like an ant crawling on the ground."

She turned and looked at him. His face was hidden in deep shadow, but she could feel his eyes on her. "When I had the accident and I was trapped in the car, I remembered my father and me fishing at camp. I was eight. It was one of the few times I ever felt connected to him. Suddenly, in those last few moments, I wanted to see him one last time, tell him I loved him. It was then I realized some things really do matter, that life isn't about going through the motions." She fell silent.

Neil drained the rest of his wine. "You're right. Life isn't about going through the motions." He stood up. "This stuff is running right through me. Be right back."

Janet heard the sliding glass door swish open behind her. After he came back, she said, "So, what drew you to become an architect?"

He sat down with the bottle and refilled his glass. "Tell you the truth, it wasn't my first choice. I wanted to be an artist, work for one of the big ad studios in the city. I had excellent grades so I applied to Cooper Union."

"Cooper Union! Wow, you really shot for the top."

"Yeah, little did I know how high the top was. I knew I was screwed when I went down to the city for a visit and saw what I'd be competing against. I was good, but not that good." He sipped his wine. "So, after much brooding and feeling sorry for myself, I started exploring other areas and found architecture ... or it found me."

"I never viewed architecture as art before," she said. "I always thought it was just about construction: how you put a building together; engineering stuff."

Neil laughed. "That's what most people think. They don't realize buildings say a whole lot about a culture, a people. Take for example, the Empire State building. When you see it, you think of New York City. It's more than a building. It's a place, a presence people identify with. Same's true with the Eiffel Tower or Notre Dame Cathedral. Architecture is an expression for how we see our place in the world."

"I read a history book in high school that said no building in medieval Europe could stand taller than a cathedral spire."

"That's right." He set his wine glass down on the deck rail beside him. "In fact, architecture owes much to the religions of the world."

"Why's that?" Janet said.

"They pushed the envelope of engineering with their desire to create a house worthy of God, or gods, depending on what religion you're talking about. Take Notre Dame again. You walk inside, and marvel at the space. It's huge and yet you don't find any columns to speak of that support the roof which, by the way, is vaulted."

"How's that?" Janet said.

"They created what is known as flying buttresses. The columns supporting the roof and preventing it from spreading are on the outside. And then, there's the Pantheon with its dome of concrete spanning a hundred and fifty feet, give or take."

Janet eyed him suspiciously. "A hundred and fifty feet?"

"I'm not kidding." He paused and crossed his legs. "Only the religions of the world with their desire to please their gods could drive us to go beyond the bounds of accepted practice. And because of that, we have buildings like the World Trade Center, the Sydney Opera House, and domed stadiums.

The sounds of a car pulling in the driveway made them cock their heads. Barney sat up, ears pricked. "I think that's Megan," Neil said, getting up. "I'll be right back."

Janet glanced at her watch. *Wow, we've been out here for two hours.* She leaned back and relaxed as the doorbell rang. Barney barked at a strange voice murmuring through the house. Janet frowned. *Why's Megan ringing the doorbell?* Rising, she slid the door back and stepped inside. As Barney raced past her down the hall, she heard Neil's distraught voice.

"What? When? Is she all right? Where is she?"

8

After Janet shooed them off, Brad and Neil piled into Brad's truck and peeled out of the driveway, following the patrol car to the hospital. Megan had been found stabbed and raped near the dumpster at the back of the *Reporter's* parking lot.

Janet sat on the couch over the last three hours, nibbling her fingernails by the phone waiting for news. As she did so, the memory of what had happened to her years ago in a dark little room in her uncle's barn played over and over in her head.

Fucking monster! Janet bit back rage and tried to focus her thoughts on her friend. *Megan you have to be all right!* The baby cried out. She went to his room and cracked the door. In the sliver of the soft, gold light bolting in from the hallway, she saw him turn his head to look at her through the slats of the crib.

His deep blue eyes locked onto her. "Momma, momma."

Oh, God! She never thought she'd ever hear those words directed toward her. Children were never part of her life plan. But something deep inside stirred and she closed her eyes. Gathering strength, she opened them and went in. When he saw her close up, he cried, "Where momma? Momma?"

"She's not home right now, Kyle." She sniffed and felt his bottom. "You're wet. How 'bout we get you changed?"

He balled his hand up and rubbed his eyes as she laid him on the changing table. While she unbuttoned his layette, his innocent gaze penetrated her defenses, melting her anger and fear and the ugly memory that had taunted her for so long. In that moment, the child reached a part of her no one had ever touched, and a sudden tear leaked out of her eye.

The phone rang, rousing Janet from a fitful sleep. Lurching upright, she glanced at Kyle snuggled up in a blanket beside her on the couch with his hand clutching a little black, plush bear. The clock over the TV pointed to 3:05 AM. She braced herself and picked up the receiver. "Hello?"

"Janet ... Brad."

"How is she," she said, holding her breath.

"Stable. Just came out of surgery. No major damage, but she lost a lot of blood. How's Kyle?"

She ran her hand lightly over the little boy. Felt the rise and fall of his sleeping body. "He's fine."

Brad's reedy voice sounded strained and tired. "Good ... we're gonna be here awhile more. There's cereal in the cupboard above the toaster. Formula's in the cabinet under the silverware drawer. Three scoops to a bottle."

"Don't worry. We'll be fine." She paused. "You guys all right?"

"We're doing." He paused then said, "It's late. I better get going and let you get some sleep."

Janet yawned. "I'm okay. Say, what about the party? Can I call anyone? Let 'em know it's off?"

"Shit! I ... yes, if you wouldn't mind. Their numbers are in the address book on the kitchen counter. Wait, you don't know who's coming."

"You can let me know in the morning."

"Oh, duh! It's the middle of the night. Shit, look, I gotta go. And hey, thanks."

"No problem. Bye."

Brad hung up, and in the wake of the dial tone, Janet heard an unsaid, '*What if she doesn't make it?*'

Janet put Kyle down for an afternoon nap when she heard the front door open. She tiptoed out of the room and met Brad shuffling down the hall. Their eyes locked briefly, and a quick hello followed before he slipped into his bedroom. A moment later, she heard the shower turn on. *I'll put a pot of coffee on. He looks like he could use a cup.*

Her back was turned when he stepped into the kitchen twenty minutes later. She looked over her shoulder as she drained her third cup of coffee. Brad was shirtless and kneading his neck. A large black tattoo of a cobra sprawled across his chest. She never liked tattoos, so she averted her gaze.

"Meg hates it, too," Brad said, edging up to the island countertop.

Yeah! I can understand. It's hideous. "How is she?"

"Holding her own. She has multiple stab wounds. One of them grazed a blood vessel in her leg. Doctor called it ... a fem-a fem-something."

"Femoral artery," Janet said.

"Yeah, that's it. Anyways, she lost a lot of blood like I said, but she's gonna make it." He stretched his muscular arms out, gripped the edge of the countertop and stiffened his jaw. "They caught the asshole though. A convicted sex offender! Apparently, he saw Meg, Char, and Clancy come back from dinner last night. Staked the lot out and waited."

Brad blinked and Janet saw rage fill his dark brown eyes.

Trembling, he cleared his throat. "Meg parked near the dumpster, so obviously, she was his first choice."

He took a deep breath, releasing his savage grip on the countertop and tilted his head back. "How's Kyle?"

Janet drifted to the coffee maker, pulled a mug down from the cupboard and poured him a cup of coffee. "He's good. How's Neil?"

"All right, I guess," Brad replied, taking the mug. He slugged back a gulp and snuffed. "I'll be heading back up soon as I get changed and find his meds." He shook his head and stared into space. "You know what's sad?"

"What's that?" Janet said, watching him struggle to keep his composure.

"We had this fight yesterday afternoon. I was pissed 'cause she volunteered to work overtime. Which meant I had to pick up Kyle from daycare." He bit his lip and turned back to face her. "You know what I found in the back seat of her car when I went to pick it up this morning?"

Janet shook her head.

"A brand new set of clubs! Pings! She bought me fucking Pings! She'd been saving up for 'em all year. Am I an asshole or what?" He sucked down the rest of his coffee and ran a hand over his brow. "Anyway, Thanks for taking care of Kyle and for making coffee. Meg was right. You're aces." He set his cup down. "I guess it takes shit like this to find out who your friends are. I was wrong about you."

"Oh?"

"Well, yeah. You were never in my top twenty list."

Janet smiled dimly. "Well yeah, don't feel too bad. You weren't on mine, either." *And still aren't, but you're moving up.* "You better get going."

"Right." He turned and stepped out of the room.

Later that night, Janet set Kyle in his playpen and sat on the couch, watching him play with his toys. Her leg bothered her more than usual today. She rubbed it as Kyle looked up at her through the mesh of the playpen. He was quiet, studied her a minute then went back to playing.

She dragged the evening paper over from the table beside her. Glanced at the front page. Tried to take her mind off things but realized too late the paper was the last thing she should have run to. In the bottom, lower right hand corner, a headline in bold letters said, 'Reporter Employee Attacked in Parking Lot.'

She folded the paper up and tossed it in the trash.

Two days later –

Janet heard Brad's truck pull into the driveway as she sat on the back deck. The truck door shut and a minute later, she saw Neil raiding the refrigerator through the screen of the open sliding glass door.

"Hi. Let me make you a sandwich or something," she said, getting up.

"That's all right. I got it," Neil answered.

"You sure?"

He looked up while slathering jelly on a piece of bread. "Yeah, really." He slapped another piece of bread on top and stepped onto the back deck, sandwich in hand and went to the railing. She watched him while she played with Kyle. His worn eyes looked out over the yard.

After a minute, he turned and settled his bleary gaze on the baby. "You having fun with Janet?" he asked. The little boy looked up at him and then returned back to his growing pile of blue, yellow, and red blocks stacked around him.

"I think he wants to follow in grandpa's footsteps," Janet said. She picked another block up and handed it to Kyle. "How's Meg?"

"Better." Neil glanced out over the yard and took a bite of his sandwich. "She has some nerve damage in the right leg that'll need physical therapy. Other than that, they say she's fine..."

Janet glanced downward, recalling the difficult months she had gone through with rehab. "And you?"

He shrugged, and she saw him swallow hard. "I've been better." He watched his grandson play at her feet. "They're gonna discharge her tomorrow. Can you hang out a little longer?"

"Sure." *You have to ask?* "Hey, I was about to go in and get a glass of iced tea. You want one to go with that?"

He eyed his half-eaten sandwich. "Sure." After a deep breath, he drew his lips into a strained smile and went over to Kyle. Setting his sandwich down on a table, he said, "Can I play blocks with you?"

Kyle looked up. A beaming smile spread over his rosy cheeks as Neil lifted him into his arms. Janet watched them coo together then went inside. When she returned, Kyle was standing in Neil's lap and they were face to face. The little boy squealed and laughed as Neil tickled his ribs. When Neil saw Janet, he set Kyle back down on the deck.

"He's a good boy," she said, handing him his drink.

"Well, that's because he's easy to love," Neil said. He took a sip of his iced tea. As he set it beside his sandwich, the smile on his face faded. "I remember when Megan told me she was pregnant with him. I said to myself: Meg, you just got married. What're you thinking of? But inside, I was jumping up and down. I was going to be a grandpa."

Janet sat and buttoned her lip.

"I remember the day Meg was born. She was such a peanut. The nurse's nicknamed her 'the banshee.' Didn't believe them until one day Sharon calls me at work." He shook his head. "And all I hear is this raging scream with Sharon's voice somewhere in the background, saying 'We need formula—now!' Then a click."

Janet chuckled.

"My teeth rattled all the way to the store and back home. But this little guy over here ... he's a quiet one."

They watched Kyle stack blocks. "And a little builder, too," Janet put in.

"Yeah, he is," said Neil. "At least I'm able to see him more often now."

"Meg told me she has a brother, Trevor, is it? Have you called him yet?"

Neil drained the last of his tea and sighed. "Trev and I don't talk." He said, getting up and stepping to the railing.

Janet watched his gaze stray out over the yard. "Don't you think you should let him know?"

Neil turned, and for a moment she thought he might lash out, but he said nothing.

"He's her brother," she went on.

"I know that!" Neil snapped, furrowing his brow. "It's not like I don't want to. He won't take my calls."

"So, try again."

"No, I don't think so," Neil muttered, turning away and running a hand through his hair.

"This is his sister!"

"Yeah, and I'm his father," he spat back. "I'm sorry you're in the middle of this, but I'd rather you stay out of it." He turned his gaze back out over the yard.

Janet took a deep breath, fighting the powerful urge to tell him to grow up, and spun for the door. As she opened it, she heard Neil quake behind her. Turning, she saw his face buried in his hands. She looked upward at the overcast sky then walked to him. Standing with her hands hovering over his back, she debated what to do. Finally, she reached out and put her arms around him.

The next morning, Janet rolled over in bed, rubbed her eyes, and focused on the alarm clock. It was 5:15 AM. The night before had been a long one. Kyle had come down with the croup, and the little guy had been up most of the night keeping his father busy.

Megan was coming home today. That meant it would be the last day Janet would take care of Kyle. Not that she had minded. It just felt uncomfortably, too comfortable. She pushed the feeling away and thought of home and her bed with its nice fluffy pillows and familiar smelling sheets.

Flipping the covers back, she got up and slipped into her robe. As she tiptoed into the kitchen to make herself a cup of tea, she saw the faint outline of Neil's body on the sofa. He hadn't bothered to pull the sleeper out. She watched him as she waited for the water to boil and pressed her lips together, refusing to compare him with her own father. When the teakettle started to whistle, she whisked it off the burner so it wouldn't wake anyone.

After fixing her tea, she padded to the sliding glass door and stepped into the first dim light of dawn settling on the valley. Sipping her drink, she went to the back of the deck and watched the approaching sunrise lift the muted grays from the trees.

Several minutes later the glass door behind her swooshed open. She turned, half expecting Neil, but found Brad bare to the waist heading toward her in old tattered blue jeans. She turned and looked back out over the yard. "Couldn't sleep?"

He stepped up beside her and stretched his arms over his head. "Nope."

"Long night," she said.

"That, it was," he mumbled. "I was thinking some coffee might be in order?"

She ignored the implied order for her to wait on him and eyed him as he reached into his pants pocket. Pulling a pack of cigarettes out, he put one to his mouth and lit it.

"Don't say nothing to Meg 'bout this, okay? I promised her I'd quit." He shook the match, snuffing the flame and dropped it over the rail.

Janet shrugged. "So give it up."

Brad smiled crookedly. "I will. Just not right now." He took a drag and blew out a ring of smoke. "She's different. Barely says a word. It's so not like her. Like someone came and took her place, someone I don't know. I keep telling myself she'll snap out of it. She'll be back to jabbering. But then I go back up there, and she's still the same."

He sucked in another drag and laughed bitterly. "You know, I used to wish she'd shut the hell up and take a breather once in a while. Right now, I'd give my fucking right arm to hear her motor mouth."

He drew another drag and flicked the ash-head over the rail. "She's never gonna be the same, is she? I mean, how could she be?" He paused, knotting his brow. "I love her, but I'm not sure I can do this."

"One step at a time," Janet said, feeling her radar go up.

"Yeah, I suppose," Brad said. He took a deep breath.

Meaning what? Janet thought. She suppressed her urge to tell him to be a man, and said, "She needs you. Be there for her."

His sighed. "I'm trying. It's hard though. I mean, how do ya deal with being afraid to touch your own wife?"

"You do it by remembering why you married her in the first place," Janet said, quietly.

"Yeah," he muttered. His gaze went inward then and Janet could see him debating some unknown thought. At last he cleared his throat, and tossing his cigarette over the rail, said. "Well, guess I better get showered."

Brad and Neil pulled in the driveway with Megan at noon. Janet scooped up Kyle from his playpen and scurried to the door. When Kyle saw his mother, he put his arms out. Megan smiled while she hobbled up the front walk.

Janet's heart drummed. *This can go really good or really bad.*

"Hi baby," Megan said. She leaned forward, and with a slight grimace, pulled her son out of Janet's arms. "Were you a good boy while Mommy was gone?"

Kyle shook his head and coughed.

Megan wrinkled her brow and pushed a lock of Kyle's hair off his face. "You're not feeling well, are you pumpkin?" She glanced at Janet.

"He has the croup. Started last night. Brad called the doctor. I took him in this morning." To Brad, Janet said, "There's a script on the kitchen table that needs filling."

"Well, I'm home," Megan said as though that implied everything would get back to normal. Janet glanced at Brad, but he looked away and went around them through the front door. "Let's get inside," Megan said.

9

Janet nibbled on a piece of toast while watching Megan gaze out the sliding glass door. It was just after eight. The steady drizzle pattering the deck since dawn had finally given up. In the distance, an island of blue peeked through a slate gray sky. Brad had left for work an hour ago. Kyle sat in his highchair munching animal crackers while noisily playing with his food.

Megan turned her attention onto him. "Eat your cracker, honey," she said, wiping a line of drool off his chin. The little boy took a nibble and went back to humming loudly. Megan smiled and looked back out the window, a lock of hair coiled around her finger. "Rained hard last night," she said.

"Yes, it did," Janet replied.

"Did it wake you?"

"Once."

"I couldn't sleep," Megan went on, her gaze still fixed on the sliding glass doors. "I used to love listening to the rain and the low rumble of thunder. When I was a kid in Akron, I'd get in my bathing suit and run around in it."

"I still do," Janet said, curling her lips into a smile.

Megan was quiet a moment then said, "So, what time you leaving?"

Janet set her cup down. "Around one."

Megan nodded. "I'm not going back to the *Reporter*."

"I know," Janet said.

"I mean, I just can't," Megan whispered. "Just the thought of stepping outside right now scares the hell out of me." She buried her head in her hands and burst into tears. "I keep seeing his face, his eyes."

Janet reached across the table and put her hand on Megan's shoulder. Megan flinched.

"What am I gonna do? I can't sleep, I can't take care of Kyle, I can't even take care of myself," Megan cried, hunched over. Her trembling fingers groped for Janet's hand, and when they found it, squeezed tightly. "I'm such a fucking mess."

Janet bit back tears.

Megan tilted her head up, her bleary eyes desperately seeking answers Janet knew she couldn't give. "My father, he tried to put his arms around me yesterday, but I pushed him away," Megan said. "I pushed my father away! What the hell is that all about? What am I gonna do? Everything has gone to shit."

Kyle dropped his bowl, shattering the moment. Janet leaned over and picked it up. As soon as she put it on his tray, he picked it up and dropped it again.

"Okay, Kyle, up you go," Janet said. She lifted him out of his highchair and took him into the other room to play in his playpen. When she returned, she pulled Megan up out of her chair. "Come, there's something I want to share with you."

Janet pulled the sliding glass door open and led Megan onto the deck. "I never told anybody this until now," Janet said, "but we now share something together."

"What?" Megan muttered.

"I was raped," Janet said, and paused while the words hung between them. "I was thirteen. We, my mother and father and Craig, used to go to my uncle's farm in Redfield on the weekends. One day my uncle cornered me in the barn." She took a deep breath and forced herself to go on. "No one knew what happened. I mean, how could I say anything? He was my uncle. No one would believe me. I still remember every second of it."

"So he got away with it?"

"Not entirely. Life evened things up with a stroke not long afterward."

"Well, I guess that's something," Megan said and chewed her lip. She was quiet a minute then said, "So, you got over it then?"

Janet shook her head. "Get over it? You don't. You survive it, get a little stronger every day. Beat it back because if you give up, he wins!" There was a long silence between them while they stood looking out into the distance. Somewhere, beyond the patchwork of fences, a dove could be heard cooing.

Megan broke the quiet between them. "I'm not sure I can."

Janet turned and took Megan's hands in hers. "Yes, you can! And you will." Megan shook her head, but Janet lifted her hand, held Megan's chin and looked deep into her frightened eyes. "Look at me! You're not alone. I'm here! I know you can't see the future right now; neither could I, but I made it," she added, and pulled Megan into her arms and held her fiercely as all the old memories flooded back. "You can, too."

"I don't know," Megan said.

Janet pulled back, looked into Megan's tragic gaze. She had no magical answers for Megan only that she was going to be there for her. "I want you to know, I love you, Megan. I've never had a real best friend before, until now. You are my best friend."

Megan blinked back tears. "And you are mine."

After they all ate lunch, Neil went outside. He had been quiet all morning. Janet watched him through the living room window. He sat on the porch steps, elbows on his knees. He lifted a hand, ran it through his hair, and looked down at the steps. She wished there was something she could say to ease his pain, but there weren't any words nor would there ever be for times like these. She turned away and put her overnight bag next to the door.

Megan was in the kitchen, staring out the window. It was time for Janet to go, but how could she take Neil away in a time like this? She thought about leaving him there and coming back for him or maybe Brad could bring him back.

She opened the door, went out, and sat beside him. "I was thinking maybe you'd like to stay a little longer. I have to go, but I could return later on."

"Thanks, but no. I have to get back for a meeting."

"Look, I know it's none of my business, but I think you should stay."

He looked up and considered her with a bleary gaze. "If she were alone, I'd agree. But Brad's here. The kids need some time alone."

She hadn't thought of it that way. "Then can I make another suggestion?"

"Sure."

She cleared her throat and screwed up her courage. "I don't know for sure, but I can almost guarantee it that if you go in and wrap your arms around her, she wouldn't push you away. She needs to feel safe, Neil. She needs to know there's someone in the world she can trust again. And that person is you. You're her father. Be that father. For her!"

Two hours later, they were on the road listening to the murmuring radio. As she drove, Janet could still see Megan's head buried in her father's shoulder. She allowed herself a tiny smile as she turned onto Route 22.

Neil looked at her. "I want to thank you."

"For what?"

"For pushing me to do the right thing. It's not like I didn't want to, I just didn't know how."

She smiled. "Not many of us do."

"But you did. So what gave you such insight into my Meg?"

Janet shook her head. "Intuition."

"You continue to surprise me."

"Oh?"

"Yeah. Just when I think I have you pegged, you do something that throws it all out of whack."

She laughed. "Well, that's good to know. So, what did you have me pegged for?"

He looked at her sidelong. "You really wanna know?"

"Well … on second thought, no." She cocked her head and drummed her fingers on the steering wheel as James Taylor's, 'Fire and Rain' came on. An idea had been simmering in her mind for the last hour. *He could use some time away from the world and so could I. Why not?* "Hey, I just had a thought."

"Wow—just one?"

She smacked him on the arm. "Very funny. Anyway, I'm thinking it might be fun to take a drive out to the coast."

"Now?"

"Why not?" She glanced at him. He wasn't frowning, so she pressed ahead. "It's only an extra hour and a half. And the way I look at it, it'd be good for both of us. Ever been to Depoe Bay?"

"Can't say as I have."

"Then it's time you saw it."

After they dropped Barney off, along with Janet's overnight bag, they headed down toward the coast. They came to Lincoln City as traffic was picking up. Her gaze bounced around as she aimed down the four-lane main route bisecting the ocean-side city. Neil's gaze strayed toward the ocean, which now and then peeked through whitewashed one-story buildings. Parked cars angled up to the curbs as they drove through what her father called a 'one light town.' Here and there, a mini mall or a grocery store popped up. Beyond them, steep muted tors ran down to unseen beaches. Their ragged tops lined with naked, wind-blasted cypress.

She pulled up to a stoplight.

"There's a restaurant ahead," Neil said. He pointed to a rustic wood shingled building with neon lights in the window.

"You hungry?"

"I could eat."

She nodded. "Okay, but I've another place in mind in that case."

They followed the road as it wove back and forth along the coastline through Gleneden Beach and past Fogarty State Park until they came to the little harbor town of Depoe Bay. At the north edge of town stood a modest A-frame restaurant overlooking the water. They pulled in next to it and parked. Neil got out and strode to the wooden rail running along the ocean side of the lot. Beyond it was a precipitous drop.

She joined him, her gaze panning the wide sweeping vista. To her right a peninsula of rock dotted with scrub and a few spindly pines ran out to the crashing waves. She followed its out-stretched crooked finger to the restless waters. In the past, she'd seen Humpbacks and Rights migrating north off this point. There were none today.

"Shall we?" she said, nodding toward the restaurant behind them.

He glanced at her and they headed for the door. "Sharon would've liked this place."

Janet considered him a moment. "Can I ask you a question?"

"Shoot."

"Have you ever imagined life with someone else?"

He opened his mouth, but nothing came out. Finally, he said, "No, not really."

"Why?"

He shrugged. "Never had the time."

"Or wanted to?" she added.

"I guess, maybe. Like I said, I don't really know," he replied.

"Maybe you should start," she said.

After dinner, they went north to Fogarty State Park. It was turning dusk when they pulled into the empty lot. After they parked, they trudged under the overpass of the highway out to the beachhead. A snaking path through the high, soughing grasses led them to a giant desiccated log under a canvas of battered and mottled clouds.

"Sometimes, I feel like such a clod," he said, popping his shoes off and rolling up his soiled pants legs.

"So what? You spilled coffee on the table. It's been done before."

He looked at the stain on his shirt and pressed his lips together. "Right."

She rolled her eyes, tossed her sneakers under the log they sat on and got to her feet. She reached her hand toward him. "Come on slow-poke. Time to get your feet in the water."

He frowned. "Slow-poke?"

"Yeah." She laughed, and it brought a dim smile to his face. Their eyes locked for a moment, then he turned away and stashed his shoes next to hers under the log.

They walked past the dunes to the water a hundred yards away, pressing their feet into the shifting sand. As they went, the weight of last week lifted from Janet's step.

He said, "I feel like a kid again."

"Good, it's the way you're supposed to feel."

"You come here a lot?"

She pulled a lock of hair away from her face. "As often as I can."

"It's nice. I like it."

"Better than nice. Oh, look, a seal. See him? Just beyond those rocks." She stopped and pointed out to a dark spot stabbing through the roiling water. "They come ashore sometimes during orca migrations. Safer here than out there."

He watched the animal bob in the water until the creature barrel-rolled and disappeared. They walked a little further until they came to a wet sandy mat fleeing to the water's edge. At length, she turned and said, "Remember when we were talking about God and stuff?" When he nodded, she went on, "Well, this is my Church, and the spirit of the water is my God."

He gazed out over the water to the setting sun veiled in cloud. "Do you think your prayers are heard?"

She shrugged. "Maybe, sometimes. I think the question is more, 'do we want to hear the answers?' "

"Right," he said, companionably.

They walked a bit more and as they did, Janet felt the urge to have a little fun. "Race you to the water?"

"Seriously?"

She winked at him. "Loser buys dinner next time."

Neil eyed her sidelong then glanced at the surf twenty yards away. "I think you're trying to weasel a free meal here, but okay, you're on."

They stopped and lined up, then burst ahead. But Janet had no intention on winning, and as soon as he got ahead of her, she came to a halt and watched him rush into the surging foam. "Damn, but it's cold," he cried.

"It's the ocean," she yelled back. She watched him splash around in the water.

He turned around. "Why do I get the feeling I was just had?"

"Probably because you were," she called back.

He batted at the waves piling around his legs. "You brat!"

Grinning, she watched him dance around in the surf, then set off for her special place. Hidden in shadow behind her, the massive rock of sandstone dug deep into the sloping bluffs. She climbed its craggy side and sat in its crook.

After a little while, Neil joined her. They sat and talked about Megan; how she brought out the best in him, teaching him patience, showing him the simplicity of life through the eyes of a child. And then the conversation shifted to Sharon; how he missed her. He knew he had to let her go, but he couldn't figure out how to do it. Janet listened, offering her silence and attention as he spoke, until at last he rubbed his neck and looked up. The sky was dark, but a pale light coming off the street lamps above the bluff bathed them in its glow. "Well, it appears we've yammered into the evening." He nodded back toward the overpass. "We ought to get back."

She conceded reluctantly. She had enjoyed her time with him today more than she could've thought possible. She forced away the subtle impulse to let him know how much she was beginning to like him and climbed down.

He scrambled after her, but the last step down off the rock to the sand was tricky and he lost his balance. He put his hand on a ledge to steady himself, but it was too little, too late. Without a thought, her hand shot out and grabbed his arm. The next thing she knew, they were rolling in the sand and laughing. She stood and brushed her blouse off as he got to his knees. When he looked up, his expression lost its smile and melted into a tender gaze. Her breath ran away, and her heart thudded as she looked back at him, understanding his unsaid words. It was all she could do to turn her gaze away.

The following week slid by without further word from Neil. Janet scolded herself as the thought of him entered her mind for the umpteenth time. She pulled down her travel case from the shelf in her bedroom closet and plopped it on her bed. In an hour, she'd be off to Crater Lake for two weeks. *Should I call him? Let him know I'm out of town. What if he tries to get a hold of me for another shoot?*

Oh, stop. If he has a job, it'll wait 'till you get back. What you really want is to hear his voice. Admit it, you like him. A lot! Christ, he's Megan's father though! This is nuts. Pack! You have a four-hour drive ahead.

October 13, 1981 -

Janet returned home from Crater Lake two weeks later. On her answering machine were several messages. She unleashed Barney and set her bag in her room. After she fed the dog, she hit the replay button. The first message was from her father. He had called to let her know he found a place a few miles west of her in Dallas. He would be moving out west next month.

She deleted the next few messages from telemarketers promising free trips and merchandise, then heard Megan's voice on the machine. She pulled a chair up and listened. Things were a little better at home. Brad was trying hard to be supportive. She had been offered work at a local non-profit paper in Salem. But there were still elements of grief and isolation in her voice. *I need to call her, see about getting together, maybe next week,* she thought.

Janet went to the fridge and grabbed a cola off the top shelf as the machine announced, "Wednesday, October 7, 1981."

"Janet, Neil here."

She jerked around.

"Give me a call when you get in. I have another project for you. Talk soon."

October seventh was six days ago. Another message followed. She moved closer as the machine announced the next date. "Friday, October 9, 1981." "Janet, Neil here again. You must be out of town. If you get this before Monday, give me a shout. Thanks."

"Shit," she muttered. She dug her address book out of her purse and flipped it open to Neil's number. As she was about to pick up the phone, it rang. She jumped. "Hello?"

"Janet, Mick."

"Oh, hi," she said. She knew it was silly, but she was hoping it was Neil then remembered she was out of a job.

"You sound excited to hear from me," Mick said with a note of sarcasm in his voice.

"Sorry, I was expecting someone else."

"Right ... anyway, I was wondering if you'd like a gig. It's not a big one, but I thought you might want it. That is unless the other rag down the street has you roped in."

Janet paused. "Actually, I never checked them out."

"Where you been then? I called a couple of times and no answer."

"You did? There wasn't anything on my machine."

"You know I don't leave messages. So ... umm, where ya been?"

"Crater Lake."

"You're working then?"

She hesitated. "Sort of."

"For who?"

"Mick!"

"All right. So what about it?"

"What about what?" *And why isn't he saying anything about Meg?*

"The gig. You want it or not?"

She drummed her nails on the counter. "Sure, I'll take it."

"Humph ... Don't go nuts over it."

She shook her head. "Have you talked to Megan lately?"

He was quiet a moment. When he spoke, his voice dropped. "Yeah, I called her shortly after she got home from the hospital. She's left the *Reporter*."

"Yes, I know." *And that has to do with ... what?* She paused, letting the silence speak for her.

She heard Mick clear his throat. "I can't believe what happened. I should've walked her out. I mean ... that could've been Vicky." He paused. "They got the bastard, though, and I'm watching how it's all handled. One screw up, and I'll splash it all over the paper."

Janet could understand he was angry but it wasn't going to help Megan. "Let's hope they lock him up for a long time."

"Ditto." Another pause, and Janet could hear the sound of a cigarette being lit. "Guess I can't blame her for leaving."

"No, you can't."

"Say ... look, I better let you go."

"Wait a minute," Janet said. "When do you want me to come in?"

"Oh, yeah. Next week. How's Monday? Around ten?"

"That works."

"Okay, see you then. And take it easy." There was a click on the other end. When the line went dead, she pushed the button down and waited for a dial tone. It wasn't until the third ring that she realized it was 3:00 PM. Neil wouldn't be home for another hour and a half.

She thought about hanging up when his machine picked up. She didn't like leaving messages, but it was just business, so she waited for the beep. "Hi, it's Janet. I'm back. Too late it seems, but give me a call anyway."

After showering and emptying her travel bag, Janet sat at the kitchen table going over her receipts from the trip. Her bank account had taken a heavy hit, and if she couldn't sell anything, she'd be eating spaghetti and sauce for the foreseeable future.

She sighed and pulling her budget sheet next to her, played musical chairs with the numbers. An hour later, she was no closer to making things work. Crumpling the sheet of fuzzy math work, she tossed it into the trashcan. Suddenly, the phone rang making her jump. She picked it up, and answered.

"Hey, you're in! Where you been? I've been trying to reach you."

"Neil!" She leaned back against the chair and tried to compose herself. "I'm sorry I missed your call. I was at Crater Lake doing a shoot. So, what juicy job did I miss out on?"

He chuckled on the other end. "I don't know about juicy, but I do have another one if you're up for it."

She took a deep breath, trying to suppress her excitement. With forced calmness, she said, "Of course ... Where, when?"

"Next week, in Seattle."

"Seattle?" She blinked and let out another breath. "Umm ... That's a haul."

"Oh, we won't be driving."

"So we're flying?" she said. When he confirmed it, she added, "For how long?"

"Probably three, four days, tops."

She squeezed her eyes shut. "I can't. I have no place to put Barney."

"What about a kennel?"

"No way. I'm not leaving him in one of those places."

"I see," he said, and she heard the disappointment in his voice. "Well, I suppose we'll have to pass on this one then. Oh, by the way, I trust you got my rent check?"

The rest of the air went out of her. "Yeah, I'll deposit it tomorrow. Gee, I'm sorry I can't do it. I really want to. It's just that Barney's family, and putting him in a kennel, even for one day would—"

"Don't worry about it, okay?" He didn't say anything for a minute, and she wondered if he was still there. "Hey, I was ... umm, thinking on heading over to Jake's. Would you ... would you be interested in joining me?"

Janet blinked and sat forward as her heart began to beat again. She eyed her beleaguered checking account. Even with the rent check, she'd be scraping by the rest of the month. *I'll have a salad ... and a glass of water.* "Ummm ... yeah, sure. When?"

"Half hour. Meet you there, say around seven?"

"Seven, oh, okay." *That leaves me what ... about twenty minutes to put myself together. And what am I gonna wear?* "By the bar, right?"

"Sure. See you then."

When he hung up, she ran for the bedroom. *Okay, I have the white top with the lace around the collar. It might work with my new jeans. Or, or ... the light blue blouse. Yeah, that's it.* She tore through her chest of drawers while Barney watched from the doorway. *It's just business; nothing more. Oh, my God, what am I doing?* Her hand reached for the phone to call him back and cancel then pulled back as if she'd been bitten.

10

Janet lay in bed, staring up at the ceiling. The spray of the soft pale light came through her window, casting dim shadows across the room. For the last hour, she wrestled an unaccustomed persistent feeling she was not used to: wanting to be more than just a man's bed buddy. Neil's parting words at Jake's last night lingered in her mind, and she still felt his friendly hug. *Why am I so drawn to him? And does it show?*

She gazed at Barney, who lay on the foot of her bed. She never thought she could feel anything more than a passing attraction for anyone. She didn't want to, or have to for that matter. There were always guys at Jake's available for the occasional romp when the urge took her. But now, things were different. Megan's rape and her accident showed her how quickly things could be taken away.

She took a deep breath as her thoughts swept back to Neil. *Fine, I'm attracted to him. But there's no reason to rush it. Hmmm ... I wonder what it would be like to kiss him.* She blinked, surprised at the thought, and smiled.

The following week, Janet headed to Lincoln City to see Tom. She called him the other day and his distant responses raised a silent alarm in her heart. As she drove past shops and fast food joints, she wondered what was going on with him.

She turned left and followed a narrow paved road bordered with tall waving grasses that melted into a one-lane dirt road. At the end of it stood a small A-framed house atop a ragged bluff that overlooked the ocean. As she parked, Tom came out the side door, carrying a bucket.

He set it down when he saw her. "Well, hello. How's my girl?" he said, marching over to greet her.

She eyed him. He hadn't shaved in a while, and wore a paint stained flannel plaid shirt. Through the front window she saw an easel. He was painting again. There was also a hint of alcohol on his breath. She wrinkled her nose. "I see you've taken the brush back up."

He shrugged. "A little. Something ta pass the time." He slapped his hands against his pant leg, raising a cloud of dust. "Come inside. Got a pot a Joe on if you're interested."

"Well, actually, I thought we'd go out for a bite. To that little diner off Seashore Drive you like."

"I'm not much on going out these days," he said. He considered her with his flashing gray eyes. Rubbed his grizzled face. "But I guess I could for you."

She reached out and put her hand around his bony wrist. "Are you all right?"

His gaze slanted out over the rolling hillside. "Yeah, sure." When she cocked her brow, he eyed her defiantly. "I'm old." He blinked, and a far away expression swept over his thin, windburnt face. Finally, he came back to himself. "Well, I better get changed if we're going out."

She followed him through the side door. When he left her to get changed, she drifted into the living room. The last time she was here, there was a couch and chairs on a large oriental blue rug. It had since been converted into a studio.

She spread her gaze out over the wooden floor littered with half-painted canvases and charcoal study sketches. In the far corner sat the easel she had seen from outside. She crept over and looked at the face taking shape on the canvas.

On it, deep brown eyes stared back at her. They were grave and focused, as if they looked straight through her. *She's beautiful.* Suddenly, Tom was beside her. He pulled the sheet over the canvas, gave Janet a firm gaze that was neither angry nor sad, then left the room.

Janet frowned; then it hit her. *That's his daughter.* Her thoughts drifted back to June telling her about the girl's suicide. Janet suddenly felt like an intruder, and as she looked around, realized the room had been turned into a private memorial.

"Okay, I guess I'm ready," Tom said. He had shaved and put on a denim shirt that hung loosely on his boney shoulders. A pair of faded blue jeans hugged his slender hips.

Fifteen minutes later, they sat in a booth at the back of a quaint little diner. It was a favorite of Tom's because he knew the waitresses, but more than that, he liked looking out the windows over the busy little harbor, watching fishing boats putter back and forth over the dark turbid waters. They ordered, and as they waited for their meals, she told him about her new gig with Neil's firm. He smiled and congratulated her, then his gaze drifted off around the paneled, pine walls dotted with watercolor paintings of the northern pacific coastlines.

"I went to the doctor last week," he said quietly. His eyes bent back onto her. "I've got a problem with my prostrate." He sighed. "I've decided to move back to Kansas to be near my brother and his wife. Time to give up the life of a vagabond. Hope that's not gonna put you in a bind."

"No, of course not," Janet said as the waitress brought their drinks.

He nodded, doctored his coffee and took a sip, then sat back as the waitress came with their orders. After they were alone again, he doused his french-fries with catsup and said, "Paintings are yours if ya want 'em."

Janet sighed. This was not the conversation she wanted to have. She steeled herself, and leaning forward, searched the old careworn face across from her. "Don't you want them?"

He ate another French fry. "Not really."

"What about your kids?"

He looked up at her. "They have plenty of 'em, 'sides, I know ya like 'em."

Janet didn't know what to say. Finally, she cleared her throat. "Thanks, I'll treasure them. When you planning on moving?"

"Next month, I think. You can sell what there is of my furniture. I won't be needing it." He leaned forward and gave her a crooked smile. "I'll be okay. Can't say I won't miss ya though. You've been a daughter to me." He averted his gaze then, and Janet knew why. The loss of his little girl so many years ago still gripped him like a fisherman's knot.

After Janet got home, she picked up the phone and dialed Neil's number. As it rang, she thought about Tom. Already, she missed him. Perhaps Neil could take her mind off it.

"Hello?" Neil said, sounding as if he'd been woken up. She peered out through the window at the veiled moon that was drifting in and out of clouds and looked up at the clock. It was going on ten.

She paused. "Hi."

His voice brightened. "Janet?"

"I'm sorry. I just noticed what time it is."

"No, it's all right. What's up?"

She eyed Barney, unsure of how to continue without sounding like an idiot. "I'm sorry. I'll call back tomorrow."

"No, no. Go ahead, please," he said in an encouraging tone.

"Okay." She looked up at the ceiling. "The reason I called was to ask if you'd like to get together sometime soon, so I can pay off that dinner bet."

"Sure. You sound odd. Everything okay?"

"Umm … Yeah. I just feel like having someone to talk to."

"Okay."

She bit her lip. "Not over the phone. My place?"

"Sure. When?"

"Tomorrow night?"

"I have a meeting in Corvallis at four tomorrow," he said. "I could be there around seven."

"That'll be fine," she replied. "See you then?"

"I'll be there. You need me to bring anything?"

"No, just yourself."

"Okay. You have a good night, now."

"Thanks. You too. Bye." She hung up and ran her hand through her hair. *Oh, my God, what does he like?* She went to her cupboards. There wasn't much there. She hadn't cooked for anyone in a long time.

"That was great," Neil said, pushing away from the table. "I haven't had salmon in a long time."

"It's my favorite," Janet said, rather proud of herself but a little nervous. She got up and started clearing the table.

"Sit down," he said companionably. "You've been running around since I got here."

She forced herself to sit, eyeing the dirty dishes and the butter crying to go back in the fridge. "You don't mind the mess?"

"Mess?" he said. "It's just a few dirty dishes. Relax. I'll help you clean up afterward." He paused, sipped his wine, and looked at her speculatively. "So you wanted to talk?"

"Let's go outside," she said, partly to get away from the clutter on the table, but mostly to buy some time to think about how much she should say about Tom. When they were sitting on her deck, she said, "I … I went to see Tom yesterday. Do you remember him?"

Neil swished his wine in the glass, his gaze never leaving her. "Sure."

"He was my aunt's tenant, and he's like a second father to me. Anyway, he's umm ... he's moving back east to be with his kids."

Neil was quiet a moment. At last he said, "What're you gonna do?"

She nodded. "Not sure."

"And now you have another empty house to contend with?"

"Yeah," she said. "Right now I'm debating whether I should keep the cottage or sell. I'm curious; what would you do?"

Neil rubbed his chin. "Oceanfront, right?"

She nodded.

"It'd fetch a good penny."

"My father's sentiments, exactly."

Neil shrugged. "You want to keep it?"

Janet's thoughts went to the expense of up-keeping the property and the taxes. Up until now, the rent had always covered the money end of things and Tom had covered the rest. "I'd like to."

"Then keep it," he said.

She looked off over her yard.

"Ah, now we come to it. Cash flow," Neil said.

"Something like that," Janet replied.

Neil downed the rest of his wine. "Why not rent it out again."

Janet shook her head. "I really don't want to. Being a landlord to one tenant is enough."

Neil curled his lips. "So, I'm just a tenant."

"You know what I mean," she said and reached over and cuffed his arm.

He feigned injury. "I think I deserve another glass of wine for that. Want some?"

She rolled her eyes. "Sure."

He got up and went inside. Through the glass door, she could see him gazing back at her. She stood and went to the railing, thinking about what he said.

Neil stepped back out and came beside her. "Here," he said, handing her a glass.

"Thanks." She offered him a smile. "You really liked the meal?"

"It was great," he said. "In case you don't know it, I'm not exactly prime domestic material, so this was a real treat. Nice place, too." He put his hands on the rail and looked off over the back fence toward the hills. "You know, married people forget what it's like being single."

"Oh?"

"Yeah. You're it when it comes to taking care of things," he said, listing off his routine chores.

"You forgot cleaning," Janet added.

"Yeah, that too." He gave her a sidelong glance. "You like movies?"

She shrugged. "They're all right. Why?"

"There's one I've been wanting to see." He cleared his throat and casually said, "Thought maybe we could go together."

"Really?" she replied, fighting the impulse to grab her purse and drag him out the door. She eyed her watch. "We'll have to hurry."

"Actually, I was thinking of tomorrow."

"Sounds like a date?" she said. "You sure you wanna be seen with a younger woman? People might talk."

A devilish grin played on Neil's lips. "You said I needed to get out, remember? So, what about it?"

"I don't know. Depends."

"On what?" he replied, raising his brow."

"On what your expectations are. I don't kiss on the first date. I have my reputation to think of, you know."

He laughed, but the idea of being on a date with him made her heart pound. She jabbed him with a friendly elbow, praying the grin on her face hid the giddy terror thumping in her chest.

11

Janet patted her bed signaling Barney to hop up and join her. It was around ten. Neil had dropped her off an hour ago. They had driven to Lincoln City and spent the day window-shopping in gift shops lining the streets along the harbor inlet. Neil looked for artwork to brighten up his living room walls. She went along because he wanted to make sure he wasn't paying too much, but she knew it was because he wanted her company. After much teasing, he grudgingly admitted to it on their way there. They ended up at Jake's on the way back for dinner.

"Did you have fun driving around with Mommy and Neil today?" Janet said to the dog as he licked her neck. "Mommy did." She gazed off toward the window into the star spattered sky, wondering if Neil had wanted to kiss her on the doorstep but didn't know how to approach it.

She let go of the dog and turned the night-light off. As she lay in the darkness, she debated the merits of her growing fondness for Neil. *I like him. He's fun ... and nice, and he doesn't try to fix me. And another thing–he's not a wolf looking for a piece. That's nice. And what's wrong with hanging out with him anyway, even if he is older? Okay, a lot older! It's not like we're sleeping together. He is cute in a cuddly sort of way, though. Oh, shit, where did that come from? No! Stop it! He's Megan's father.*

But the thought of being in bed together, of feeling his calloused hands caressing her was staring straight back at her. Would he be any different than other men she'd known? Sex was just sex to them. You lost yourself in the moment, and when it was over, you both rolled over and went to sleep or you got out of bed, got dressed and left.

She flipped the light on. Barney looked up. *I need to stop thinking about this. Maybe get something to read.* She padded over to the bookshelf in her room. *Capote? No, it's a little late to be terrorized by him. Bradley? Too dense. I need something light: Keats, too flowery; Frost, maybe ... nah. What's this?* She pulled a small box off the shelf and opened it. *Oh, the letters Tom gave me the day we cleaned June's house out.*

She brought the tattered box back to her bed, climbed up beside it, and sat with her legs crossed yoga style. Pulling the lid off, she saw an old manila envelope faded to almost white. She reached in, took it out and unwound the string that held the flap shut, and slid the contents out. As she sifted through it, she saw several letters between her aunt and father. Curious, she picked them out and read them one by one, and as she did so, felt a frown come to her face. Something about her mother having an affair with another man. She looked at the dates the letters were written, but they offered no clue regarding when it had happened. She picked another one up that was addressed to her father. It was a recent letter, the paper crisp and white. Unfolding it, she read:

William

I've thought about this for a long time and I've decided it's time for you to let Janet know the truth. You owe it to her, and if you don't say anything, I will. I know this will upset you and I also understand I'm stepping out of line, but you and Janet will never have a chance to start healing until she's told you're not her father.

Her sight went dim, and the letter fell from her hand. She sat motionless, grasping to make sense of what she'd just read. Picking it back up, she reread the words again and again. Suddenly, her whole life was a lie, and she didn't know who she was. Mindlessly, she dropped it to the floor and walked out of the room in a daze.

She wanted to run–to disappear–but to where, and did it matter? Grabbing her keys, she stepped into the garage careless that she only had a sleeping shirt on and opened the car door. Forty-five minutes later, she stood beside her mother's grave. Her father wasn't her father anymore. She wasn't sure who he was, except that he wasn't hers.

In the twilight, she knelt on the grass wet with dew staring ahead into the nothingness, wanting answers. More than that, she wanted to pound her mother's chest, to scream at her, but only a muffled cry came. "Why did you lie to me? You all lied to me! Why, Mom? Now I know why Dad always looked at me like I was an intruder. Except he's not my dad. I don't know who he is."

She glared at the flowers she'd planted a year ago, waving in the gentle breeze caressing the grounds. They were like bratty children sticking their tongues out, making fun of her. She bent over them, and one by one, ripped them from the ground.

The next morning, Janet woke on her living room couch under a soft blanket to find Neil asleep in the recliner next to her. She bolted upright and blinked into the shadows, wondering if she was dreaming, but no, he was there, gently snoring. *What, why ... oh, shit.* She shut her eyes tight as the memory of last night suddenly crashed around her, crushing her all over again.

"Janet, you all right?" Neil said, sitting up.

He leaned forward as she curled into a fetal position and buried her head in between her arms. A moment later, she felt the blanket being dragged over her shoulders, heard Neil shuffle off into the other room. *Oh, God, he must think I've lost it. And why not, look at me? I'm a mess. I don't know who I am.* Tears gathered in her eyes while she lay staring into empty space. Her throat tightened and her body quaked in a racking, silent sob until, mercifully, sleep overtook her again.

Several hours later, she sat at the kitchen table opposite Neil. The burger he made sat half eaten in front of her, the tea in her mug, lukewarm. She took a sip, looked out the sliding glass door toward the swaying Gary oak and said in a voice she barely recognized, "I feel like an orphan."

Neil leaned forward and looked at her with gentle kindness. "But, you're not alone. You have friends, people who care about you."

But she couldn't see any clear way out of the hole she had fallen into and shook her head.

"Janet," Neil said, "I know you don't believe me right now, but you will get through this."

She looked up. "That's easy for you to say. But you're not me."

He shrugged. "No, I'm not. But I care about you, and I'm not going to let you be left alone in this."

She leveled her gaze on him. "Don't try and fix me."

"I wouldn't presume to," he said. "I'm just letting you know I'm here for you."

Suddenly, she realized he was looking at her as more than just a friend, except she didn't know 'what more than just a friend' looked like to him. She got up. "Why don't you go home? I'll be fine."

"Is that what you want?" he said.

Unable to meet his imploring gaze, she nodded.

"Okay," he answered softly. "If you need me, call, okay?"

She watched him from the corner of her eye while he pulled his jacket on. *Please turn around. Don't go. Say something, anything.* She swallowed hard, felt her throat tighten for the umpteenth time. *I'm not going to cry.* "Thanks for coming."

She heard him linger by the door, felt his eyes on her then he opened it and left.

Two days later –

It was early morning, around six when Janet emerged from the underpass leading to Fogarty State Park beach. The ocean was at high tide and was washing the shoreline. Yesterday and the day before had been a giant blur. She peeled off her socks and shoes as the surf thundered against the rocks and wind battered the sandy dunes. The beach was empty, save for birds and Barney by her side. At length, she struck off under the slate gray clouds. As she walked, she thought about the man she had always known as her father.

When her grotto came into sight, she veered away from the water's edge toward it. Behind her, the waves rolled in, their rhythmic rise and fall echoing the throbbing emptiness inside her. She climbed the gentle slope running up to grotto, wanting the world to go away, seeking refuge. But now, the place she had always run to in the past felt cold and indifferent.

Barney picked his way up to her and nestled against her side. She pulled him onto her lap and hugged him fiercely. All her life, she had wanted a father to love her, to be proud of her. Except now, she had no father. For the first time in her life, she really felt alone.

She took a deep breath of the ocean air, trying to figure out where to go from here. Neil was right. She had friends. There was Megan, and there was always the crowd at Jake's. But now, she realized she needed more. She needed to feel connected to someone. Was that someone Neil? She had been struggling with the growing bond between them because it scared the hell out of her. Was it because of the vast difference of years between them? No! It was because of the fear of letting a man into her heart.

She turned her gaze upward, felt a soft warm zephyr caress her face and leaned back. All she wanted was to be happy. Didn't she deserve it? Why was it so hard? And then it hit her. She had been happy. A couple weeks ago she had been on top of the world because of Neil. The warmth in his smile, and the way he looked at her made her feel worthwhile, that she was beautiful and cared about.

An hour later, she headed up the coastal highway in a light soaking rain that made the fields and trees glisten. As she drove, she nibbled her lip. *Please be home, Neil. I don't know if I can do this again.* Her heart thumped as she pressed down on the accelerator.

As she turned onto Neil's road in the driving rain, she held her breath until she saw his truck in the driveway. Pulling in behind it, she looked up to see a light go on in the living room. She sat in the car, gathering courage. Barney moved close, his velvet brown eyes searching her. She ran her hand over the dog's head and along his muzzle. "Stay, Barney. I'll be right back."

With an effort, she got out of the car, ran to the porch and knocked. The rain beat down on her head, matting her hair to her face.

When Neil opened the door, she stood there unable to open her mouth. Everything she rehearsed fell away.

"Janet. What's wrong?" he said, pulling her inside.

She looked at him, studying his face and the alarm in his expression. "I ... I feel so alone." The words were a whisper. He gazed at her, and all she could see was his gentle heart, his acceptance of who she was, and it drove her into his arms.

Janet spread the letter from her aunt out on the table in front of her. Outside the window, a waning sunset cast a warm saffron glow on the rooftops. She read the letter twice and debated what to say to the man she had called father for so many years.

Does he know who my real father is? Will he tell me? Do I really want to know? The answer to the last question was complicated.

She turned toward Neil sitting on the couch, reading the paper. "Hey."

He looked up. "Yes?"

"Can I ask you a question?"

He folded the paper and set it in his lap. "Sure."

"What would you do if you were me?"

"About what?"

"William. My father. I'm so ... so, I don't know what I am. I mean the way he treated me growing up all makes sense now. But then he comes out and takes care of me after the accident. Tells me he loves me. I mean, what do you do with that?"

Neil got up, came to the table and sat. "Is this the letter you found?" he said, looking down at it.

Janet nodded.

"I assume you read the rest of the letters?" Neil said.

Janet cleared her throat. "Yeah."

Neil shrugged. "Then I guess I would try and put myself in his shoes. Ask what I would've done."

"I wouldn't have lied."

Neil looked at her, and she could feel the unsaid, *'are you so sure,'* words written on his face. He leveled a thoughtful gaze at her, and said, "My family has a history of early onset dementia. When Meg was little, she asked me once why grandma lived in a hospital when she didn't look sick, and I told her that grandma preferred living there. Later, after she figured things out on her own, she asked me why I'd lied to her. I said, telling you grandma wasn't right up here would've changed how you felt about going to see her and you both would've lost out on some wonderful times."

Janet thought about that a moment. "It's not the same, but I think I know what you mean. I guess the question is: do I think life would've been better if I'd known." She sighed, reflecting on what her life would have been like growing up knowing William wasn't her father.

Neil reached over the table, patted her hand and stood. "When you can answer that, you'll know what to do."

Janet picked up the phone, dialed, and listened to the ringing on the other end. After talking with Neil the night before, she came to the conclusion on where to start the dialogue with her father. Yes, he was her father. He had been there during her growing up, had mentored and provided for her.

When she heard him pick up, she took a deep breath and braced herself. "Hi Dad."

"Hey, Skeeter. I was just thinking about calling you."

"Really?"

"Yeah. Got my affairs almost in order. Should be ready to move pretty soon."

Janet nibbled her lip. "I have something to ask you, and I want you to tell me the truth, okay?"

"Sure."

She wrapped the telephone cord around her finger. "Are you my real father?"

His reply took a long time. "Why?"

"Just answer the question, please."

Again, he said, "Why?" And the tone of his voice was guarded.

"Because, I need to hear the truth from you."

"You know, don't you? I'd hoped you'd never find out."

She bit her lip. Even though she knew it for a fact, there was still a small part of her that wanted it not to be true. "So you kept it from me?"

"I'm sorry," he muttered.

She weighed that in her mind. "It must have been very hard for you. Why didn't you divorce mom instead of playing this ... this charade for so many years?"

"I loved your mother. Leaving her would've been like tearing my heart out." He sighed. "I did everything I could to jump-start our marriage. To convince myself I could forgive her. But in the end, I couldn't. I'm sorry. I never meant to hurt you."

Janet was quiet, then said, "I know you didn't. Does Craig know?"

"Not that I know of." His voice broke. "I want you to know something. When you got into your accident, I realized how important you were in my life. I want to be your dad. Can you please forgive me?"

She got up, went to the window and looked off over the neighborhood. Mrs. Ganderson was gardening in her yard. Little Jeffrey played next door in his sand box. Finally, she said, "Yes, I forgive you, but I'm gonna need some time."

He cleared his throat again. "I love you, and there'll be no more secrets between us, I promise."

"I know. Look, I have to go."

"Right," he said, and told her good-bye.

Two weeks later –

Janet sat at Neil's kitchen table sipping a Coke and watching him throw a couple of burgers on for lunch.

"His name is Kevin," she announced.

"Who?" Neil said, popping the top off his bottle of beer.

"My father, my real father."

He looked back at her, his brow raised. "Your father told you then?" He adjusted the burner below the frying pan.

"Yes. I called him this morning and asked."

He nodded. "You all right?"

"I'm okay." She paused. "It was hard asking."

"I bet. You want cheese on yours?"

"Yeah, sure." She debated her decision to look for her real father as she tried to gather her thoughts. Finally, she said, "If you were me, would you try to find him?"

Neil shut the burner off and turned around. "First off, I'd ask myself: if I did, what then?"

"Yeah, that has crossed my mind," she said. "I would like to meet him, though."

"I know," he said in a careful tone.

"Is that wrong?" she said, suddenly aware of his cocked brow.

Neil sat beside her and reached for her hand. As he took it, he looked her in the eye. "No, but what if he doesn't want to be found. He may not want you barging into his life. And if he has family, they may not appreciate it, either."

"Right."

Neil nodded. "Why don't you give it some time? Think about it," he said. "Oh, by the way, I told my daughter about us."

Janet's heart leapt into her throat. "You did? What'd she say?"

"Not much. She mentioned she'd call you later." He grinned. "I think she wants to know your intentions, sort of like the good old days. I must say; it's amusing to be on the other side of that."

"Very funny," Janet replied as her stomach knotted.

"So, you gonna ask her permission to date me?"

Janet forced a smile. "You'd like that, wouldn't you? What I might ask her is if you have any annoying habits I need to know about."

"I don't know if I like that," he said.

"Well, that's the price you pay."

When Janet arrived home, she checked her answering machine and sure enough, a message waited for her. She hit the play button and listened to Megan's voice ringing out. "Hey Janet, give me a call."

Janet looked up at the clock. 9:00 PM. As she debated whether to wait until morning to call her, the phone rang.

"Hello?"

"I had an interesting chat with my father earlier."

Janet sat and took a deep breath. "Hi, Meg. Yes, he told me."

"I guess you've had a rough couple of days. You okay?"

Janet wondered how much Neil told her about her father. "Yes, thank you."

There was a brief pause. "Anything else you'd care to share? Like how you two are getting pretty chummy these days?"

Janet felt the bait being set. "Your father's a good man. He was there for me when I needed him."

"Hmm ... Sort of like the father you never had."

Janet let the insult pass. "Meg, please. It's not what you think."

"Then tell me, please. I'm waiting."

"Can't we do this later? I've had a long day, and I'm tired."

Janet felt a frown on the other end.

"All right. When?"

"How about lunch next week? My treat. I'll be up in Salem to see Mick."

"Okay, I guess that works. What day?" Megan asked in a flat tone.

Janet double-checked her calendar. "Tuesday?"

"Tuesday it is. I'll let you go. Sleep well."

Meaning what? That I've done something wrong and you think I'm sleeping with a clear conscious? "You, too." Janet hung up the phone and closed her eyes. *It's not like I expected her to accept this, but really?*

12

Janet gave Barney the required speech about behaving while she was gone then shut the front door. She'd overslept and would just about make it to Salem in time to drop off her submission to Mick. As she got in her car, she waved to Neil, who was standing next to Barney at her front door. He had stayed over last night, and they had fallen asleep on the couch together. When she woke up in the middle of the night and felt his arms around her, it felt like she belonged there.

She was carrying that feeling with her today like a shield against her impending conversation with his daughter. Would Megan understand how she felt? Janet doubted it, but it didn't stop her from hoping. She didn't want to lose Megan's friendship, but didn't Neil deserve some happiness, and didn't she? She turned the radio on and tried to put the thought of a knock down, drag out fight with Meg out of her mind.

An hour later, she pulled into the restaurant parking lot. She found a spot and sat a moment before getting out. A few spaces away she saw an old VW beetle. *She's here.*

She checked her face in the rear-view mirror and got out. Megan stood inside the front entry of the stone and brick building.

"Hi," Janet said, shutting the door behind her.

"Hi, yourself. How was the trip?"

"It was all right."

A crooked smile crossed Megan's lips. "Good. Hungry?"

"A little. You?"

"I could eat," Megan said. They followed the greeter past pictures of local celebrities to a booth at the back of the room. "So, how's Mick?" Megan said, tossing her purse on the seat.

"Don't know. Haven't seen him yet." Janet slid into the booth and pulled a menu in front of her. "So what's good?"

Megan shrugged. "The Linguini with clam sauce isn't bad. Caesar's pretty good, too."

"So," Janet said, deciding on her entree, "How are you?"

"I'm doing."

Feeling the chilly tone of Megan's response, Janet braced herself and looked up. "And work?"

"It goes," Megan said. "Not what I'm used to, but it's safe." Her gaze narrowed on Janet. "Okay, what's going on between you and my father?"

Janet took a deep breath and was about to answer when the waiter appeared. Megan pasted a smile on, and they both ordered. When the waiter left, Janet said, "It's not what you think."

"And I'm thinking what?" Megan said. She glanced out the window beside them.

"That I'm flirting with him or something."

"It's not that, that I'm worried about. He likes you a lot. This isn't one of the guys down at Jake's. This is my father, Janet. I don't want him hurt."

Janet blinked. She'd forgotten she'd told Meg about a couple of romps. She steeled herself. "Neither do I."

"He's old enough to be your father."

"I know."

"Well, I don't know, Jan. Look, I owe you for all you did and for sharing what you went through, but I'm not comfortable with this. I mean, in my world, friends don't date their friend's father. It's … it's … weird."

"Yes, I know, but you can't always control how you feel."

"It doesn't mean you act on them, though. You look at him and see this worldly older man. But what about in twenty years? Is it going to be the same? I don't think so. I think you're going to look at him and wonder why you're there. You're going to feel trapped. And then what?"

"Looks aren't what I'm interested in, Meg."

"Really? Okay, what about if he can't take care of himself anymore? Hmmm? What about that? I don't think you're thinking this all the way through."

"So, you'd have him be alone the rest of his life?"

"No. I just think he should find someone his own age. You're drop-dead gorgeous. He looks at you and sees himself back in his teens. It might work for a little while, but sooner or later the novelty's going to wear off. Then what? He'll see the longing in your eyes to be free and it'll torture him."

Logically, Janet knew Megan was right. But what Megan assumed wasn't going to happen. It had taken ten years for her to find a man she felt any kind of real bond with. At last, she said, "I can't expect you to believe this, but it'll never happen."

Megan looked at her with obvious skepticism. "You're right, I don't believe you. But there's nothing I can do about it." Her gaze hardened. "You better not hurt him! You understand me?"

It was as close to a stamp of approval as Janet could expect to get from Megan. She met the pointed glare staring back at her and said the words she had yet to admit to Neil. "I love him, Meg. I will never hurt your father."

Megan leaned forward. "I hope not, but if you do, you'll have me to deal with." She sat back. "So what's next? You two gonna move in together?"

Janet set her fork down. "We haven't talked about it yet."

Megan eyed her sidelong. "I see. Well, we'll just take it one day at a time then, I guess."

"That's my plan. Meg? Can we still be friends?"

"For now, let's just say, I'll think about it and leave it at that."

Later that night, Janet and Neil were sitting down to burgers and fries at his place. It was a Tuesday night. The National League pennant race between the Brewers and the Dodgers murmured on the TV. Janet didn't know the first thing about baseball, other than it was the most boring game man had ever devised. But Neil enjoyed it. Thought of it as a chess match. That was all well and fine, but she didn't see a lot of chess matches on TV.

"So, how was lunch with Meg," he asked.

"Lunch was good," Janet responded carefully.

He eyed her dubiously. "Meaning?"

She managed a thin smile. "Meaning, we had a nice long chat about you."

He bit into his burger, then wiped his mouth. "I bet you did. If I know my Meg, she's all gun-ho on us. But she has her life with Brad."

If you only knew!

He winked at her. "I think it's time for this old man to start living again."

Yes it is, for both of us. Janet took a drink from her chocolate milkshake and regarded him. "I have something to tell you. It's hard to know how to say it, except to just come right out with it." She paused, and summoning her courage, said, "I want to share my life with you." She searched his face for a reaction. For a moment there was nothing, then it melted into a beautiful smile. He reached out and took her hand.

"I never thought I'd hear those words again from a woman." He searched her with a probing gaze that went to her very core. "Are you sure?"

"Yes."

He took another moment with that answer, as if savoring it. "I'm so much older than you."

"I don't care. I love what's in here," she said, touching his chest.

He reached up and cupped her cheek with his hand. "You have made me very happy."

But do you love me back? Janet thought, holding her breath.

He got up and bent his face down to her, placing a soft lingering kiss on her lips. "I didn't know how I felt about you until that day on the beach. I knew I liked you, but you were so much younger than me. I was afraid you'd think I was a dirty old man." He smiled. "I'm terrified."

"Me, too." *But do you love me, Neil?*

He kissed her again and cleared his throat. "Hey, what do you say we celebrate?"

I guess he needs a little more time to say the words. Okay, it's been a long time for him. I can wait. She smiled. "I'd like that."

"Great. Let's do something crazy."

"Crazy? Like what?"

"Like, bowling, or something. Wait a minute, I know. There's a miniature golf place down on twenty-two. It's lit up at night. We could go play a round."

"Golf?"

"Sure. It'll be a hoot."

Not exactly what I had in mind, but it will be memorable. "Okay, but I've never played before."

"Neither have I ... well maybe once or twice when I was a kid. Oh, by the way, I went to the library yesterday. The woman at the desk told me there's a group that meets there about lost relatives every Monday."

"Really?" Janet beamed and any further doubts vanished about him loving her.

The next day, Neil called her from work. "I want you to get dressed up tonight. We're going out somewhere nice. And no, I'm not telling you where, except that it isn't Jakes."

"Okay. When do I need to be ready?" Her mind swirled with thoughts of a proposal. Part of her gushed at the thought, another was anxious. *Am I going too fast here? But how can I say no?*

"Seven. I'll pick up you after I run an errand."

Her heart jumped. *A ring? But it could be anything. Don't get ahead of yourself, girl.* She took a deep breath, trying to put it out of her mind, and looked at the clock. It was a little after three. Did she have time to go get a quick trim down at *Curls*? And what to wear?

"Janet, you there?" Neil said.

"Yes, sorry. Just thinking. Yes, that works. See you then."

At six-thirty, Janet was still deciding on a dress. She dragged yet another one out of her closet and hung it up over the top of the door beside the other four. The dark maroon wrap-around with a 'v' neck collar had been bought last spring for a swank award ceremony put on by the *Reporter*. *Over the top?* She lifted the material up in her hands and over her arms. It slipped over her skin like a cool breeze. She tilted her head. *Why not?*

Twenty minutes later, she opened her front door and let Neil in. She stared at the elegant, white flower corsage in his hand whose stem and leaves had been woven around a circlet of braided gold. Her heart confirmed what she'd dared to believe all afternoon. As she pinned it on her dress, she said, "What's this all about?"

"Oh, just a little something I thought you might like." A smile turned the corners of his lips.

"It's beautiful, thank-you."

He nodded toward his truck and held his hand out. "Your limo awaits."

A half hour later, they sat at a secluded table near a large picture window looking out over the Willamette River. They barely noticed it, though, because their gazes were locked on each other. *I could exist here forever*, she thought.

At last, Neil stirred. "You are radiant." The waitress suddenly appeared at their table. He turned toward the woman. "Give us ten, would you?" The waitress' glance passed between them and a subtle smile came to her lips. After she left, Neil cleared his throat. Janet sensed him screwing up his courage. At last, he said, "I suppose you're wondering what's going on?"

"The thought has crossed my mind," she said. When he took a deep breath, she braced herself. *Okay, here it comes.*

He chuckled lightly, reached over and squeezed her hand. "I imagine it did. Okay, two things. One, I wanted to celebrate a year of getting to know you."

"A year?" *We met in '79.*

He shrugged. "Give or take. And the other is ... well, I was thinking, we've been spending a lot of time together lately ... and I was wondering if it made sense ... if you thought it might be a good idea to combine households?"

Ok, I think I know what he means, but does this combining households include a ring and wedding vows? He often says one thing and means another. She leaned forward, laying her other hand softly over their entwined fingers. "You mean move in together, as in right now?"

"Well, not exactly right now, but as soon as you're comfortable with it," he said with an anxious tone in his voice.

Well, I guess he's trying to ease into this. In a way, I can't blame him. Truth is, I sort of feel the same way. She patted his hand. "I'd love to."

He broke into a broad smile. "Great."

Suddenly, it occurred to Janet there was a problem. Her eyes widened and his brow rose. "Something wrong?" he said.

"Umm ... yes."

His shoulders sank, and his smile faded. "What?"

"Tom's moving out at the end of next month, remember?" she said. She shook her head. "I still don't know what I'm going to do with the cottage. And there's all the furniture, and Tom's art, not to mention all our stuff."

His mouth opened, and his gaze turned inward as the words hung between them. He tapped his fingers on the table and looked off into space. "What about an auction?"

Janet shrugged. "You mean sell all the furniture and stuff?"

"Well, yeah, or maybe sell it with the cottage."

"Not the art, though."

"No, of course not." He pursed his lips. "Hey, on second thought, why not keep the cottage as a retreat for us?"

She hadn't given any thought to that. "I don't know. It'd be nice to be by the ocean."

He grinned. "Good. As for your other property, Ms. Trump, you could rent it."

She frowned, not keen on the idea. "I don't know. To tell you the truth, I'm tired of being a landlord."

Neil was quiet. "There's always your father. He is coming out."

Janet looked off through the window. "I know."

"Have you made up with him?" Neil said.

Janet turned back and looked at him. "We've mended fences, but–"

"Sweetie, don't carry that stuff around with you forever. I'm not saying forget it all; just don't let it get in the way of your happiness."

He was right, and Janet knew it. Living in the past had never served her. It was time to start living in the present, and the present was with Neil. At length, she nodded. "I'll give him a call."

During the next three weeks, Janet talked with her father often, and little by little, the sting of finding out the real truth subsided. In retrospect, Janet felt for him. Will had never asked to be cheated and walked out on. Yes, he could be difficult, stubborn and callous at times, but overall, he was loyal and generous. And he wanted to be out here with her. As for which house to rent to him, Janet couldn't help choosing the house her mother left her. In the meantime, Tom got his affairs in order and moved out of the beachfront cottage. For the next five months, Janet and Neil spent every available moment moving and painting. By St. Patrick's Day, her father had settled in her Salem house.

Now came the hard part. Janet wasn't used to having people underfoot or having to discuss financial decisions. She had her way of doing things, and Neil had his. He preferred lists. She preferred a laid-back approach. He was a creature of habit. Doing things the same way all the time. Throw one little extra thing into the mix, and he struggled to deal with it. He called it the tried-and-true method. She called it OCD. These two traits, easygoing and regimental, were a conundrum that baffled her.

And then there was Megan. Janet lamented how their friendship had deteriorated, and though she tried her best to bridge the widening gulf between them, nothing seemed to work. After a while, Neil sensed something was wrong and pinned her down about it. He tried to convince her to give it time. That Megan would come around. But Janet knew it bothered him.

He sat in bed reading the paper. He looked up and winked when she came in. "Hi, beautiful," he said.

"You like," she said, turning around.

"Yes, I do." He patted the bed. "Come over here and sit beside me."

"No way," she said, ducking into the bathroom. She pulled her hair back, tied it up in a ponytail. "I have stuff to do today, and weren't you going into the office this morning?"

"Changed my mind," he said, suddenly behind her. He kissed her neck softly.

"What are you doing?" she said, fighting the warm, tingling sensation running down her body.

"Appreciating my wife," he murmured behind her.

"Is that a proposal?"

His smile left him and his deep blue eyes glistened. He took her hand and gazed softly at her. "Yes, it is. I love you."

Her heart stopped, and her breath caught in her throat. *Oh, my God! He said, he wants to marry me!* She put her hand to her mouth and her legs wobbled.

"Well? What about it?" he said softly. "You want to marry this old man?"

She studied his large round face. Felt the slight trembling of his hand. Heard his breath being stolen from him. Felt his palpable fear of uncertainty. She tried to untangle the knot of sudden emotions washing over her. "Yes. Yes I'll marry you."

He blinked and kissed her tenderly. "You trying to kill me?"

She grinned, and a giddy sensation rose inside her. "No. Not until I'm your beneficiary." She hugged him fiercely, and they tumbled back into the bedroom and onto to the bed.

13

Eight months later -

Janet spooned up to Neil and draped her arm over him. She hadn't slept well for the last three days since she'd gotten the news from her doctor. *How could this have happened? I've been careful. More than that, do I want a baby, and how do I tell him?* Her gaze slipped out the window toward the ever-brightening dawn sky. Their wedding was planned for mid September. She would definitely be showing by then. Everything would have to be changed. And how would it look to his family, Megan especially, if things were escalated to accommodate her condition? She wasn't so concerned for herself as she was for Neil. He was a private man, and she didn't want to embarrass him.

He stirred and rolled over onto his back. His arm lifted up and ran under her pillow. A hand touched her shoulder. His fingers softly brushed her skin. She saw him blink and then he rolled a lazy eye toward her.

"Morning," he muttered.

She buried her head into the warmth of his shoulder. Listened to his beating heart, rode the undulation of his chest as it rose and fell. "I love you," she said. Her hand grazed over his chest. Her stomach churned. She wanted to hide, to pretend her pregnancy was only a dream.

"Love you too," he replied.

He pulled her tighter, and she heard him yawn. She said, "I have something to tell you."

Another yawn. "What's that?"

She gathered her thoughts. No matter how she put this, it would change everything. "I went to the doctor on Monday."

"What about?"

She took a deep breath. Summoned her courage. "I missed my period." She closed her eyes. "I'm pregnant."

Dead silence.

"Neil?"

"Yeah."

"Say something?"

He pulled his arm out from underneath her and rolled onto his side, facing her. "I'm not sure what to say. A child, wow! How do you feel about it?"

"I don't know."

He studied her. "Do you want one?"

"Yes ... and no." Her throat tightened. "I mean ... I've never seen myself as a mother. I love kids, but the thought of having one terrifies me. And then there's all the plans we made for the wedding. They'll have to be ditched. And what will your family think?"

He put his hand under her chin and lifted her face toward him. "There's nothing for us to be sorry for. We're both in this together. And don't you worry about my family. It is what it is." He kissed her forehead and was quiet a moment. At last he said, "Sometimes life throws you a curve ball. And when it does, you roll with it. You'll be a fabulous mother. And wedding plans can be changed."

"You're not upset?"

"Why would I be?"

"I didn't think you'd want any more children."

"I wasn't planning on it. But then again, I wasn't planning on falling in love again, either." He grinned. "Wow, I can hardly believe it. I'm gonna be a dad again." He pulled her into his arms and they entwined with a tender kiss.

The weeks rolled past at lightning speed. Janet felt like she was on a roller coaster. The worst of it had centered on her up and down emotions. Tears flowed often when she was alone. She couldn't see any clear end to all the wedding re-arrangements. But it was the over-powering fear of suddenly having a child that terrified her most.

She stepped out of the shower and stood, viewing her blossoming body in the mirror. She was now four months along and the ever-present background nausea of the last month had finally subsided. Hopefully, she wouldn't outgrow the wedding dress in the next two weeks.

She toweled off and dressed. Neil had already left for work. Her father was due within the hour. They were going to get him a new suit for the wedding. He'd be giving her away.

She envisioned him walking her along a flower-laden path on the beach to Neil. Could almost feel his hand on her arm. See the look in his eye. He had softened and opened up in subtle ways over the last few months. She liked the changes and she was changing too. Yes, she'd get past the secrets and the lies. She'd do it because she wanted to.

Twenty minutes later, the doorbell rang. Her father was in what he called his west-coast attire. White socks and sneakers, navy-blue polo shirt and tan slacks. A flat-brimmed navy blue cap rode over his receding hairline.

He gave her a hug. "Morning Skeeter. How's my girl?"

"I'm good." She led him to the kitchen. "I'm almost ready. Coffee?"

He shook his head. "Nah. Have you eaten?"

"Just a bagel."

"Well, let's go for breakfast then. My treat."

She looked sidelong at him. Took a gulp of tea. "You're bound and determined to fatten me up aren't you?"

"Just want my grand–" He cleared his throat and looked away. "Your son to be healthy."

Janet sighed and went to him. "Dad, it's okay. He's your grandson!" She looked him straight in the eye. "Okay?"

"I ... I didn't want to be presumptuous."

Haven't we had this conversation before? She took his hand and held it. "Look, the past is the past. You're my dad, and I want my baby to have a grandpa. So you start thinking of him like that."

His face brightened, and his eyes glistened. "Will do, boss. Let's go eat now."

They ended up in a small café in town. Her father ate while she looked out the window beside their table. Her thoughts were a million miles away, envisioning life with a baby. How it would change her. She thought of Megan. Saw in her mind's eye how she fussed with Kyle. All the kisses and hugs. Then remembered the night Megan had been raped and how she had been left alone to take care of Kyle while his mother fought for her life. At one level, Janet knew she could handle a child, but this was her baby, not Megan's, and there was a lot more to it than playing and changing diapers.

"Hey, you've hardly touched your food," her father said.

She smiled. "I'm not all that hungry, I guess."

"What's wrong?"

"Nothing. Just thinking."

He frowned. "Everything'll be just fine."

"I know." She pushed a chunk of hash browns around her plate with her fork. "So, you excited about shopping with me for a suit?"

He broke into a devilish grin. "As long as you don't drag me all over creation."

She giggled then decided to break into something that had been on her mind all morning. "You think I'm rushing into this?"

"What? Getting married?"

"Yeah. I mean, I love him, but..."

"But what?"

"You know—the baby and everything."

Her father set his fork down. "You were planning on marrying him anyway, right?"

"Yeah, but it wasn't supposed to be like this. You know..." She took a sip of her tea.

He sat with her comment a minute, then said, "I guess the question is: what's changed? I mean, what's changed in how you feel about him?"

Didn't Neil ask her this same question once before about her father? Ironic! She nodded. "It just feels like we're doing this to make things look right. It doesn't feel good."

"Look Skeeter, I'm no expert on this stuff. But to me, it boils down to how you feel about him. Set this baby aside a minute and ask yourself why you wanted to marry him in the first place. If the answer's still the same, then what difference does it make?"

"Do you like him? I mean, you've never really said much."

Her father eyed her and sat back. "He's a little old for you. Then again, you were always more comfortable with older people. Yeah, I like him. He's a good man from where I sit."

"Megan's not too thrilled."

"Yeah, I noticed. But you're not marrying her."

"No, I'm marrying her father."

He smiled. "I can imagine she's not thrilled having a mother-in-law only a couple of years older than her. She'll get over it."

Right Dad. And pigs fly. "One can only hope."

He reached over and took her hand. "As long as you love him and he loves ya back, it'll be all right. Now, come on. Eat up. We have shopping to do."

Her father dropped her off at home around three. They had bought him a conservative brown suit and tie. Since he refused to go bare foot, she had to talk him into a pair of sandals. She shut the door and watched him pull out of the driveway.

"Come on, Barney. Mommy needs to lie down." She went up stairs to the bedroom with the dog padding behind her. Along the way, she passed a stack of boxes outside of the bedroom that was being renovated for the baby. She grabbed the top box then peered into the empty room waiting for trim work and a new coat of paint. In her mind's eye, she saw the white crib with a Teddy Bear mobile slowly spinning over it. Then, as if the baby inside her sensed her thoughts, she felt it move. She smiled.

She went to the bedroom, set the box on the bed, pulled her shirt up and stood in front of the mirror, profiling her belly. Excitement raced through her, and with it came a strong urge to call Neil, but he was working. She'd tell him when he got home. Right now, she needed a nap.

She kicked off her shoes, moved the box to the floor and crawled onto the bed. Dragging the blanket over her, she closed her eyes only to open them again as the writing on cardboard box registered in her brain. She sat up, pulled the box up onto the bed with her and read, 'PERSONAL STUFF'.

She pulled the flaps back and before her lay a pile of photos and a stack of neatly tied letters.

Shutting the flap, she reread the prominent lettering. She sat there a moment, debating. Slowly, her hand pulled the flap back open, and crept into the box then quickly came out. *This is none of my business, except...* Except that part of her wanted to know what he was like under the mask he showed the world. She closed her eyes. Again, her hand went back into the box. *Maybe just one or two letters.*

An hour later she was deep into the stack. With every word she read, her throat tightened. The letters weren't addressed to anyone, but rather they were his thoughts poured out about the pain he went through after Sharon's death. Suddenly, she was frightened. Could she ever fill that void?

"What are you doing?"

She startled and looked up. "Neil! You're home. I didn't hear you come in."

His face knotted. "Put them away please."

"Yeah, sure. I ... I'm sorry. I was just looking for a place to put stuff and I—"

He came in and gently took the letters from her and put them back in the box. "Why would you do this?"

Her shoulders sagged, and her stomach flipped. "I ... I don't know. I just ... I'm sorry."

He looked at her like a wounded animal, picked the box up, and left the room. Sudden tears welled in her eyes. *Oh, God, what have I done?*

That night as they lay in bed, Janet replayed her invasion of Neil's privacy over and over again in her head. Of all people, she knew the sacredness of one's private writings. And yet she'd violated it. She felt awful not because she had been caught or that she had broken her own commandment, but because she knew she had lost Neil's trust.

Neil lay on his side, turned away from her. He had never turned away from her before. She didn't know what to do or say. A deep chasm had opened between them. He was unreachable and she was terrified.

"I love you," she said into the moonlit silence and waited for a reply. There was none. "Neil, if you're awake, please say something."

"What do you want me to say?" he said at last.

Janet clenched her eyes shut. "I'm sorry. Please believe me."

"Why did you do it?"

She thought about it a long time before she answered. "I wanted to know if you were the same inside as you are outside with me."

His voice flattened. "And did you find what you were looking for?"

Her throat tightened. She wanted to feel his arms around her, wanted to feel safe in his love. "Yes."

He rolled over, and she felt his eyes on her. "I trusted you. You, most of all!"

She twirled the engagement ring on her finger. "Do you still love me?" She held her breath.

He didn't say anything for a moment. Then finally, "Yes."

Janet bit back tears. "You want to push the wedding back?"

He rolled back onto his side away from her. "We'll talk about it in the morning, okay? We should get some sleep."

She felt tears gather in her eyes, and she buried her face in her pillow as her body quaked in fear of losing everything.

14

A terrible silence enveloped Janet. Neil had barely spoken to her since that night three days ago. She felt isolated and abandoned and began to entertain giving him back the ring. She shuffled into the den. Pulled out the album of photos she'd put together of them. It was supposed to be her gift to him on their wedding day. Shots of places they had gone. Things they had done. She looked at them. It seemed years had passed in a span of days.

She could hear Neil moving around in the upstairs room he'd converted into an office. The last two days, he had spent all evening up there after getting home from work. Said it was because he had a large proposal due. She didn't believe him. He was avoiding her.

A knock on the front door brought her out of her dark musing. She got up and went to answer it. Found her father standing outside. "Dad, what're you doing here?"

A boyish expression was on his face. "I've come to collect your fiancé for a round of golf."

Janet knitted her brow. "Golf? Neil's never played golf."

Her father came in and took off his hat. "Then it's high time he started. Consider this his bachelor party. Besides, I'm tired of playing alone."

"Well, I'm afraid now's not a good time. He's working."

"His car's here."

She pointed toward the ceiling. "Upstairs."

"It's a Saturday for crying out loud." He pushed by her and marched to the landing. "Hey Neil, get away from that crap and come down here."

A door opened and a moment later Neil was at the top of the stairs. "Oh, Will. What's up?"

"I came to rescue you from my daughter, but it seems it's work you need rescuing from."

Neil eyed Janet. When he looked back at her father, he said, "Now's not a good time."

Her father glanced back and forth at them. It didn't take a genius to see he knew something was wrong. He said, "It's never a bad time to get out in the sun. You can take an hour or two off. Work'll still be here when you get back."

Neil shot Janet another sidelong glance, as if accusing her of setting something up. "I really don't have time, Will."

But her father pulled him aside. Whispered something into his ear. Neil's tight expression faded. "Okay, okay … you shamed me into it."

Janet felt a stab of fear. *Dad, please don't get in the middle of this. It'll only make things worse.* "Shall I set another plate at the table when you get back?"

"We'll be home when we get home," her father said, escorting Neil toward the door.

It was near dusk when they returned. Her father didn't come in, though. She watched them say good-bye through the front porch window then skated into the kitchen. The last thing she wanted to be accused of was spying. After the front door opened, she heard Neil take his jacket off. She waited for the familiar sound of footsteps heading up the stairs, but instead, turned around to find him standing in the doorway.

"Hi."

"Hey."

"You have a good time?"

He shrugged. "It was different."

"My father can be a little much sometimes."

Neil sucked his lower lip and shuffled into the room. "That he is. He's pretty smart, too. We had a long chat."

"About what?"

He took her hand. "I know you didn't mean it, reading my letters; it just caught me off guard. I've been a real bear to live around lately, haven't I?"

"It's okay," she said.

"No, it's not. We need to talk."

He led her into the living room, motioned her to sit on the couch as he strode to the window. Looking out at the large Gary oak, he said, "I know this sounds like I'm holding onto the past, but part of me feels guilty for the way I feel about you, as if I'm betraying her somehow. I know it's foolish, but I can't help it. Guess I didn't realize what was really bothering me until I saw you with my letters."

"I didn't know you were feeling bothered," Janet said, fighting to keep her heart from going into free-fall.

"Neither did I." He turned around and looked at her with despairing eyes. "She lives inside me. You know that. You can't change it. When she died, she took a piece of me with her."

Janet pressed her lips together. Her chest felt as if it might collapse at any moment. "You miss her?"

"Yes." He turned around. "But she's gone. And I need you to accept that."

"I'm trying. I love you." *Please say you love me back.*

"I know," he replied.

"I'm not going anywhere, unless..." Suddenly, her heart stopped, petrified of what she was about to offer.

"Unless what?" he said quietly.

She saw him gasp and felt the palpable fear in his voice. "Unless you want me to."

"Of course not!" He came to her. "I just don't know what to do right now. I mean, how do I deal with the memories? How do I love you the way you should be loved? I don't know anything anymore, except that the thought of losing you scares the hell out of me."

"So don't," Janet said, standing up. She put her arms around him, molding her body around his broad thick chest.

His arms enfolded her. "Okay," he whispered.

Janet pulled her head back and studied his large round face. He was fighting so many demons, yet she couldn't imagine any other man she'd ever want to be with. *We'll fight them together.* She smiled, then reached up and kissed him. "You take your time. You have my heart." When he nodded, she continued, "Can I ask you a question? Is that why you've been single all these years?"

He shrugged. "After she died, I tried to ... date ... you know. But my heart wasn't in it. And after a while, I just forgot about it. Besides, I had Meg to think about. I didn't need complications in my life."

"And then I came along," she said.

"And then you came along. And for the first time, I felt alive again. You made me smile."

Janet grinned. "You made me smile, too." She patted his shoulders, and said, "Look, there's no rush. We can hold off on getting married."

He shook his head. "No. I want to marry 'you'. I just need to find a place for her to live inside of me that won't get in the way of us."

September 20, 1983 –

Well, today's the day, Janet thought. She sat on the porch lounge, looking out over the fields across the road. A dome of blue sky kissed the tall pine and hazelnut on a distant hillside. In less than six hours, she'd be exchanging vows with Neil on the beach. He was staying with her father right now. Left the night before. They both had a lot of things to do apart from each other. She sipped her breakfast tea and stroked Barney's head. The dog looked up. "It's been a rough couple of days, hasn't it little man?" she said into the quiet, still morning. He bent his head forward and lay down on his out-stretched paws.

Am I doing the right thing? She wondered. *He's still in love with her. I can't compete with a ghost. Will she always be there? Like a shadow over me? Over us? I wish I knew. The only thing I do know; is that I love him. And now, in a little while, we'll be married. And there're so many plans we've made.*

She took a deep breath. The war of 'what ifs' raged in her heart. But it was the thought of being alone again, of not feeling him by her side at night when she slept, that scared her more. At last, she summoned her courage. *I love him. I want him. I'm just blowing this all out of proportion. Get a grip, girl. You're getting married today and you've got a million things to do.*

Lilies and daisies decorated the windswept beach right up to Janet's beloved grotto. Gulls swooped under thin, white braided clouds above. Janet stood at the far end of the flowered path that would take her to meet her husband and clasped her father's hand. He squeezed it and eyed her. A proud and adoring expression beamed on his face. Ahead, Neil stood in his brown suit looking back. Their family and friends tightened at the edge of the sandy aisle. Cameras clicked.

As she took the first step, she smoothed down the sides of her cream satin dress. A guitar played in the background. Neil's favorite song: *'And I Love You,' by the Beatles.* This day was as she had imagined it for the last year. She passed faces as her father led her down the sandy aisle. She knew them all, but they were a blur. Her gaze was pointed in one direction. At Neil.

Suddenly, she stood beside him. Everything around them disappeared. Neil held her in a tender gaze. His face rimmed in sunshine, radiated into a beautiful smile. Janet studied him a long time and turned to her father. His eyes sparkled as she smiled back. "I love you, Daddy," she whispered.

He took her into his arms, kissed her cheek tenderly, then pulled back and placed her hand in Neil's.

From that point on, she was in a dream, watching Neil as he repeated the words the minister said. His rich, deep voice filling her soul, and in between his words she felt the magic of his love.

"Do you promise to love and cherish this woman, forsaking all others?" the minister said.

"I do," Neil said.

"In sickness and in health?"

"I do."

"For better or worse?"

"I do."

The minister turned to Janet. Repeated the vows. She gazed at Neil. Studied his beautiful, round face. There was a depth in it that she'd never seen before. At last, she answered with a faltering voice to each question the minister asked. "I do."

She took Neil's ring out from a small hidden pocket inside the sleeve of her gown. Placed it on his finger. Heard herself say, "With this ring, I thee wed." There were more words, but she didn't hear them. The only thing that mattered stood right in front of her.

Finally, the minister presented them to the gathered friends and family and proclaimed them, 'Man and Wife.' Neil brushed her veil aside and pulled her gently into him. Kissed her like he'd never kissed her before. Tender and sweet, it lingered on her lips like morning dew on the grass. A wave of euphoria rushed through her. There were no words to describe the emotions welling up inside her heart. She knew this moment would live in her for the rest of her life. No one could ever take it away.

15

Janet and Neil left two months later for Alaska. They had planned to go the following year for their honeymoon, but the baby changed all that. Neil managed to get an earlier flight and also arranged it so they had a week to recover after they got home.

Janet watched Neil as he looked out the window of the plane. He was like a kid going to Disneyland. He had always wanted to go to Alaska, and she had no objection. Her camera would get a good work out. She pulled a magazine out of her carry-on bag and flipped through the pages.

"Look at that," he said, nudging her. "Incredible!"

She leaned over and took in the vast dun landscape studded with snow-covered peaks, deep crevices, and sprawling glaciers. "It's beautiful."

"Awesome," he said. He looked at his watch. "Another forty-five minutes and we'll be down."

"Uh-huh."

He pulled his self-made itinerary out of his vest pocket and studied it for the hundredth time. "We'll grab a bite to eat when we get to the hotel then get to bed early. Long day tomorrow."

"You're cute."

"What?" he said, shooting her a perplexed look.

"The way you think and plan things."

"I just like being prepared." He looked at her and smiled. "Okay, I go a little overboard sometimes."

"A little?" Janet said, creating a tiny space between thumb and forefinger. "You want something to drink? The flight attendant is coming around again."

He shook his head. "I'm caffeined out." He turned back to his itinerary.

They dove into their own musings. Janet turned back to her magazine and was halfway through an article when her stomach fluttered. *Hi baby*. She took a deep breath, enjoyed feeling the infant moving in her womb, and decided tonight would be the night she'd share her little secret with him.

"It's okay," Janet said.

Neil rolled off of her and lay on his back. The sunset was in its final throes outside their hotel room. They lay there quietly as the clock ticked on the nightstand edging toward 10:00 PM.

At last, he said, "I'm sorry."

She turned on her side toward him. Draped a leg over his knee and put her head in the crook of his arm. "For what?"

He sighed. "You know."

"It's been a long day. Don't worry about it." *But it's more than that. He hasn't been able to finish in a week.* She worried. With each failed attempt, Neil seemed to withdraw a little further away from her.

"Yeah, right," he said.

She tapped his chest with her finger, debating whether she should tell him his baby had started moving in her like she had planned on doing earlier.

"What?"

"Umm ... just wondered what the cruise director had in mind for tomorrow."

He brushed her shoulder with his finger. "Cruise director?" His dark tone lifted a little.

"Yeah, you're the cruise director. So what's the plan?" She tickled him.

He squirmed. "Stop that!" He shifted his arm, and she felt his fingers burrowing into her ribs.

"Don't you dare," she said, reaching back and seizing his hand. "Now come on, tell me. Where're we going?"

He pulled his hand away, and she felt it move up under her shoulder. "Well, if you must know. Once we get the camper, we'll be heading to Denali. I was talking to the bartender in the hotel. He said, on a clear day, you could see the mountain all the way from Palmer. A hundred and thirty miles away."

"Wow."

"Yeah. Thought we'd stop in Talkeetna, too. There's a pretty lake there. Lots of nice views. Your camera will love it."

"I'm sure it will."

He grew quiet and a moment later said, "I'm sorry. I thought I was dealing with it. I thought once we got married and were up here, things would return to the way they were." He sighed. "I just don't know. Sometimes, when I close my eyes, I see her on the hospital bed. Her eyes shut as if she were just sleeping."

Janet's heart sank. She didn't know what to do for him. She sighed. "It's all my fault. If I never–"

"No. Things happen. We'll get past it."

"Right." *Should I say this? Should I tell him about me? Would it help him?* She took a deep breath and lifted her head so she could see his face. "We all have things in our past that hang with us, honey. Sometimes they're nice, and sometimes not so nice, and we wish they'd never happened. Like me reading your letters."

He opened his mouth to say something, but she put her finger to his lips. "I want to tell you something that happened to me a long time ago. It's not anything like what happened to you and Sharon, but it might help you understand that I know a little of what you're going through."

"Okay."

Janet steeled herself. "When I was thirteen, we used to go down to my uncle's farm on the weekends. He had a big place down near Uniontown. Anyway, I used to love going into the barn, watching the cows and playing with the kittens. There was always a ton of them. One day–it was a week after my brother's birthday–I was out around back alone feeding the chickens when suddenly my uncle shows up. He watched me with this really weird look on his face. It felt strange, but he was my uncle so I figured it was just his being a grown-up, and grown-ups did and said odd things.

"Anyway, he asked me to come into the barn. Said he had something to show me." She paused and looked away into the darkness. "He led me to his shop and shut the door behind us..."

She heard Neil's audible gasp. He reached up and touched her face. "Oh, Janet."

"Yeah." She paused. "Like I said, it's not the same, but there it is."

He was quiet a long time. Finally, he said. "I guess you're thinking that sharing painful memories can draw us closer."

"I was hoping so, if that makes sense."

"Maybe you're right. I wish I'd known, I'm sorry."

She peered up at him through the murky shadows. "Know what? That he forced himself on me? And if you had known, would it have made a difference with us?"

She lifted her head up and looked down at him. "No, I'd still have fallen in love with you." *Should I say this? Careful Janet, this is thin ice. But I need to say it.* She put her fingers over his hand caressing her cheek, and said, "Are you sure?"

He was quiet a minute. "Yes, I would've still fallen in love with you." He cleared his throat. "So you never said anything?"

"No. I was thirteen. My parents were fighting like cats and dogs. They never would've heard me. Besides, there was enough going on without me making things worse."

Neil sighed and she sensed a shift in his mood, but she wasn't sure what it was. "Does it bother you when I–"

"No," she said emphatically. "Making love with you is bliss." She paused, letting him absorb her words. "But it's not the end-all. I love you, for you. You don't have to perform for me to be happy. Okay?" He nodded. *Did he believe her?* But it was out of her hands.

"Let's go to sleep," she said at last, laying her head back down and nuzzling his chest. "You are so beautiful; do you know that? You make my life so much better than I ever thought it could be. And I love you to pieces for it."

A week and a half later, Janet stood on the dock, looking out over Cooke Inlet. Their honeymoon was drawing to a close, and though part of her wanted to go home, another part wanted to escape into the wilds with Neil and live in a mountain cabin away from the world. She looked out across the bay toward the thick heavy mist clinging to the rising mountains. The tang of the ocean hung over the dark water. Neil came up behind her and pulled her close. She leaned into him and laid her head back against his shoulder.

"So, dear, are you having fun?" she said.

He drew her a little tighter, and she felt a smile. "Yes, are you?"

"Immensely." She breathed in the clean, fresh air and let it mingle with her thoughts. "So this place we're going to, Seldovia, is it? Tell me about it."

"It's an old Russian village, settled in the 1800s. The brochure says there's a trail leading out of town into the wild. There's an old church there, too; Russian Orthodox."

"Sounds like fun. How much longer 'til the ferry leaves?"

He lifted his arm and checked his watch. "Another twenty minutes. You want to go sit? There's a bench over there."

"No, I'm all right here," she said. Her eyes drifted toward a raft of otters bobbing in the water on their backs, cracking crab shells for their morning breakfast. She thought about her camera, but dismissed the idea. She pointed out toward them. "Aren't they graceful?"

"What?"

"The otters. I'm always amazed watching them." She fell quiet. Listened to the lapping of the waves against the wharf. Finally, she said, "When I was little, my father took us to Vancouver. I remember going out on this boat looking for whales. The only thing we saw though, was these little guys. Everyone was disappointed 'cept me. I loved them. I could have watched them all day."

"They are fun, aren't they?"

She paused as the memory flooded her thoughts. Saw her mother in her mind's eye. Remembered how they had argued that day over something insignificant. She spied a mother and pup a hundred yards out in the channel. She said, "It's more than fun though … at least for me. See that one out there with her pup?"

"Yeah."

"Look how she fusses over the little guy. You can almost feel the connectedness between them." She turned around and looked up at Neil. "I never had that. Not that I remember anyways. Don't get me wrong; my mother loved me. There was just this distance between us."

"I'm sorry."

"It's okay. Do you think I'll be a good mother?"

He stroked her hair. "Of course you will."

"Hmm … I worry sometimes. I mean, until I got pregnant, I never saw myself having a baby."

He turned her around. Looked into her eyes. "You know why I think you'll be a great mother?"

She gazed back, expecting some cliché. "No, why?"

"Because you know what it's like not to feel the bond."

How does he know what to say? It's like he's in my head some-times. "But if I never felt a bond, how do I know it's there? I have nothing to go by. Do you think it'll just come and I'll know how to do the right things?"

"Yes. And I'll be right there beside you."

She buried her head in his coat, sheltering her face from a sudden gust of cold wind. *Promise?*

A horn blew behind them. The moment shattered. "All aboard," cried a loud voice.

They made their way onto the gangplank, meshing in with the gathering crowd. After they found a seat at the stern, they huddled close together while waiting for the ferry to push off. A dark haired woman sat with a man across from them, and her gaze was direct: first on her then Neil. There was no smile on her pencil thin lips. Janet could tell what she was thinking but didn't care. Love knew no boundaries, age least of all.

Forty minutes later, they pulled into Seldovia's harbor. The tiny port was littered with boats. Most were fishing vessels that bounced up and down in the water as the wake of the ferry slipped under them. On the hillside, old tar-papered buildings and weathered clapboard houses stumbled down to the water's edge. Dark smoke rose from their metal flue chimneys, staining the gray sky. A hint of a road snuck around them. The sound of children playing floated over the water. She felt her baby squirm.

Neil suddenly looked at her. "You okay?"

She took a breath and drew a smile across her face. "It's the baby. It's moving."

His expression exploded into a vision of wonder. "Oh, Janny! Really?" He put his hand over her abdomen and held it there gently.

The woman across from them frowned. Janet knew it was childish, but she couldn't help staring back and enjoying the moment. She turned her attention back to Neil. "Move your hand up a little and to the right. Feel him?"

"It's a he?"

"I don't know. It could be a girl. I've just been coming to think of it as a 'he' for some reason."

"So you've felt him before?"

"Yes ... I meant to tell you several times, but they were just flutters that I knew you wouldn't be able to feel. This is stronger. Did you feel that?"

Neil's face blossomed into a smile. "Yes, I felt it!"

There were no words in Janet's heart to describe watching him as he experienced their baby moving inside her. It was as if all the dark clouds that had been haunting him for the last two weeks had parted and there he was, shining like a bright, copper penny.

They grabbed a cone and a map at one of the little shops in town. Headed for a trail at the far end of the village. Along the way, they passed children playing in the street. Janet watched a little one toddle along after the older children. He had short curly brown hair and large brown eyes. He turned his ruddy face toward her and flashed a beaming smile. Her hand went to her belly again, felt the subtle roundness.

"Your cone's dripping, sweetie," Neil said.

She stopped walking and looked up. Saw a tiny stream of chocolate running over her thumb. Licked it away. When she turned back to look at the child, he was in his mother's arm and heading down the street. At last, she said, "Do you ever think of what our little one might look like?"

Neil wiped his chin with a napkin. Waited for her to catch up to him. "No, I haven't. Have you?"

"Not until just now." She followed him across the village square and recalled the face of the little boy she'd passed a moment ago. She melded it with Neil's broad and sturdy nose spattered with freckles, his full lips and square jaw and saw her son in her mind's eye. "I think he'll look like you."

He eyed her sidelong. Chuckled. "God forbid."

"Oh, stop. Oh, look! An art studio. Want to go in?"

Neil shot her a reluctant smile. "Maybe on the way back?"

"Okay, but it'll cost you." She shifted the strap of her camera bag over her shoulder and took another bite of her cone. "You ever think about your son ... Trevor?"

"Some." He popped the last of his cone in his mouth. "But I'd rather not talk about it right now."

"Sorry."

"It's okay," Neil said. He checked the bright colored paper map and pointed ahead. "There's the sign for the trail. Let's go have some fun!"

An hour later they emerged from a winding dirt path onto a rocky horseshoe beach littered with driftwood. The clouds had parted and a ray of sunshine poked down through the trees huddling around the ragged cove. Janet removed her shoes. Rolled up her pant legs. Waded out into the icy, shallow water. Neil planted himself on a log near the mouth of the trail and watched her splash around. A moment later, he had her camera out, taking pictures of her. She wasn't used to having her photograph taken. It was always the other way around. She sort of liked it and struck a couple of poses.

"Hey you," she called back. "Take your shoes off and join me."

He shook his head. "I'm busy."

She rolled her eyes. Splashed around a little more. "You're such a stick in the mud sometimes." She bent down and lifted a shell out of the water and turned it over in her hand. After studying the purple hued stain in its center, she headed back to him.

"Look what I found," she said, offering Neil the shell.

He set her camera down beside him. Took it and held it up. "Wow, nice."

Janet frowned. "Camera goes in the bag, sweetie."

"Right. Sorry 'bout that." He gave her back the shell and picked the camera up.

"It's okay. Just have to be mindful of it. That's my livelihood there." She ran her fingers over the rippled surface of the shell to the smooth center. "I'm gonna keep this."

Neil tucked the camera into its compartment and looked up. "Okay."

"You want to know why?"

"A souvenir?"

She sat beside him. "No. It reminds me of you."

"Okay. I can hardly wait to hear this one."

She playfully swatted his arm. "Oh, stop already. It reminds me of you because it's rough on the outside and beautiful on the inside." She turned his face toward her with a finger. "Are you happy?"

"Yes, very much."

"Good." She closed her eyes. Breathed in the cool brine air. "This place reminds me of my beach."

"Does it?"

"Yes." She took another deep breath. "There's a quiet spirit about this place. If you close your eyes, you can feel it." She paused. "I could stay here all day. Do you remember the time when I first took you to my beach?"

"Yeah." A faraway look came to his face. "We talked for a long time. You helped me get past what happened to Meg."

But it's where we fell in love with each other, too. Why did he pick that thought to remember? "Yeah, right. I'm sorry, I shouldn't have brought it up."

"It's okay." He put his arm around her, pulling her close. They watched the waves roll in and scour the beach. Finally, he said, "When did you know?"

"Know what?"

"That you were falling in love with me?"

"I'm not sure. It just sort of happened," she lied. She glanced at him and smiled. "Besides, even if I knew, I wouldn't tell you."

"Really?"

"Yes." She eyed him playfully. "It's one of the mysteries we keep to ourselves. Can't give away everything."

"You're an 'itch'!"

"I have to be. Keep you in line." Her hand shot out around him and dug into his ribs. He tried to grab it, but she was too fast and found another spot to tickle, and then another and another. A moment later, they were on the ground with her sitting on his chest, knees pinning his arms down.

"Okay, okay, stop already," he cried, looking up at her. His laughing gaze shifted into a soft penetrating stare, as if he were tracing every line of her face. "I love you."

"I know." She bent her head, enclosing them in a curtain of long, dark hair. "Do you know why I love you?"

He gazed up at her, and she thought she would melt. "No, tell me."

"Because when you look at me like that, I feel as if I'm the only person in the world that matters. No one has ever made me feel the way you do. For the first time in my life I feel like I belong somewhere, that I'm not this kid looking in through the glass of a candy store, watching everyone else live their lives. Thank-you for stopping on that winter night and being there for me."

"And I will always be there for you."

16

"Push!" Neil cried.

Janet squeezed her eyes shut as the contraction seized her with a savage grip. Her breath stuck in her throat. Neil put his hand under her back and bent her forward. She no longer felt his hand under her. All she knew was the unbearable pressure that pushed out from inside her. She grunted then yelled out in a voice that seemed to come from nowhere and everywhere at once.

"Okay, Janet. The baby's head is crowning. One, maybe two more good pushes and we'll be there," the doctor said.

She caught her breath as best as she could. Her body felt as if it were about to split open. A cloth wiped her face. She opened her eyes and saw Neil watching her. He stroked her hair and shot her an encouraging smile. "We're almost there, sweetie. We can do it."

She panted. Not because she had learned and practiced it for the past three months, but because she had no choice. She shot him an indignant smile, and between breaths, said, "What's this … 'we' stuff?"

A giggle came from somewhere in the room.

"Okay, Janet," the doctor said. "Home stretch now. Next contraction, give it all you got."

Like I haven't been giving it my all? She swallowed. Forced a deep breath. Narrowed a stern eye at her husband. *And you're getting a vasectomy.* Clenching her face, she braced herself for another ferocious effort and dug her fingernails into Neil's hand.

"Ahhhhhhhhhhhhhhheeeeeeeeeeeeeeeeeee…"

"Push! Keep pushing, Janet!" the doctor encouraged. "You're almost there!"

She grit her teeth. Her head felt like it was going to explode. Stars appeared in front of her eyes, and then all at once, her body opened up and for an instant, she felt like she was emptying out her insides. Her eyes rolled back in her head and with it, she had a sensation of leaving her body. The next thing she knew, she was looking into the beautiful gaze of her husband. Tears collected in the corners of his eyes as she heard their child's shrill squalling.

"It's a boy," Neil said as the nurse lifted the child up for her to see before taking him out of her sight. A moment later, the nurse was back and she laid the child on Janet's sopping breast. The baby curled his legs, grabbed at her gown with tiny hands, as if climbing a mountain.

Janet let go of Neil's hand and cradled the child against her. Ran her fingers through the child's fine copper hair. Peered into his tiny blue eyes. Felt the bond solidify. It was instant, unbreakable, and in that moment, everyone in the room disappeared except her and her baby. She studied him like a photograph, checking his fingers and toes. Inhaled his newborn scent. Imprinted him on her heart. He was perfect and he was hers.

Neil bent over her. Kissed her brow softly and laid his hand over his child's back. "He has your nose."

"And your hair," she said, without looking up.

From the corner of her eye, she saw a nurse edge beside the bed, clipboard in hand. "What a beautiful baby. Have you picked out a name for him yet?"

"Yes, we have," Janet said. She nuzzled the child. "His name will be Nathan Alexander Porter."

In August of that year, Neil's right hand began to shake. It was barely noticeable at first, but by Thanksgiving, it had developed into a significant tremor. Janet worried. Begged him to go to see the doctor. But there was always some excuse from him that he was too busy with this or that. As soon as things lightened up, he'd make an appointment. Except that things never seemed to lighten up.

Janet knew the real reason. He was afraid. Although he rarely talked about the vast difference in age between them anymore or his concern over what could happen someday, she knew it was on his mind.

She put Nate down for a nap and went across the hall. Neil's office had taken over June's old studio space. Where June's studio had always been a cluttered cornucopia of art brushes, paints, and canvases, Neil's office was a neatly organized affair. Every pencil, piece of paper, stapler, picture arranged just so, and they never left their spots except for use or cleaning.

Even the books on the bookshelves were in alphabetical order. A baseball signed by Mickey Mantle and a picture of him with Reggie Jackson sat front and center on the credenza behind his 'Pilgrim' oak desk, which had been passed down through generations. He was sitting at it, pencil in hand, as the afternoon sunlight poured in over his shoulder. A drawing was rolled out in front of him. A yellow legal pad sat on top of it. Janet watched the pencil jerk back and forth erratically as it hovered over the pad. Oddly, when he wrote the shake went away.

Suddenly, he looked up and set the pencil down as if he'd been caught with his hand in the cookie jar.

"Yes, dear?"

"I want you to see a doctor about that tremor, and I mean it this time, Neil!"

He frowned. "It's just a little thing."

"Little thing, my butt. Come on, Neil. This isn't just about you anymore. You have Nate to think about."

"Yeah, I know."

"So!"

He got up and came around the desk. "I just hate having people poke and prod me, is all."

"As if I don't? Look, you make an appointment, or I will." She went to his desk. Picked up the phone and offered him the receiver.

He took it from her grudgingly. Punched in a number. She knew he wanted her to leave, and usually she gave him privacy on the phone, but she wasn't budging. At last, he cleared his throat and hung up. "The answering service picked up. Must be out golfing or something. I'll call tomorrow, first thing."

She measured his words and looked hard at him. "Promise me."

His voice rose an octave. "I said I would, didn't I?"

"The baby's sleeping," she said in a stern half whisper. He looked off through the window. "Can you look at me please? I want you to promise."

"Fine, I promise!"

"Why are you being like this?"

"Like what?" he said, furrowing his brow.

"A jerk!"

"A jerk?"

She crossed her arms in front of her. "I believe that's what I said."

"I'm tired and I have a ton of work, okay?"

"You always seem to have a ton of work when you're avoiding something. You know, I begin to wonder if you're more interested with your job than us?"

"What's that supposed to mean?" he shot back.

"You spend most of your time working lately. You have a son, too, you know."

He huffed. "I'm well aware of it."

"And Christmas is coming. Not to mention, I have a shoot down in Big Sur next week."

"Yes, I know. Look, I don't want to argue."

"Neither do I, Neil, but I begin to wonder sometimes what's more important."

He looked down at the floor. She knew the accusation was unfair, but it was how she felt. She didn't wait her whole life to meet this man only to see him crumble before her because he was afraid to see a doctor. At last, he said, "You know that's not true. It's just ... well you know."

She held him with a pointed stare. "No, I don't. Tell me."

He cleared his throat. Walked to the window and looked out. "It's just that lately I've been thinking about my mom a lot. I told you she had Alzheimer's, remember?"

Janet tried to shoo away the ominous reminder. "Yes, I know. It doesn't mean you're going to get it, though."

"Well, no." He shrugged. Turned around to face her. "It's just when you tell me I'm too serious sometimes, that I need to be a kid once in awhile, I see her. She was so serious. Drove my father nuts. He said she got it because she never allowed herself to have any fun." Neil paused and shoved his shaking hand in his pocket. "Are you angry with me?"

"No, Neil, I'm not angry. I just want you to take care of yourself."

He nodded, and they fell silent as the mantle clock ticked on the shelf. Finally, he said, "I don't want to be shoveled around in a nursing home like a bag of rotting potatoes. My mother disintegrated right in front of me. Every day she went a little further away until one day she didn't know me at all. Sometimes I'd go up and find her sitting in a dark corner somewhere, strapped to her chair. I'd wheel her back to her room and sit, having these surreal conversations with her about black leather shoes and how she wished she knew where she'd put them. After a while, I stopped going. I just couldn't do it anymore. Dad stayed to the end. He found her lying stone cold in her own shit."

Janet went up to Neil as the words she wanted to say crashed up against each other. She took a deep breath and gazed into his tragic face. "I promise you ... no matter what, I'll never put you in one of those places."

He blinked. As his finger traced her lips and ran down over her neck, he broke into an expression that said, *I love you for it, but you don't know what you're saying.*

Three weeks later, Janet and Neil sat reading magazines in the spacious mint green waiting room of the Neurologist. They waited for over twenty minutes along with several others who sat with them on the third floor of the Physician's Office Building. Janet wondered what was taking so long. Her nerves were frayed from waiting so long to find out about Neil's battery of tests. She glanced at him out of the corner of her eye as he read his magazine. The door opened beside them and his name was called.

They followed a short blond haired assistant down the carpeted hall to the end and were shown into the doctor's office. When the door was pulled shut behind them, Janet heard Neil take a deep breath as he sat in the upholstered brown cloth chair.

Dr. Childe's office was spartan. A simple cherry desk sat in the center of the room. A matching credenza with a few photos and a clipper ship in a glass bottle sat behind a wingback leather chair. A blue and white Persian rug ran over a hardwood floor.

Dark purple painted walls were dotted with accreditations and diplomas and a cream colored blind held the outdoor sun at bay.

Neil tapped his foot on the floor and pinned his shaking arm underneath his leg. Janet took her seat and looked straight ahead. At last he cleared his throat. "I wonder how Nate's doing with his big sister?"

Janet glanced over at him. Saw the tension in his face. "I'm sure he's having fun with her. You okay?"

"I'm doing. Just wish this was over with."

"It will be … soon."

The door opened and the doctor stepped in with a folder in hand. Neil stood up, offered his hand into the man's long fingered grasp. Janet smiled politely. She had only met Dr. Childe once. Had forgotten how tall he was. The man had them sit back down then climbed in behind his desk like a pilot into a cockpit. He loosened his dark red tie and opened the folder. After a brief moment of consulting with it, he took his glasses off and looked up, staring at Neil with deep-set black eyes. "Well, Neil, it's confirmed. You have Parkinson's. But it's early yet."

"Catching it early. That's good, right?" Janet said.

"Yes, it is," the doctor said, leaning back into his chair. He looked at Neil. "If we keep a close eye on it and medicate appropriately, there's no reason why you can't keep a healthy lifestyle for a good long while."

"So, it won't get any worse?" Neil said.

The doctor bent forward. "I'm afraid it will. Parkinson's is a progressive and degenerative disease." He got up and went over to a bookcase. Took a volume down and opened it on his desk to a plate showing the brain. He pointed to a part near the center of the organ. "This region here, called the Substantia Nigra, is where things are going wrong for you. What essentially happens with Parkinson's is the nerve cells here that secrete Dopamine, which are critical in motor control, deteriorate. For some reason, which we don't totally understand, they are easily damaged more so than in other parts of the brain. Since you've never been a drug user or been in a serious accident, I can only surmise it may have happened during your bout with pneumonia a few years ago."

Janet's brow flew up. "Pneumonia!"

Neil shrugged. "Never thought about it really, until the Doc here questioned me on it." He turned back to the doctor. "So, what now?"

"Well, for one thing we're going to put you on *Parcopa* and *Madopar* right away and I want to start seeing you regularly every other week until we're comfortable with how things are going. Also, I want to see you on a wellness maintenance program of physiotherapy, exercise, and an appropriate diet. Weight often times plays an important role." He sat back down and opened Neil's chart again. "I want to see you drop at last thirty pounds, more if possible."

Neil coughed. "Thirty?"

"Yes, that would put you right around 215. I'd prefer 195, but I'll take whatever we can get."

Janet could see her husband's shoulders sag. No more of his beloved potatoes or lasagna or baked goods. The loss of apple fritters with his morning coffee would be the hardest.

The doctor pulled out a script pad from his drawer and wrote down his orders on four separate sheets.

"This, here," he said, sliding the first one toward Janet, "is a referral to a physiotherapist. And this one is for a nutritionist. The last two are your medications."

Neil nodded. "What about my job?"

"I see no reason you can't continue to practice."

Neil smiled then a puzzled expression came to his face. "Why is it when I write or draw, my hand doesn't shake?"

"That, I haven't quite figured out," the doctor said. "But it might be the brain having something to do, rather than just idling around. Is there anything else I can answer for you?"

Janet spoke up. "What about me, what can I do?"

Dr. Childe tore off another script sheet and scribbled a name and number on it. "This is a support group that meets monthly. They're wonderful, and you two should both go. As I said, the disease isn't far along, and we can keep it moving at a snail's pace if we treat it right. And don't be afraid to call me at any time."

The doctor stood up. An obvious sign the consultation was over. They said their good-byes and went out of the room and down the hall. When they were in the lobby waiting for the elevator, Janet said, "You okay?"

"I feel better. But thirty pounds?"

"Yes, I know. You want your last supper before we go home or do you want to start your diet right now?"

He thought about it for two seconds. "Let's go eat at Jakes! I'm having the Italian platter."

17

May 11th, 1991 –

Janet put the groceries in her car while Nate sat in the front seat munching a cookie. A sea of cars flowed over the supermarket parking lot on a bright, warm Saturday morning. Janet felt glad to be getting out of the store and away from the foraging crowds. She shut the hatch door of their new Dodge Caravan, pushed the cart to the side, and joined her son. He was getting bigger, and every day took on more of his father's looks. He eyed her attentively and knotted his face the way children did when thinking deep thoughts.

"Mom, are you mad at Dad?" he said as he put his seat belt on.

The question caught her sideways. "No, Nate. Why?"

He bit his cookie, and as he chewed, said, "I heard you and Dad yelling last night."

Janet regarded him and felt as if she'd been struck with a sledgehammer. "We were having a little disagreement, sweetie." But it was more than that. In fact, it was getting to the point she couldn't even talk to Neil anymore without enduring another round of him doubting himself and using it to make her feel guilty. It was manipulative and stupid. Why couldn't he see what he was doing? Yes, his forgetfulness was frustrating, but his moping about it and then using her frustration against her was worse.

The memory of last night's argument replayed itself in her head. It really wasn't so much an argument as it was a scolding, and she was the one giving it. *Am I really a bitch? Debit cards aren't all that difficult to get replaced. But, it's getting old, and I'm beginning to feel like an idiot calling the bank for, what, the third time in six months to get the damn thing replaced.* She shook her head and forced the memory away. They were going to Fogarty State Park to take in the ocean today. Why ruin something she and Nate had looked forward to over the last week?

She threw a smile on. "Are you excited to be going to the ocean?"

Nate beamed a smile at her. "Yes, Mom. Can I wear my new swim suit?"

"Of course you can." She leaned over and kissed him on his forehead. Inhaled his fresh-washed essence. Suddenly, it hit her that she hadn't felt a connection with Neil for a long time. She looked up and away from Nate as the uneasy thought drove itself into her. *Are we drifting apart? Are we turning into my parents?*

The deep blue dome over the gray waters of the Pacific was without a single cloud, and in it shone a molten sun. Janet forced Nate to sit on the large *Bugs Bunny Roadrunner* terry cloth towel and slathered sun block on his back, arms, legs, feet, and face. The boy squirmed, anxious to go play at the water's edge while Barney, who now, a step slower than he used to be, paced beside them. At heart, he was still a puppy. Neil sat next to them in his baggy, red swimming trunks reading *Awakenings*. His legs, thin and bony from losing so much weight over the last seven years, were stretched out over the towel. His back was propped up in one of the new style beach chairs that had no legs. He had been quiet all the way to Fogarty. She covered the last square inch of Nate's back and sent him off to play.

Offering the bottle of lotion to Neil, she said, "Want some?"

He dog-eared his page, set the book in his lap and looked up. "Thanks." As he dabbed lotion in his palm, he added, "Sorry about last night."

"Me, too." She paused. She had been playing with an idea since that morning's grocery shopping. "I think we ought to take a vacation. We haven't been anywhere in the last three years."

He shrugged. "I know, and I'm sorry. Work's been a real bear. When did you have in mind?"

She could feel the oncoming resistance, and braced herself. "Soon. Maybe August."

He rubbed his chin. "I'm not sure if I can get away then. It's a busy time for us."

"Then when?" she pressed.

"I don't know. I'll check my calendar when we get home."

She painted a false smile on her face and made her voice thin and demanding. "Well, make it a priority, okay?"

"I'll do my best. Any place in mind?"

"I don't know, anywhere ... but a long ways away from Salem. And I want it to be just the two of us."

"A second honeymoon?" he said, raising his brow.

"Yeah. We need time away together. I need time away ... with you."

"I wasn't aware of that," he said. "Is this about last night?"

"Partly." She sighed. Sometimes he was so one track. "But it's more than that. Neil, we've been going through the motions for a while now."

"It happens."

She bit down her anger at his reply, hating it when he made such pat remarks about really important stuff. It was almost like he didn't care and wasn't interested in doing anything about it. Finally, she said, "Yes, it happens. But it's more than that. I feel like we're drifting apart. And lately..." She fell quiet, letting the words hang in the air between them.

"And what?" he said, looking at her hard.

Her voice was but a whisper. "And I feel like, I don't know ... that the romance and desire we had isn't there anymore. It's like we're just going through the motions."

"I see." He looked away. "And, so what happens if this vacation doesn't work?"

"I don't know. I can't see that far. But I want to try. I don't want to go through the rest of our lives this way."

"We won't. But you can't always be on top of the mountain, Janet."

She looked up. *How can I make him understand?* "Neil, you won't let me in anymore. You drop into these moods, and when you do, you disappear."

"Mom, look what I made," Nate said, running up with Barney.

"What did you make, sweetie?"

"Come see!"

"Okay." To Neil, she said, "Coming?"

"Yeah." He got up and followed them to Nate's sand castle. They stood around the simple, but well thought out sculpture, praising Nate's artistry. Their son had constructed a perimeter rampart wall, and inside it were sand pail formed turrets that had windows and doors etched into their sides.

"That's good, honey." To Neil, she added, "Isn't it?"

Neil dropped to his knees and studied the castle closer. Nate watched him, his eyes telling her that he needed his father's approval. *Please Neil, don't look for ways to improve it. Just let him bask in your praise for once.* At last, Neil said, "It's very good, Nate. What's this supposed to be?" He said, pointing to a square ridge inside the rampart wall.

"It's a landing place for the dragon," Nate said as if it should've been obvious.

"Oh, a dragon. Is he a like a sentry?" Neil said.

Nate looked at him puzzled. Janet said, "A guard."

"Oh. No, Dad, he's for riding."

"I see. So, he lands here and they get on?"

Nate bent down beside him. "Yeah."

"Well, if he's big, wouldn't they need a tall platform right here so they could get on?" Neil said.

Nate frowned. "I guess."

Janet sighed. Neil looked up at her. A questioning expression was on his face. She shook her head. "I'm sure you were going to put one there, isn't that right, Nate?"

The boy shrugged. "I guess."

"Why don't you do it then and when you're finished you come get us." She bent over and tapped Neil on the shoulder, letting him know she wanted to talk with him privately. When they were out of Nate's earshot, she said, "Why do you always have to point out things like that to him? Can't you tell him it's good and let him be happy about it?"

"I did tell him it was good," he said. "I was merely suggest-ing–"

"But to a seven year old, suggesting is the same as criticizing. Neil, he worships you. You need to let him have a few victories without suggestions every once in a while. God knows he'll get enough criticism in his life without you adding to it right now."

Neil frowned. Looked off. "Yeah, you're right. You're always right," he said, his voice thin and clipped.

"What's that supposed to mean?"

"It means I don't seem to be right about much of anything anymore," he said. His hand began to shake more than usual. A sign that he was upset. "I wonder... " he dropped off and turned to go back to their towel.

She chased after him and grabbed his shoulder, turning him around. "Wonder what, Neil?"

"Never mind. Look, I really don't want to get into anything right now. I'm tired of arguing," he said. He blinked and looked away. When he spoke, his voice was strained. "Sometimes, you make me feel like I'm a child who can't take care of himself, let alone my son."

She closed her eyes and kicked at the sand under her feet. The long silence between them was filled with the arguing of gulls, the chatter of other people around them, the sounds of children playing and babies giggling and bawling. Finally, she said, "I don't think you're a child. You just don't think sometimes. He's seven years old. It's been a long time since you were seven. You've forgotten how to get down on his level and play."

He sucked his cheeks in and nodded. "Guess you have the advantage there."

She wasn't sure if that was meant as a teasing jab or a biting remark. She let it pass. "I want to go with you the next time you see the doctor."

He turned and looked at her startled. "Why?"

"Because, I want to ask him some things."

"Such as?" he said.

"I want to know if Parkinson's affects memory and mood."

"And if it does?"

"Then at least I'll understand what the hell's going on." As she said it, it occurred to her that every day, Neil's job demanded a good memory in order to juggle the six or seven projects he was working on. How was he doing it? And if he had a strategy, why wasn't he using it at home? And if he didn't have a strategy, was he being covered for at work, or worse yet, was he screwing up and no one had noticed. The thought of him losing his job made her stomach flip. Finally, she put out her hand and said, "Look, we've got to get this figured out. I can't keep going through this, and neither can Nate. Do you want us to be a family?"

"Yes, of course I do! What kind of question is that?"

"Well you're certainly not acting like it lately. In fact you haven't acted like much of anything for the last few months."

"Meaning?"

"You brood all the time. You live in that fucking office in Albany, and when you're not there, you're upstairs with your head buried in a set of drawings."

"It's my job, Janet!"

"Yeah, right." She shook her head then continued, "It's more than that, and you know it." She paused, debating her next move. She felt trapped with no way out but to go nuclear. Now her hands were shaking and it felt as if her lungs might burst. She gathered her strength and forced herself to look him straight in the eye and said, "Either you let me come with you or–"

"Or what?"

"Or we're through. I've had it."

His eyes grew large. Another long stretch of silence ensued between them, and it seemed as if everything around them had been sucked up into a dark hole. Finally, he said, "Is that a fact?"

She felt her heart thud. Part of her wanted to take back the words, to go back and start the conversation over. But it was too late now, and if he was willing to let her walk away, then what did it say about their marriage? She crossed her arms in front of her, and said, "Yes. I will not live in a shroud of secrecy anymore."

"Secrets? I don't keep secrets from you."

"Don't you? You don't talk to me. I ask to go with you to see the doctor, and you stonewall me. Your moods are up and down like a yoyo."

"I've got a lot on my mind," he protested.

"So don't we all. You know what I think?"

"What?"

"I think you're obsessing you're going to end up like you're mother, and it's eating you up ... eating us up. Is that what you want?"

"No, it's not what I want. It's just that..."

"Then what, Neil?"

"I don't know. I try the best I can."

She eyed him. "Really? Well, you're doing a piss poor job of it lately. What is it with you? Can't you see I'm trying to help you? Can't you see I love you? Can't you see that Nate needs you? Put away your stupid pride for one God damned minute and consider us for once."

He frowned. "I do consider you and Nate ... all the time."

"It certainly doesn't feel like it. So what's it going to be?"

"What's what going to be?"

"Are you going let me come with you to see Dr. Childe or not?"

He stood there looking at her, and in his eyes, she could see him trying to figure out whether she was serious or not. *I hope you don't call me on this Neil because as much as I want us to work, I'll walk if I have to.* Finally, he said, "Very well, you win. I hope you're happy."

He started to turn away, and she reached out and put her hand on his shoulder. "This isn't about winning. It's about taking care of each other. Remember our vows, Neil? In health and in sickness?" She held him with a penetrating gaze for a moment and then turned and went back to Nate.

"Hi Neil," Dr. Childe said, entering the exam room. "Oh, Janet, you're here, too." He gave her a friendly smile and took a seat across from Neil, who was dressed and perched on the examination table. The room was small and painted a mute tan. A poster on the wall beside her showed a color cut-away section of the brain.

They chatted about the weather and the Gulf War for a bit. Finally, Dr. Childe turned to Neil and said, "So, what's going on with you?"

Neil shrugged. "I seem to be having more problems with my memory."

The doctor crossed his legs and scanned Neil's chart. "What kind of problems?"

Neil's glance darted over to Janet. "I set things down and five minutes later can't remember where I put them. Or someone'll tell me something and before the conversation's done with, it's gone right out of my mind."

"This happening all the time?" the doctor said. He looked up and gave Neil his full attention.

Neil pressed his lips together. "Not all the time."

Dr. Childe wrote in the chart. "Any disorientation? Not know where you are all of a sudden?"

Neil shook his head. "No, none of that."

"Forget phone numbers of people you know by heart? Names of family?"

"No." Neil's gaze drifted toward the window.

Janet remained silent, content to just listen for the time being. The doctor turned his gaze to her then put it back onto Neil. "How are you sleeping?"

Neil bent his eyes back onto the doctor. "Good ... most of the time."

"Appetite?"

"All right, I guess."

"Well you look good," Dr. Childe said. "Still doing South Beach?"

"Most of the time."

The doctor looked down at his notes. "Any depression?"

Janet saw Neil catch his breath. He shot her a wary gaze and slowly moved his hand and put it under his leg, pinning it to the papered surface of the examination table. "A little," he muttered, and she saw him swallow hard.

Dr. Childe's gaze darted back and forth between her and Neil. "Is there something you want to tell me, Neil?"

Neil hesitated. Janet knew he didn't want to tell the doctor the truth, but with her there, he was forced into it. At last, Neil said, "I've been sort of struggling, I guess. At least that's what she says."

Janet piped in. "His moods bounce around like a ping-pong ball. Some days he's bright and cheerful, and others he sulks like a child."

Neil shot her a glaring look but kept silent. The doctor set his pen down and Janet could see him drawing conclusions. Finally he said, "You're worried you're becoming your mother, aren't you, Neil?"

"The thought crossed my mind," Neil conceded.

Understatement of the year, but at least now he's admitting it, Janet thought.

"Okay, we're going to do a little test here. I want you to look at the three words I'm going to write on this sheet of paper then give it back to me. Later, I'm going to ask you what they are." He scribbled the words down and handed Neil the sheet. "Got them?"

Neil nodded and gave him back the paper.

"Okay. First question, and these might seem mundane and idiotic, but bear with me. Where do you live?"

"7785 Hazelwood Road."

"And what day is today?"

"Wednesday."

"What is your daughter's name?"

"Megan."

The doctor drew something on his pad and handed it to Neil. "What is that a picture of?"

"A bicycle."

"What's Janet's birthday?"

"Careful, Neil," Janet said, grinning.

He gave her a crooked smile. "May 23rd."

"And who is president of the United States right now?"

"Bill Clinton."

The doctor looked down at his chart. "What are the three words I asked you to remember?"

Neil's eyes suddenly grew wide. He licked his lips. "Sand, water and … and … and … shit … and bone? Bone right?"

"That's right," the doctor said. He smiled and got up. "And don't worry about it. There's no failing the test." He extended his hand, palm up, and waited for Neil to put his hand in it. "How's your tremor?"

"Not bad. 'Cept when I'm stressed, it gets worse."

The doctor checked his reflexes along with the usual things doctors did: blood pressure, heartbeat, peering into the eyes with his pen light. As he palpated Neil's shoulders, he said, "You're taking your meds regularly?"

Neil nodded.

The doctor stepped back. "You're in great shape." He clicked his pen and stuck it back in his lab coat. For a moment Janet thought that was it, but he sat back down, put his hands together and steepled his long fingers upon his lap. Finally, he said, "I think the loss of your short-term memory and depression is related to your knowing too much about your mother's dementia. Sort of like a reinforcing causal loop that feeds on itself, and so you always end up in the same place you started, fearing the worst with each and every incident of forgetting and that is what is making you miserable, and I might add, your wife."

"Sort of like a self-fulfilling prophesy?" Janet said, piping in.

"Yes, exactly," the doctor replied. "That isn't to say we shouldn't keep an eye on your forgetfulness, Neil. And from now on, I want Janet with you when you come to see me."

"Just wonderful," Neil said with a grunt. "A spy. You don't know what you've just done to me."

"I'm quite sure you'll live," Dr. Childe said, and he wrote out three scripts and stood.

"What are these for?" Neil said, taking them.

"Routine blood work and a CAT scan. I want a base line in case I need it later on." He offered his hand to Neil and after they shook, excused himself.

Janet felt better. Now, if only Neil would believe what Dr. Childe said, perhaps his moods would level out and they would find each other again. She said, "Well?"

He shrugged. "Okay, so you told me so." He looked at her out of the corner of his eye. "So go ahead and gloat, you earned it."

"I'm not gloating. Aren't you relieved?"

"I guess," he said, and a tiny smile came to his face. "Now you'll really have a reason to yell at me if I lose something. Or maybe you'll just hide things from me and watch me run around like a rat in a maze trying to find it."

She was buoyed by Neil's comedic attempt. "Not me. You think I would do something like that?" she said, ushering him out of the exam room.

"In a New York minute if you thought it'd be entertaining." He laughed.

She squeezed his hand. "Hungry?"

"Ravenous."

"Nate won't be home from school for another hour and a half. Let's celebrate."

"Celebrate what?"

"That there's nothing wrong. Want to go to Jakes?"

His eyes lit. "Don't tease me like that."

Janet put her arms around his neck and gave him a lingering playful gaze. "Oh, I think we can make an exception this time."

He smiled. "That, I'm definitely in town for."

"Good. And you can tell me over a burger where we're going on vacation this summer."

"That's entrapment!"

"I know." And she kissed him playfully.

18

June 19th, 1994 –

Janet stepped out of the bathroom and back into the bedroom where Neil was lying in bed, writing in his medical diary with Barney by his side. She wrapped a towel around her hair and sat at her dressing table. In the mirror, she saw him watching her. "Good morning. Did I wake you?"

"No, I was awake." He set the diary down on the night table beside him. "Well, it's Nate's big day. I hope he doesn't try and over reach himself on the mound."

"He'll be fine. You worry more than he does."

"Maybe, but I know him. When he gets hyped, he tries to throw the ball harder than he should and then he gets in trouble."

"Do me a favor? Keep that to yourself." She unraveled the towel around her hair and started combing the snarls out. She looked in the mirror and saw fine wrinkles around her eyes. She frowned and looked closer, as if doing so would make them go away. "I'm getting old," she complained.

"Oh, please. Don't talk to me about old. You're quite lovely."

"You're biased." She shook her head and sighed. "So, did you sleep well?"

In the mirror, she saw Neil pick up the diary and start writing again. "Yeah. You?"

"Tossed and turned." She thought for a moment as she watched him write in the journal the doctor had given him. It started out as an exercise to help maintain his motor skills and over the last three years had turned into a haven for his dark thoughts to be exercised and worked out. She looked back remembering how she had gutted those trying times out between them, and couldn't say whether she had done it because she loved him or because she had simply gotten used to it. In fact, she wasn't sure where the line between being in love and loving someone was anymore. Did it matter? She turned around and said, "How much am I in there?"

He looked up. "In where?"

"Your journal," she said.

He twisted his body, as if in discomfort, and said, "Some, why? You never asked me about it before. How come now?"

"I don't know," she said. "Anything wrong?"

"No."

She shrugged and combed another snarl out of her hair. Looking back over her shoulder, she said, "You ever write things about what could've been?"

"Like what?"

"I don't know. Like what if we had never met? Or what life would be like if I were older or you, younger?"

He set his pen down and ran a trembling hand through Barney's graying fur. "Not really. Although, there are places I suppose where I thought about it a little."

"Right." She pushed the idea away, plugged in her hair dryer and said, "Do you love me?"

He straightened up and eyed her quizzically. "Of course I do. Something wrong?"

"No, never mind."

Neil frowned. "Now it's my turn to get tough. Everything's not all right. Come over here."

"I'm fine, really," she lied. But everything wasn't all right. She wanted to feel the fire that had been there when they first fell in love. But it wasn't there. They just existed together, each living their own separate life. She studied his face in the mirror. It had thinned over the past few years. "Tell me, when you look at me, what do you see?"

"My best friend," he said. "Talk to me."

"About what?"

"What's going on?"

She set the hair dryer down, walked over, and crawled up on the bed next to Barney. "I don't know. I just feel like we're drifting apart again. We don't do anything anymore."

"We're just in a little rut, Janet. It happens. We'll climb out. We always do."

"But we've been in this rut for months." When he cocked a skeptical brow, she added, "Well, it feels like it to me. And I feel so apart from you sometimes."

He removed his hand from Barney and put it over hers. "Don't we talk now?"

She looked away. "Yeah, but–"

"But what?"

"I don't know. I mean we talk, but we don't say anything really. Just, how are you? How do you feel? Did you sleep well? It's all trivial stuff."

He patted her hand and put his finger under her chin, raising it up so she was looking at him. For the first time, she noticed a slight jiggling of his head, as if he were one of those animal toys whose head bounced around whenever they were touched. He said, "Okay, let's talk then. What do you want to know?"

She let out a tragic laugh. "It's not that easy. You just can't order up a conversation."

He sighed. "Now, who's disconnecting? Look, you want to talk? I'm listening. But I'm not a mind reader."

She looked at him, and her heart sank. How did they get here? It was as if they were on separate planets. Finally, she said, "I want us back. I want to feel the excitement of being with you again. I want us to feel alive again. The way it is right now, I feel like we're just going through the motions all over again."

He considered her with a long, probing gaze. "Then maybe we need to do something about it." He paused and she watched him brainstorming. "What about a weekend away for us? But, hold on—I'm planning it and you're not going to know anything about it."

"Really?" *What an intriguing thought.*

"Yeah. Get your calendar and mine from the office, and let's get it booked."

She slipped off the bed and stepped into the hall to see Nate shuffling toward her, hair running in all directions over his head and face. "Hi honey. Ready for your big day?"

He yawned. "Is breakfast ready?"

"That depends on what you want. If it's cereal, you know where it is."

"Can we do French toast?" he said, giving her a fetching smile.

"Alright, why don't you go get dressed and wash your face and hands? Dad and I are figuring something out and as soon as we're done, I'll be right down.

Twenty minutes later, Neil walked into the kitchen. "So what time again do we pick up your father?" He sat down at the table and balled his hand into a fist and opened it up, stretching his fingers out like a starfish. He did this several times every morning, working the muscles and tendons in his tremulous hand. The exercise kept the muscles strong and helped resist the growing tremors.

"Noon," she said. She spied Nate shoveling a large fork load of French toast into his mouth. "Nate, slow down," she said. To

Neil, she continued, "I think grandpa's more excited than Nate is about this game."

"He's a big sports fan," Neil said. "Trevor was into basketball. He was pretty good at it, too."

Janet raised a brow. Neil rarely talked about Trevor. She wondered if she should encourage him to say more, but as she thought about it, he glanced off through the window into the morning sunlight. "Coffee?" she said.

"Yeah, thanks." He pushed his cup toward her and pulled the morning paper off the counter.

"Is Megan coming?" she said, turning off the burner under the skillet. She dished the last three slices of French toast on top of the small stack on the platter and set it on the table.

The paper rustled in Neil's hand as he sipped his coffee. "Said she was." He scanned the headlines and then helped himself to some toast and doused a healthy portion of maple syrup over it.

She waited until he was done. "And Brad?"

"Yep." He reached for the bacon and plucked a slice off the grease-soaked paper towel. As he put it in his mouth, his eye twitched and an odd expression flashed across his face. He looked down as if trying to catch his breath.

Janet stopped what she was doing. Studied him. Felt a shiver run through her. "Neil, you alright?"

He looked up. "I feel a little dizzy." He took a deep breath and all at once, his gaze turned inward as if he were deep in thought. His hand jerked several times and he started to get up. The chair slid back and before she knew it, he tumbled to the floor.

Neil!" She flew around the table. Kneeled beside him. Barney started barking.

There was no answer, only a confused expression on his face. He tried to get up but couldn't.

"Mom, what's wrong with Dad?" Nate cried, kneeling beside her.

"I don't know, honey. Get the phone. Hurry! And Barney, shut up!" She pulled Neil toward her.

"Here Mom," Nate said all at once gliding back down beside her. He handed her the receiver.

Janet punched in 911 then put the receiver to her ear. *Hurry up, hurry. Answer, answer! Come on, come on.* "Yes! I need an ambulance. My husband just collapsed ... Yes, he's breathing. Yes, he's conscious, but he's not alert." She eyed Neil anxiously as she gave her address to the woman on the other end. A line of drool ran out of the corner of Neil's mouth. Finally, the woman came back on. "Yes, I'm still here," Janet answered.

"An ambulance is on the way," the woman said. "How old is he?"

"Sixty-five ... No, no history of heart disease ... No strokes either ... yes, yes. Right." She eyed Nate. "Get a pillow and a blanket."

The two of them gently coaxed Neil to lean back onto the floor and rest his head in Janet's lap.

"He's gonna be alright, right Mom?" Nate said as the color drained from his face. "Nothing's going to happen to him, right?"

"No, nothing's going to happen, Nate. He's gonna be fine," Janet said, and she prayed to God she was right. "Now get those things I asked you for."

Janet stepped into the ER exam room where Neil lay on the gurney with his back propped up while chatting with a nurse. When he saw her, he put his hand out. She went to his side and studied him. The skin below his left eye was drawn down slightly, but he smiled. With a mild slur, he said, "This wasn't the surprise I had in mind for you."

She felt the heavy fear that had dogged her since he collapsed that morning slip away, and she managed a tiny grin. If she had any doubts about whether she loved him or not, they had been thoroughly extinguished. She said, "Some people will do anything for attention."

He squeezed her hand. "How's Nate doing?"

"Much better. He's with grandpa out in the waiting room."

"The doc said I had a petite stroke. Nothing serious."

"I know. How do you feel?"

He shimmied himself up so he sat erect with his feet out in front of him. "All right, I guess. I could use another blanket, though."

The nurse turned around from whatever she was doing. "I'll bring one right over after I'm finished."

Janet cupped her hand to Neil's cheek. "You scared the hell out of me."

"Sorry about that. Scared myself a little, too. Did you let Megan know?"

"Dad called her. She's on her way." The nurse came over with the blanket and draped it over his feet. Janet waited until she was gone and put the finishing touches of tucking it in around his legs. "How's that?"

"Much better. Thank-you. Did they tell you how long I'm stuck up here for?"

"Not yet. They want to do some tests."

"Great," he said, pursing his lips. "Oh..."

"What?" Janet said, alarmed.

"Nate's game. I've completely ruined it for him."

She shook her head. "He's fine, don't worry." She turned to another nurse who had come in. "Can my son see his father? He's in the waiting room with his grandfather."

"Absolutely," the man said. "Stay here and I'll go get him."

"Thanks," Janet said. She pulled up a folding chair, careful not to bump into the I.V. pole next to Neil's gurney. "I love you to pieces, you know that?"

"And I love you to pieces, too. You know, it was so strange when it happened. I could see you, but it was like you were a million miles away."

The morning's event flashed before Janet's eyes for the hundredth time: her supporting Neil's head in her lap, combing her fingers through his hair; the drool running over his chin sending a galvanizing fear whose memory still struck terror in her heart. She pushed the memory away. "It's over now, and the doctor says you're going to be fine."

Neil winked. "Did he? That's good to know."

Nate appeared at the door with the nurse. He stood there a moment then slowly crept in. Neil looked up. "There's my guy. Sorry I screwed up your game."

"It's okay, Dad," Nate said eyeing his father warily as if he were afraid something might happen at any moment.

"Well, am I going to get a hug then?" Neil said, letting go of Janet's hand. He opened his arms and pulled the boy into his arms as the doctor arrived.

"Hello, I'm Dr. Faharo," said a stocky man, maybe a little taller than Janet. His aquiline nose and smooth, dark olive skin gave him an exotic look, Indian or Middle Eastern maybe. He held out a thick hand to Janet that had a broad gold wedding band and stood by as Nate disengaged himself from his father's arms. "How are you feeling, Mr. Porter?"

Neil shrugged. "Pretty good."

"You had a small vascular event this morning. Nothing too serious, but it needs to be looked at very carefully to make sure it is not a harbinger of things to come. I am scheduling you to have a CAT scan and some more blood work. I see here you have Parkinson's disease. How long have you had it?"

"Nine, ten years," Neil said.

"And you are currently taking Parcopa and Madopar?"

"Yes," Janet answered.

"Any history of heart disease in your family?"

"No," Neil replied.

The doctor nodded. "And no stroke or vascular disease either?"

"Not that I know of," Neil replied. He reached over and grabbed the glass of juice the nurse had set on his tray earlier.

"Trouble sleeping?"

Neil took a sip and set the glass down. "Sometimes. Not often, though."

"Okay then, that is all the questions that I have for now." He reached into his lab coat pocket and pulled out a penlight. "Could you please to look straight over my shoulder?" The doctor bent forward and shined the light into Neil's eyes, first one then the other. "Good, and good." He picked up a small tuning fork from the counter behind Janet, banged it against his hand and put it to Neil's leg. "You feel that?"

"Yep."

"And here?"

"Yep."

The doctor put his hand to Neil's face, turning his head one way and then the other. "Well, you have a little paralysis on the left side, but nothing too noticeable. Now, I have called your neurologist, Dr. Childe. He will be coming to see you tomorrow. For now, depending on what comes back from hematology, I think I will be putting you on a blood thinner called *Coumadin*. It will help to make sure that if there are any further small clots that they will be dissolved, so we will not have any more unfortunate events."

"So, I'm up here for the night?" Neil said.

"I am afraid so. But our kitchen is much better now I am told, so you will not go hungry. I will see about a room for you as soon as we are done. Are there any questions you would like to ask?"

"Yeah," Neil said. "How long am I out of commission–from work that is?"

Dr. Faharo thought a moment. "You are an architect, no? So could be a week or maybe two, just to make sure. We shall see. We do not want to rush things." He smiled and turned toward Nate. "This is your grandson?"

Janet cleared her throat. Nate frowned. Neil said, "He's my son."

"Oh! I am so sorry. Please forgive me." He gave Janet a second look then. "And you are his wife?"

"Yes," Janet said. "Don't feel bad. Everyone makes the same mistake."

"Well, I will leave you now. Have a good day." He turned and left the room, just as Megan showed up.

"Dad, are you okay," Megan said, rushing to his side. She put her arms around him and hugged him tightly.

"Careful, girl! My I.V."

"Oh, sorry." She looked at Janet. "So, was that the doctor just then?"

"Yeah."

"And?"

"I'm fine," Neil said, breaking in. "Just a little mini stroke."

Megan's eyes widened. "A stroke!"

"Nothing major. The doctor says I'm gonna be just fine."

Megan shook her head. "But what are they doing about it?"

"They're gonna run some tests," Neil said. "Sit down and relax sweetie. You're making me nervous. And say 'hi' to your brother."

"Oh, hi Nate," Megan said. She came over and kneeled down in front of him. "I'm sorry. How're you doing guy?"

"I'm okay."

"Good. You're father's gonna be just fine."

Janet stood. *I think I'll get out of here and let them be alone.* "Nate, you hungry? Let's go down to the cafeteria and let your sister have some time with your father, okay?"

Nate shoved his hand in his pocket and followed her out of the exam room. On the way, Janet collected her father and the three of them melted into the busy corridors of Salem Hospital.

19

Three months after Neil collapsed on the kitchen floor with a minor stroke, Janet noticed changes. Where in the beginning he laughed often and was extremely attentive, now he had become quiet; almost secretive, and over the last three weeks had worked a lot of overtime. Janet worried. The last thing she needed was for him to have another stroke, and who knew how bad that would be. He wasn't driving yet; instead, he rode into work with one of the guys. Alan, she thought his name was. So that was good. As for who brought him home at all hours of the evening–that was usually whoever was available.

What really bothered her was his avoiding her inquiries about what was going on at work that required his attendance so late into the evenings. Aside from that, tomorrow was their eleven-year anniversary, and he hadn't mentioned a word about it.

She pulled into the parent drop-off loop at Nate's school and found a spot to park. She arrived twenty minutes early because the outdoor shoot of a building in town had been cut short by sudden rain. As she sat in her car looking through the rain-spattered windshield, she thought about Neil's odd behavior. Did it have something to do with his stroke? Or was he reverting to old ways. She didn't know, and the more she thought about it, the more worked up she got.

She turned the radio on to take her mind off her growing annoyance, but her mind kept coming back to Neil's seeming ignorance of their anniversary. Well, she had done her part. Nate was all set to spend the weekend over at his best friend, Jimmy's house, and Barney was going with him.

She drummed her fingers on the steering wheel as the radio reeled out The Boss', *Born in the USA*. Five minutes later, the front door of the school opened and a river of sixth-graders came pouring out into the rain. Nate ran toward the car, backpack in hand and coat draped over his head. He opened the passenger-side door, threw his coat and pack in the back seat and got in.

"Hi sweetie. How was school?" she said, starting the car and pulling away from the curb.

"It was all right. Can I go to Jimmy's?"

"After dinner, Nate," she said.

"Jimmy said his mother was okay if I ate over there."

Janet shook her head. "What about homework?"

He frowned, and his shoulders sank. He looked out the window then suddenly looked back. "I could do it over there."

"I don't think so, Nate. Besides, you're going to be with him all weekend. You come home and eat, do your homework, and we'll see about you going over afterward."

He opened his mouth as if to say something then shut it. She glanced at him out of the corner of her eye. "So, have you decided whether you're going to play basketball this year?"

He shrugged. "A little."

"And?"

"I guess."

"You don't sound like you're crazy about it."

"It's okay. Except I never got to play much last year."

"You were just starting, honey. You're bigger now."

"Yeah, but so is everybody else," he said. "Do you think I'm smart?"

Janet raised a brow. "Of course. Why?"

"Eddie Dankin said I was stupid 'cause I need tutoring in math."

"And you listen to this Eddie?" she said.

"He's the smartest kid in school, so–"

"So what? And who says he's the smartest? Everyone has areas they have trouble with. Even Eddie Dankin. Don't ever let anyone make you think you're stupid. That gives them power over you." She turned onto the road that led to their house and kept an eye out for deer. It was that time of the year again.

Nate was thoughtful. "How come I can't do math?"

"It's not that you can't do math. It's just that it hasn't clicked in with you yet. It will. Give it time. You know, you could ask your father. He's pretty good with math."

"Maybe, except he's been working a lot and I don't see him much."

Which is something I'm going to remedy very soon, she thought. "We'll talk to him about it tonight." She pulled into the driveway and parked.

They got out of the car and ran for the house between the raindrops. Once inside, Janet set her satchel on the kitchen counter and noticed the red light blinking on the answering machine. *Neil!* She hit the playback button. Listened to the message she had grown accustomed to hearing over the last month. 'Working late. Be home as soon as I can. Hopefully around eight.' She punched the stop button and stood fuming.

"God damn him," she muttered. She rarely called him at work, but this was becoming too much. She picked up the phone and dialed his number. It rang on the other end and was finally answered by his voice mail. She knotted her brow. If he was supposed to be working, then where the hell was he? She hung up and a myriad of possibilities flooded her thoughts–all of them preposterous and none of them good.

She sighed, determined not to let her mind run away with her and decided to forget about it for the time being. Nate would be hungry in short order so she pulled out last night's leftovers from the fridge. As she turned the oven on, she noticed the reminder pad on the counter next to the toaster. Why was it there and not over by the phone? She picked it up, and as she went to put it where it belonged, noticed the sheet had impressions of writing from the page that had preceded it. She studied it, trying to make out what it said, and when she couldn't, remembered a trick she had learned in grade school. She opened the junk drawer, fished for a pencil and lightly shaded the paper with graphite until suddenly a name appeared with an address.

"Paula! Who the hell is she?" Janet muttered. The address was in the Heights. She tapped the pencil eraser on the page as Nate came into the kitchen.

"Got my homework done. Is dinner ready yet?"

She looked up. Rearranged her thoughts. "Done already?"

"It was only one page," Nate said, reaching for the cookie jar.

"Don't even think about it," she said, swatting his hand away. Let me see your assignment."

He rolled his eyes and thudded back upstairs.

Janet turned her thoughts back onto the mysterious name and address and put the leftovers in the oven. She could think of no one they knew in the Heights. Neil had some answering to do when he got home.

After she let Nate run over to his friend's house to play, Janet picked up the dishes and loaded the dishwasher. She was about to start it when the front door opened. She looked up. It was just going on seven. Neil walked in and set his brief case on the floor.

"Hi, love," he said cheerfully.

She leaned back against the counter. "You're home early."

"Yeah, we finished quicker than I thought we would. You eaten yet?"

"As a matter of fact, yes we have."

"Anything left over?" He peeled his jacket off and set it on the back of the chair.

"No. We finished what was left of last night's dinner, which you missed for the third time this week. Who's Paula?"

He froze for the tiniest of seconds. "Paula?"

"Yeah. Her name's written on the memo pad over there."

He sucked his lip. "I see you've been sleuthing. She's a client."

"Hmmm. Are we making house calls now?" Janet said.

He narrowed his gaze. "What do you mean?"

"Well, the address is in the Heights, and so far as I know, there's not a lot of offices or business out that way. Unless the partners at your firm have decided to do residential architecture now."

"You're good," he said, breaking into a smile. He went to the refrigerator and opened it. Stared inside.

"What's so funny?" she said. She was now both annoyed and perplexed.

"You'll see. Is there anything in here to eat?"

She went over and pushed the refrigerator door shut on him. "Neil? What the hell's going on?"

"I'm not telling you yet. You'll have to wait and find out."

Now she was completely baffled. *So this has something to do with our anniversary then?* "What are you up to?"

He patted her cheek with a tremulous hand. "You never mind what I'm up to." He pulled the refrigerator door open again. Grabbed a soda and popped the lid. After a gulp, he said, "I suppose I'll have to live with a TV dinner. By the way, where's Nate?"

"Over to Jimmy's house, playing," she said, feeling better now that she was fairly certain he was up to something good. She backed off on her inquisition and smiled. "Sit down. I'll throw something together for you."

"Buttering me up will get you nowhere," he said, taking a seat at the table. "By the way, I'm going to need you to pick me up tomorrow."

I can play this game, too, she thought. "Oh, not working overtime?"

"No," he said, volleying back a smile. "Planning board meeting, and my ride needs to be somewhere else."

"I see," she said. *Let's see how he deals with this.* "I can't be there until six-thirty, though. I have to take Nate to get him signed up for junior basketball."

He looked at her hard and she could see him working it out in his mind as to whether she was twitting him or not. Finally, he said, "That's alright. Meeting isn't 'til eight. We'll have plenty of time. Although, I imagine Nate will be bored as hell."

"He can do his homework. Oh, and he could use some help with his math if you have the time, unless of course, you're working overtime for the next six months."

"Not sure on that. I'll let you know." He yawned and stretched his legs out in front of him. Looked past her to where she had set a skillet on the burner to fry a burger. "In the mean time, do manage not to burn my supper."

She turned, saw the smoke rising up off the oiled surface of the skillet and turned down the flame. "Of course dear. Anything else I can do? Shine your shoes, press your pants?"

He shot her a devilish grin. "Now that I think of it, you could come over here and give me a massage."

"Is that so? What about your dinner?" she said. She turned the burner off, and with a slow alluring gait, walked over to him.

"I'll take my chances," he said and pressed his lips on her arm.

Janet dropped Nate off over to his friends and started for home to get ready for whatever Neil had in mind for her. It was now going on three and depending on traffic, she figured she had about forty-five minutes to throw on something decent, put her hair up and fix her face in time to pick Neil up from work.

As she drove, she thought about the night before. After Nate had gone to bed, Neil had come up behind her in her studio and seduced her with a trail of light wet kisses down her neck. Soon after, she found herself being led to their bedroom, slowly undressed and laid down and gently stroked in all the places she loved. She felt her nipples harden under her bra as she thought about the passion they shared the night before. *Easy girl. You'll get yourself into an accident.*

Ten minutes later, she pulled into her driveway and ran into the house. Barney looked up from where he lay on his blanket by the window then got up and followed her into the bedroom to watch her rummage through her closet. After much debate, she settled on a cream-colored cashmere blouse and a deep red pleated skirt–Neil's favorite–and peeled her jeans and top off. In the mirror she eyed her body, naked except bra and panties, and saw a woman flushed with love again.

An hour later, she pulled up in front of Neil's office and as she checked her face in the rear view mirror, Neil opened the passenger door. He got in, took a large white envelope out of his brief case and set it on the dashboard. It had no address but in the top left hand corner, a stamped label said, Salem National Bank. Janet wrinkled her brow.

"What's this?" she said, picking it up.

He snatched it away from her and set his briefcase in the back seat. "For my board meeting." His brow rose slightly as his gaze drifted over her blouse and skirt. "So where's Nate?"

"Over to Jimmy's."

"So no basketball try-out?"

"No. But we have to pick him up as soon as you're done," she said, watching him to see what effect her push back was having at this little game he was playing with her. "So, where we going?"

"It's a little out of the way. Hop onto twenty-two. I'll tell you when to exit."

"A little out of the way? Hmmm. Not too many places I don't know around the valley. Can't be that out of the way," she said, pulling the car out into traffic and easing onto the arterial.

"Well, it is," Neil said. "Trust me."

"Right." Janet smiled. *Let him have his little game. I have to admit it is fun, though. Wonder where he's taking me?* After they turned off the arterial and headed toward Dallas, she realized they were heading to Jake's. She glanced at him out of the corner of her eye. "Okay, either your planning board meeting is at Jake's or we're going to dinner. So, which is it?"

He smiled, and soon after, they were sitting at a table in Jake's. The restaurant was quiet. A TV murmured from the semi-lit bar at the other end of the room. Crisp, red tablecloths covered the tables. They ordered drinks and after the waiter left them, Neil pushed the envelope toward her. "Before you open it, I want to toast us."

"Okay," Janet said, feeling her heart beat a little quicker in anticipation. "You know, I think I like this new you."

"Is that so?" he said as the waiter came back. The man set their drinks down in front of them and was about to ask if they were ready to order when Neil shooed him away. He lifted his glass. "To us and our wonderful new future. Happy anniversary!"

New future? Bank envelope? Wait, oh my, a trip! He's taking me to Europe or Egypt maybe? I've always wanted to go there. Breathless, she drank a sip of wine and when she set it down, Neil nodded toward the envelope. "Now you may open it," he said.

She picked it up, ran her finger under the flap and pulled a long folded bundle of papers out. The top page said, DEED. She looked up, baffled. "What's this?"

Neil's eyes sparkled. "I bought us some property. I'm going to build you a house."

Janet sat with the bomb that had been laid in front of her a moment and read the front page of the deed. The address was the same address she'd seen on the pad at the house. "Neil, where did you get the money for this? It's the Heights."

"I know. I picked the place out myself. Nice treed lot with a stream."

"We already have three houses!" Janet said, bewildered. "What are we going to do with a fourth?"

He smiled. "Not to worry. I have a buyer lined up for our place."

"A buyer?" She set the deed down, took a deep breath and tried to wrap her mind around what was happening. They had always talked about large purchases in advance of going out and getting them, but this was way beyond that. This was astronomical. She shook her head. "I don't know what to say." She gritted her teeth, trying very hard not to get mad. "Where did you get the money? It's not like we're rolling in it."

Neil reached across the table and took her hand. "I never told you, but when Sharon died, I had a large policy on her. I never used any of it, except to bury her of course. I sank the rest into stocks and bonds, in case something happened to me, Megan and Trev would be taken care of. They're grown now, have their own lives. I want to use it on us. I want to build you a house."

Janet knew the property values in the Heights. The kind of money needed to buy land and build a house there ranged in the middle to upper six figures. She balled her hand into a fist and put it to her mouth as she stared at the deed. Finally, she looked up and stared at him. "How much do you have?"

Neil said, "Around a million, five or so."

Her breath caught in her throat. "A million, five?"

"Sorry I never told you. I guess I never wanted to think about using it 'til now. Never a real good reason. But after what happened to me in June, I realized life is short and wanted to do something with it instead of letting it just sit in a bank. I love you. Let me build this house for you, for us."

"Does Megan know about this?"

He shook his head. "And I don't want her to."

"I see. And just how are we going to explain building a house to her, especially there. Once she sees the area, she'll pepper us with questions. I don't like lying."

"We're not going to. Our affairs are our business!"

"Yeah, but?"

"But nothing," Neil said, sitting back. "You needn't worry."

"Maybe." Janet was of divided mind. She knew Megan. The woman wouldn't just accept a pat answer, and Janet didn't like the idea of being under a microscope, especially one Megan wielded. Still, building a new home excited her and she couldn't deny she often wished for a studio of her own.

She tucked the deed in the envelope and pushed it back to him. "If Megan gets wind of this–"

"She won't," Neil insisted. "Are you upset?"

"No. It's a beautiful gift, and I love you for it. I just want to make sure we're thinking this whole thing through before we jump in." She smiled and reached across the table for his hand. "So this was what you were up to the last month and a half. Overtime, my ass!"

"I had to throw you off somehow. It's a good thing you didn't look at the pad before, otherwise things could've gotten sticky."

"You are too much, Janet said. "You sneak! I'll never trust you again."

20

It took some time for Janet to get comfortable with selling June's house, which she had called home for better than ten years, but once she made her mind up she found herself feeling like a kid at Christmas. Of course it was a foregone conclusion she would sell the house, she just had to feel like it was her decision and not Neil's.

In the meantime, Neil busied himself around the house doing little projects on the weekend, cleaning out nooks and crannies, which hadn't seen the light of day in years. She was glad because she had been meaning to get to these little jobs for a long time and now they were being done for her.

Tonight, they would tell Nate about moving. Janet felt nervous about how her son would take the news. She remembered when she was younger how her mother uprooted her across the country. It took a long time to adjust. This wasn't the same of course, but Nate had come to be good friends with Jimmy down the street and who knew how he'd react. She set the table for dinner and went into the family room to relax by the fireplace where Barney spent much of his time lately. He looked up when she sat, pulled himself up and came over to her.

"Hey boy," she said, bending over to pet him. "How's my little guy?" The dog nuzzled her hand and flopped down beside her. It was then she saw a lump behind his ear. She got down on the floor and probed the fur around it. The lump was the size of a golf ball, and it was soft and fleshy. An anxious feeling rushed through her, and she tried to ignore it. The dog turned his soft brown eyes onto her and held her gaze for some time. It felt like he was telling her good-bye, and an unbidden tear welled in her eye. She quickly wiped it away. "We'd better get you into the vet first thing tomorrow," she said, petting him.

Over dinner, she tried to focus on the family meeting ahead where Nate would be told about their move, but all she could think of was Barney. Her gaze darted toward him often as he nibbled his kibble in the corner by the kitchen bay window.

"Everything all right, honey?" Neil said, interrupting her thoughts.

"Yeah, fine. You want some more potatoes?"

"No, I'm good." He looked at her with concern.

She glanced at Nate who was shoveling macaroni salad into his mouth at an alarming rate and shook her head. Mouthed the word, *later*, to Neil. To Nate, she said, "Slow down. It's not going to run away from you."

The boy looked up and eased the assault on his dinner. He cleared his mouth and said, "How long is this family meeting going to take?"

"I don't know, depends," she said. "Why?"

"I was thinking maybe if it's all right I could go over to Jimmy's after."

She pushed her plate away and wiped her mouth with a napkin. "We'll see," she said, which of course to Nate meant, yes. To Neil, she said, "I'm gonna start cleaning up unless there's anything else you want."

"No, I'm stuffed." He drank the last of his water, got up and scraped his plate off into the trash.

"I'll help," Nate said, trying to hurry things along. He grabbed the butter and put it away in the fridge then ran for the dishwasher and opened it.

Neil disappeared into the other room and came back with a couple of dirty glasses. He set them on the top rack of the dishwasher and stepped beside her. "He'll be okay," he whispered.

She nodded. "I know." She loaded the last of the silverware in the dishwasher, and told Neil to take Nate into the family room.

"Moving?" Nate said as if it was a foreign word.

"Yes, I'm going to build us a house," Neil said.

"Where?"

"In a place called the Heights," Neil said.

"Towards the orchards," Janet said, filling Nate in.

"Right," Neil said. "And we'll have a big yard, and there'll be trees and a stream and a large field out back."

Janet could see Nate working things out as he sat on the couch. She held her breath waiting to hear what he would say. "That's a long ways away. I won't be able to see Jimmy anymore will I?"

Neil started to tell him about new friends, but she cut him off before he said anything more. "Not as much, honey, but you'll see him. And he can come with us when we go up to the mountains every year."

"Yeah, right," Neil said, catching on. "And guess what? I'm going to design our house, and you can help me. In fact, you can design your own room. What do you think?"

Nate shrugged. "I guess. Can I do a drawing like you do, Dad?"

Neil grinned. "Of course."

Nate brightened, but Janet could see he was still unsure. She decided he'd had enough news for one night and gave him permission to go to Jimmy's.

After Nate left, Janet led Neil into the family room and called Barney over. "Put your hand right here behind his ear and tell me what you feel."

Neil bent down beside her and put trembling fingers on the dog. His brow knitted, and he looked up at her. "You just discovered this?"

"Before dinner, yes. I didn't want to say anything in front of Nate. The house was more than enough for him to deal with tonight."

Neil sighed. "You call the vet?"

She nodded. "I'm taking him in tomorrow morning, first thing."

"It's probably just one of those fleshy growths," he said getting to his feet. "My next door neighbor back east had a dog who had one of these and he did just fine."

"That's my hope," Janet said, looking up at him.

Three days passed and Janet was on pins and needles waiting to hear from the vet. Then finally, the call came. Janet stepped into Neil's office upstairs as he talked to the doctor on the other end. Suddenly, he frowned and took a deep breath. "I see. When? Yes, of course. Yeah, me too."

As Neil hung up, Janet's heart raced.

He came to her and put his arms around her. "The lump is a tumor and it's..."

"What?"

"Cancerous, and it's spread all through him."

Janet's eyes flooded with hot tears as Neil clutched her tightly. "Why is this happening?" she muttered, burying her head into his shoulder. "Why now when we're building a house."

"I don't know honey," Neil said.

"But we're finally the way I always wanted us to be. It's got to be a mistake."

Neil's body trembled. "Doctor Manning said not to wait too long. We don't want him to suffer."

Please, please, no. Oh, Barney. She bit down on her lip as Neil held her, remembering the first day she got him. It seemed like a lifetime ago.

March 1st, 1995 –

Tomorrow was the closing for the new house, but she wasn't feeling celebratory. Yesterday, she had said good-bye to her little friend and faithful companion. Outside of Neil, no living thing had heard her most deep and darkest secrets, and there was no one she trusted more to love her no matter what than Barney. Neil had bought a pet casket and had Barney embalmed and laid into it. When their house was completed, they'd find a fitting place to bury him.

Nate was utterly distraught and hadn't eaten all day or yesterday. She forced a couple of slices of toast and glass of milk down him this morning and let him stay home another day from school. Neil had already left for work, and a deathly quiet had settled over the house. From experience, Janet knew to leave Nate alone to deal with his own grief in his own way. He was a lot like her when it came to losing things you loved.

He lay in his room with the door shut. She went upstairs, peeked in on him then pulled the door shut and retreated to her studio. On her desk lay the submission for a prestigious award she'd long thought about trying for but never had the courage to enter until Neil talked her into it. She eyed the Ansel Adams entry form and started filling it out. She was half way through it when Nate shuffled in behind her. She turned around and opened her arms, and he melted into her.

Holding him for some time, she decided to get out of the house and do something. She led him downstairs, threw a jacket on him, and said, "Let's go for a ride."

"Where?" he said, pulling on his gloves.

"The ocean. I want to show you something."

They got in the car and drove to Fogarty under dark clouds with a hint of snow in the air. The beach was closed, but she didn't care. They parked along side the road, and the two of them ambled down through the tall soughing grasses to the frosted dunes.

Fifteen minutes later, they were climbing up to her grotto. Janet sat on the rim of the rocky enclosure, her hair spun out behind her in the wind. Nate joined her, and she put her arm around him. "When your grandmother brought me out to Oregon, your great aunt June, whom you never met, showed us this place. We used to come here during the summer to splash in the water and take in the ocean. Your grandmother loved it here, and so did I. As soon as I was old enough to drive, I'd come here as often as I could."

"To swim?" Nate said.

"Sometimes. Most of the time it was just to sit by the water and think."

"About what?"

"Life. Why things are the way they are."

"Like Barney?" he said quietly.

"Yes, like Barney." She was quiet a moment. "One year, just after I was out of college, I came down to do a shoot for a job, and I found this rock."

Nate looked around. "Is there something special about it?"

"Oh, yes," she answered, pulling her collar up a little more. She turned to him and zipped his jacket up as far as it would go.

He gazed up at her as if she were a beautiful queen, and said, "What's special about it, Mom?"

"It's where I made peace with myself and everything else that ever happened to me growing up."

"Like what?"

"My mom and dad breaking up. Missing my friends back east. That kind of stuff."

"And it helped."

"Yes." Her thoughts drifted back to the turbulent time in her life when it was just she and her mom against the world. It seemed like an age ago. "Anyway, this is where I fell in love with your dad."

"Really?"

"Yep. I brought him out here after your sister got hurt. He was very sad and I wanted to help him get through it."

Nate shot her a puzzled look. "Megan got hurt? How?"

"Doesn't matter. It was a long time ago, and she's all better now." *We'll, sort of.* She went on. "Anyway, your dad climbed up onto this very rock with me, and we talked for hours."

"Is that how you fell in love with him?"

Janet remembered Neil tumbling off the rock, and the two of them rolling in the sand. It brought a smile to her face. At last, she said, "Yes." She watched her son trying to work out what it meant to fall in love in his head, and she pulled him tighter. "Do you know how much I love you?"

"As much as the whole ocean?"

"More. You are the light of my life. And soon, we're going to have a new house, and you're going to have a new room with a big bed and lots of windows so you can look out at the trees and the stream–"

"Do you think there's fish in the stream, Mom?"

"Probably."

"I'm gonna fish it every day."

"I bet you will." She looked out over the gray waters and at the seagulls arguing on the shore.

"I'm getting cold, Mom. Can we go now?"

"Sure, sweetie. Hey, how about a hot chocolate on the way home?"

"And a doughnut?"

"Sure." She helped him down, and the two of them made their way back along the beach through the shifting sands. It had been what she needed, and by all appearances, Nate, too.

Neil unrolled a large sheet of paper on his desk and motioned Janet with a tremulous gesture to come have a look. She stepped up to his side and saw a sprawling plan with a broad, wrap-around porch. In the back of the house lay a large kitchen with a cooking island separating the room from a breakfast nook. A series of windows and doors raced around the two rooms and looked out onto a multi-tiered deck. A large fireplace dominated what he had labeled a 'Great Room' just off the foyer. Nate's bedroom sat on the east end and theirs on the west. Her studio lay down the hall from their bedroom past his office.

"It's preliminary for right now," he said pointing out things. "I still have to work on the master bath and bedroom. Your office, of course, will need tweaking. But it's a start. After dinner tonight, why don't we sit down and start fleshing things out?"

Janet said, "I can't believe we're really building a house."

Neil smiled. "You want me to pinch you?"

She shot him a sly grin. "You want to start something we can't finish 'til later on?"

"Promise?"

She slapped his arm. "You know, you've turned into a dirty old man."

"Thank-you," he said. "What a nice compliment." He pulled her close and kissed her square on the lips. "I'll be down in a minute. Oh, and by the way," he added with a wink, "I have an announcement to make, so a bottle of wine might be in order."

She thought about asking what it might be, but changed her mind. Not that she could've gotten it out of him, not after the way he pulled off his anniversary gift to her. Well, she had been working on an announcement of her own. Trevor had answered her letter and while his response was guarded to the idea of seeing his father again, he didn't say, 'no', either, and that was encouraging. He told her to write back or give him a call and they'd talk more about it.

"I've decided, I'm going to retire," Neil said after sipping his wine.

Nate kept right on eating, but Janet's fork froze in mid-air and she put it back down on the plate and eyed him. "Are you sure? You told me once you wanted to work 'til you couldn't lift a pencil."

"I know, but when I said it, I was in a different frame of mind. I think this new house'll keep me plenty busy, and besides, it's high time I spent time with Nate, here."

Nate looked up. "What?"

"You're father wants to spend more time with you," Janet said, "So he's retiring."

"Oh, cool." He drained his glass of milk and ran his arm across his mouth. "Can I be excused?"

"I guess," she said. "Your homework done?"

He hesitated.

"Nate!"

The boy threw his arms up. "Oh, Mom. I'll do it when I get home."

"No, you'll do it now," she insisted and shot a glance at Neil, but he was looking elsewhere, as if lost in thought, except it looked more like confused. "Neil?" she said, suddenly alarmed. "You okay?"

He came to himself. "Uh … yes. What is it?"

"Your son needs to do his homework before he goes out to play, don't you agree?"

"Nate, homework, now," Neil said, jerking his thumb toward the hallway.

Nate thumped across the room. "I never get to do anything!"

"Yeah, I know, life's tough," Janet answered. She listened for the telltale sign of Nate's footsteps going upstairs and when she heard them, said, "You're sure you feel all right? For a minute there, you had me worried."

"I'm fine. Just thinking is all."

"About what?"

He set his glass down. "What it will be like not going into work the first time. It'll be strange after all these years not having to get up and be somewhere."

The foundations went in as soon as weather permitted and the house began to take shape. Originally, it had been for just the three of them, but after some thought, they decided to add a wing for Janet's father and sell the house he lived in. Oddly enough, William didn't argue with them about moving in, except to say, not right away. He wanted to keep his independence for as long as possible as well as staying out of the middle of things. So they found him a small apartment and put the house on the market, reducing Janet's real estate empire—as Neil liked to call it—to just two properties.

Janet stood, camera in hand, on hard-packed soil leading up to their future garage with Neil by her side. A pair of carpenters were busy setting another of the long span timbers making up the vaulted roof over the Great Room. They watched the men bolt the member to the wooden column and the ridge beam above.

"So once they get all the timbers in place, they start framing in?" Janet said, pointing upward. She took a couple of shots.

"Sort of," Neil replied. "Post and beam construction is trickier than conventional construction. Things need to be worked out well in advance. Like electric and plumbing runs so you don't have exposed conduit and pipes on the inside." He pointed to a wall that had been started around the side and led her to it.

"See how it's constructed? This is called a panelized wall. They laminate rigid insulation between the interior finish and exterior sheathing in advance of installing the section. The wiring is pre-installed in the shop and when it comes to the site, they just connect it all up like a big tinker-toy set."

Janet nodded. It seemed so easy, yet difficult at the same time. "So once they get going on the exterior walls, it'll go fast."

"Lightning quick. Come along with me. I have something to show you." He took her hand and guided her through the construction debris to the other end of the house where they stepped into the high grasses running behind the property. They walked past tall Douglas fir, cedar and hazelnut until they came to a gentle rise crowned in budding buttercup and sweat pea. A slender birch bough hung above a spot overlooking a sparkling little stream. "What do you think?" he said.

"About what?"

"Putting Barney, here."

She felt her throat tighten and put her hand to her mouth. "It's perfect." She took his hand. Squeezed it. *Sometimes, you amaze me, husband.*

21

December 23, 1996 –

Janet put the finishing touches on the Austrian Pine that dominated the Great Room. The tree sparkled, showering reds, yellows, blues, and greens against the wood paneled walls. The tall windows overlooking the valley threw her reflection back at her as she stood on the upper rung of the stepladder.

Placing the silver seven-pointed star over the top spire of the tree, she glanced down at her husband. Dressing the Christmas tree had once been his job. Now, at sixty-seven, and with his Parkinson's starting to rage, he had grudgingly let the job fall to her.

"It looks splendid," he said, his mottled and bony hands tightly gripping the ladder rails.

Translated, *you can get down now dear before you hurt yourself.* She moved a family ornament, a small red teapot, to another branch and climbed down. Over the last year the rustic 'post and beam' constructed house seemed to have gotten larger.

He stirred beside her. "When's everyone due?"

She folded the stepladder. "Around five or so."

"Where's Nate?"

"Over at Jessica's. I told him to be home before things get started."

"Is he bringing her along?"

She smiled. Neil was quite taken by the pretty brunette girl down the road who had become his son's friend. He thought she was a good influence on him. "I believe so," she said, heading toward the kitchen with the ladder in hand.

"Good," he said, following up behind her. "I must say I like her much better than the rest of the kids around here."

"Do you?" Janet said, opening the mudroom door.

"Yes. She's a smart little whip–polite, too."

Janet had to agree. Kids were getting a little too full of themselves these days, not to mention down right nasty and cruel to those that didn't fit in with their self-centered world. She hung up the ladder and stepped back into the kitchen to check the turkey for the party. As she pulled it out to baste it, she saw Neil lift a cookie off the wire cooling rack.

"What're you doing?" she said.

"Having one of your ginger snaps," he announced.

"Put that back! They're for tonight. And don't look at me like that. It'll get you nowhere. By the way, did you sign Megan's Christmas card yet? I left it on your dresser."

He cleared his throat. "Not yet."

She sighed. "Well, she's going to be here in a couple of hours, so don't forget."

"I know, I know," he grumbled.

She pushed the turkey back in the oven, shut the door and stepped over to him. As she put her hand to his stubbled cheek she said, "You, my dear, need a shave."

"Do I? What if I told you I was thinking about growing a beard?"

"Really? Well, it's your face, so do what you want," she said, and kissed him.

204

An hour later, the Great Room hummed with Christmas carols and the banter of family and friends. Megan's son, Kyle, and his girlfriend, Debbie sat on the raised stone hearth sipping sodas.

Brad, along with her father and Craig and his son, Joe, inspected the variety of finger foods on the buffet as they argued over the prospects of a Patriot-Seahawk Super Bowl match-up.

As Janet sliced cheese for a cracker tray, Megan came beside her and lowered her voice. "Why hasn't my father shaved?"

Janet smiled politely. "He's growing a beard."

"A beard!" Megan said. "He hasn't had a beard in years."

"I know," Janet remarked. She helped herself to a slice of cheese and offered one to Megan as she anxiously thought about her surprise to Neil.

Megan shook her head. "I don't like it on him."

"I don't know," Janet said. "It might turn out all right. Besides, shaving's difficult for him now."

That seemed to settle the issue because Megan had no further comment. The woman picked up a knife, pitched in with the preparations and remained quiet while they worked side by side. Finally, she looked up, "So, where's Nate?"

"He'll be here shortly. He's bringing a girl from down the road."

Megan lifted her brow. "A girl?"

"Yeah."

"Really? That's nice," Megan said.

"Yes it is," Janet replied, wondering what Megan was thinking. She placed a bunch of grapes in the center of the cheese-and-cracker tray and appraised it.

Megan plucked a piece of celery from a bowl and ran it through an open tub of dip. She lowered her voice. "So when's my big brother supposed to show up?"

"He said around seven," Janet replied. "His flight was delayed in Chicago." *God, I hope this doesn't blow up in my face.*

A minute later, the front door opened, and in walked Nate with Jessica. The girl slipped out of her boots and jacket. Almond shaped eyes and a dazzling smile lit the room.

"I was just about to call you and find out where you were," Janet said, taking their coats. She pulled back and suddenly found herself wondering how her twelve-year-old son had grown up so fast.

But Janet's longing gaze didn't register, and he turned to Jessica and said, "You want something to drink?"

"Yeah, that'd be great," Jessica said, darting her dark brown eyes over the room nervously.

"And how is Jessica today?" Neil said, shuffling over.

"Hi, Mr. Porter," Jessica gushed. "Good, thank you."

"I hope you're hungry," Neil said. "We've got a house full of food. By the way, how are your studies at school?"

"They're good," Jessica said.

"Still interested in architecture?"

"Neil, honey, let's not hi-jack Nate's friend okay?" Janet commented.

"It's okay, Mrs. Porter. I don't mind," Jessica said as Nate returned with a soda.

Twenty minutes later the doorbell rang. Janet looked up at the clock. It was just after seven. It had to be Trevor. She took a deep breath, went to the door and opened it.

"Janet?"

She looked at the man with a woman standing by his side. He was tall with short-cropped red hair and a strong roman nose. Deep blue eyes peered out through wire-rimmed glasses.

"Trevor?"

"That's me, and this is my wife, Nadia."

Janet opened her arms and wrapped them around him. "Come in," she said. "Your father's out in the dining room. I can't tell you how good it is to finally meet you." *And how nervous I am.* "How was your flight?"

"Long, but we're here," Trevor said as they parted.

"Nadia, the picture Trevor sent doesn't do you justice."

Nadia smiled politely. "Thank-you. What a beautiful house you have," she said as Janet pulled the door shut behind them.

"Does he know yet?" Trevor said as he stepped out of his boots and removed his coat.

"I haven't said a word."

"I was sort'a hoping you'd tell him, but I suppose you know best. Megan here?"

Janet took Nadia's coat and hung it up. "Yes. Why don't you stay put right here, and I'll go get him." *Well, here goes.* She walked out to the dining room and found Neil at her ginger snaps again. "I thought I told you they were for later."

He grinned. "Well, later is now. Who was at the door?"

"Come see for yourself," she said. As he looked at her quizzically, she took his hand.

"I detect a bit of mischief. What're you up to?"

"You'll see. Come on." She led him around the table and across the Great Room toward the foyer. When they rounded the corner, he stopped and she felt his hand squeeze her fingers.

"Hi Dad," Trevor said.

Neil's face tightened. "Trevor." He glanced at Janet and the air ran out of the foyer as they stared at each other. Finally, Neil said, "You look good."

Trevor nodded. Cleared his throat. "This is my wife, Nadia."

"Trevor's told me a lot about you," she said.

Neil tore his gaze off of Trevor and fixed Nadia with a friendly smile. "I bet." He darted an eye back at his son then at Janet. "Well, let's get you introduced around," he said.

As Trevor ushered Nadia ahead of him, he leaned close to Neil. "I know a lot has happened between us, but I'm hoping maybe..."

Neil pursed his lips. "I loved your mother."

"I know," Trevor said just above a whisper. "It was hard to let go. I was angry ... at everyone, not just at you. And then we stopped talking and the days turned to months and I didn't know how to begin again."

"It was hard on everyone," Neil said, regarding his son watchfully. Janet knew her husband was waiting for an apology, an acknowledgement that he had done all he could.

"Yeah," Trevor said, and he glanced at Janet as if trying to gauge what to say next. He pressed his lips together. "Are you upset I'm here?"

Neil shook his head. "No ... no, I'm not. I take it Janet is responsible for your appearance?"

He smiled. "Sort of."

Neil fixed Janet with a knowing gaze. "Just what I thought." He put his arm out and pulled Trevor toward him. "It's good to have you back home."

Neil led Trevor and Nadia into the Great Room. "Everyone, I'd like you to meet my son, Trevor. He, and his wife, Nadia, have traveled all the way from Germany to be with us for the holidays."

A frenzy of hugs and patting on the back ensued, and as Trevor and Nadia basked in the greetings, Janet saw Megan's jaw stiffen. "Hey, Sis, long time no see," he said, stepping up to her.

Megan pasted a smile on her face and leaned into him for a brief hug that amounted to nothing more than a light brush. Janet sighed. *Come on Megan; let things be for just one night.*

After the table was cleared, they all went into the Great Room to open gifts around the tree. They sat in a large semi-circle, Neil on the couch with Janet beside him. Nate fished a gift out from under the Christmas tree and brought it over to his father. Neil held it a moment, looking at the wide, red bow and the card taped on top of it.

"Well, go on. Open it," Trevor said.

Neil pulled the card off the box. It was a homemade card that someone had spent a lot of time making. As Neil read the words to himself, Janet saw his eyes mist. He wiped them and fixed his gaze on Trevor.

Nadia touched her husband's arm.

Neil cleared his throat, got up and went to Trevor. And though his words of forgiveness were whispered between them, Janet could read his lips. Father and son embraced, and as they held each other, Janet furtively glanced at Megan, who was fighting some unknown emotion from across the room.

Neil let go of Trevor and turned a smile onto his daughter, and when she saw it, she put her hand to her mouth and ran out of the room.

Later that night after everyone went home, Janet and Neil lay in bed talking as they did every night before they turned out the lights. Janet glanced over at a picture on their dresser. It was taken when Nate was seven years old on the beach at Fogarty. The four of them were sitting on a blanket. It felt like a lifetime ago. She sighed.

"Something the matter," Neil said.

She shrugged. "Nothing."

"When it's nothing, it's something," he said softy.

"Just memories," she muttered.

"Well, we made some tonight. I want you to know how much your gift meant to me. You gave me back my son."

"I only brought him here. You did the rest." She looked off toward the picture. "You remember that day on the beach."

"I do." He smiled. "It was a perfect day. I do miss that little guy."

Janet nestled up close to him and put her head on his chest. "Me, too." She paused. "Nate wants a puppy."

"Really?" Neil didn't say anything for a moment. "How do you feel about it?"

"I don't know," she said. "I mean; it's not fair to Nate to deprive him of something just because I'm having a hard time with it."

"I don't know about that. You have a right to deal with your feelings just as well. Nate's young. He can wait a little while until you're able to handle it."

She looked up and flashed a tiny smile at him. *But when will that be?* "I liked Trevor's card."

"It was from his heart."

"I know. I'm glad he's back in your life."

"Me, too," Neil said, stroking her hair. "Megan had a hard time with her brother being here. You know she never really forgave him for what happened between us."

"Yeah, I know. Do you think she'll come around?"

"Hard to say. That daughter of mine can hold a grudge."

You have no idea, she thought. She looked up and studied him. "Can I tell you a secret?"

"Sure."

"You're beautiful."

He pulled her tighter to him. "Thank-you."

They lay there a minute more until he reached over and turned the light off. She rolled onto her side and he spooned up to her. "What are you doing?" she said as she felt his lips tracing tiny kisses down her neck.

"Seducing my wife," he whispered into her ear.

"It's late."

"Like we have anywhere to be in the morning." He ran his finger down her arm and over her hip.

"You're being a snot," she said as a stirring ran through her. "But, it is Christmas." She turned around and met his lips with a warm kiss and then let her desire take over.

22

September 3rd, 2001 –

The Labor Day weekend was a time of retreat for Janet and Neil, and over the past seven years since Tom moved out, they'd spent their time in the cottage June had willed to her years ago. This year, they decided to have family join them by the ocean along with Cleo, their Basset tri-color hound. The dog had grown from the floppy puppy he'd been four years ago into a fifty-five pound, nose-to-the-ground eating machine.

This year Jessica joined them. She and Nate spent much of their time together. At seventeen, Jessica had become a stunning brunette beauty. Her smile could get Nate to do just about anything she wanted, and Janet wondered more than once what that had led to despite her best efforts not to think about it.

Jessica stood beside her washing celery for their cookout. Janet peered out the window at Neil who was sipping iced tea with her father out in the back yard. Life was good. She diced the last of the potatoes as Jessica turned the faucet off.

"So, looking forward to your senior year?" Janet said.

Jessica grabbed a towel and wiped her hands. "I guess. I mean … it'll be fun, but sort of sad. Once it's over, I won't see a lot of my friends for a long time."

"Yeah, I know. But it's not forever. So, have you picked out a college?"

"Sort of," Jessica said, and shrugged. "I like Ohio State, but SFU is interesting, too."

I bet Nate's pulling for SFU, Janet thought. He had already committed to San Francisco University and having Jessica nearby would certainly be his preference. "Well, I'm sure you'll make the right decision–whatever works best for you."

"You think Nate'll be mad if I choose Ohio State?" Jessica said off-handedly. She tossed the last of the celery into the bowl and dumped the scraps into the trashcan between them.

"Don't know, but you shouldn't make your decision based on Nate."

Jessica nodded, and Janet could tell she was deeply divided about it. "I know you like my son a lot, and he cares about you, too, but if things are meant to be, they'll be. Cliché, I know, but true."

"Yeah, I guess you're right," Jessica said, giving her a tiny smile.

"It's hard isn't it?"

"Yeah. I mean, we've been together ever since you guys moved to the Heights. It'll feel weird not seeing him every day."

Oh, then you have made up your mind. Janet reached over and patted her shoulder. "You'll be okay, and so will Nate. When you gonna tell him?"

Jessica sighed. "Probably after graduation. I mean–there's no point in saying anything now. It's so far away, and who knows, I may change my mind."

"You might," Janet agreed, "but only if it makes sense. Don't let your feelings get in the way of your future. There'll be plenty of time for that later on."

"You know," Jessica said, "I've never told you before, but you're kinda like a second mom to me. And easier to talk to."

Janet smiled. "Thank you. That means a lot. And you've been like a daughter to me as well. Don't worry, things'll turn out all right," she said and pulled the girl into her arms and gave her a hug.

As they broke apart, Megan marched into the house with a sullen expression. Janet eyed her warily, wondering what had happened back home as Kyle and Debbie followed behind. After the two teens fled into the back yard, Janet said, "Hi, how was the ride?"

Megan dumped her purse on the counter. "I need a drink."

Janet cleared her throat. "I have some ice tea in the fridge."

Megan shot her a classic 'you-got-to-be-kidding' look.

Oh-oh, Janet thought. "Okay, you tell me."

"How about a Rum and Coke?"

"How about a beer?"

Megan frowned. "Fine, I guess that'll have to do."

Janet went to the fridge and pulled a bottle out, popped the top off and gave it to her.

Janet watched her from the corner of her eye as she took a long pull. "I'm going for a walk along the beach. Join me?"

Megan wiped her mouth with the back of her hand. "Sure, why not?"

They tramped down the gravel lane in silence to the main road and crossed over it onto a narrow path that dissolved into the windswept sands. When they were treading the water's edge, Janet said, "So what's going on, Meg?"

"Nothing. Just a bad day." She averted her eyes out over the crashing surf.

Janet pursed her lips. "Want to talk about it?"

"Not especially."

They walked a few more steps. "Is it Brad?"

Megan stopped with a twisted grimace clenching her face. "I don't want to talk about it, okay?"

Janet went ahead to let Megan be with her anger. Suddenly, she heard a muffled cry behind her. When she turned around, she saw Megan hunched over sobbing with her hands over her mouth. Janet went back and put her arm around Megan, half expecting her to rip it away. But Megan didn't move and so she held her while the waves washed their feet.

Finally, Megan said, "The fucker had an affair. He's been nailing a bitch at work for over a year!" She wiped her tear-stained face with the back of her hand. "I feel so all alone. Like I've been abandoned." Megan sobbed. "I mean; Kyle's moving out and getting a place with Debbie. Dad has you and Nate, and now he has Trevor back. And you, the only real friend I ever had, I lost because I was a bitch." She blinked and looked away as Janet's throat tightened.

"Megan," Janet whispered, "You never lost me. I've always been right here."

Megan eyed her, and in that moment, seventeen years of bad water between them pulled away like the receding surf beneath their feet. "I'm sorry. I was so mad when you and Dad got together. It was like he stole you from me, and you went willingly without a second thought."

"And I always thought it was because you didn't believe I loved your father."

"I knew you loved him. The way you looked at him. It was pretty obvious. The sad thing is Brad has never looked at me like that. I told myself it was his way. He loves me. He's just not a romantic. I still love him, though, despite everything. Is that wrong?"

"I don't know. That's something only you can answer."

"Right. He told me it's over between him and the bitch. That he wants just me. That it was all just a big mistake. A big, fucking mistake." She snuffed. "How can one whole year be a big mistake? I mean, in my mind, it's a whole shit load of fucking mistakes."

"What do you wanna do?"

Megan shook her head, and her lip curled into a forced half smile. "I have no clue."

Janet put her hands on Megan's shoulders. "Why don't you stay with us for a while? We have room."

Megan nibbled her lip. "I don't know."

"What's to know?" Janet said.

"I mean … I wouldn't want to get in the way."

"Nonsense! Come here girlfriend," Janet said, and a moment later they were both hugging each other fiercely.

Labor Day came bearing bright sunny skies. Kyle and Debbie took Megan's car and returned to Northgate the night before.

Janet poured Megan a cup of coffee as they sat around the kitchen island talking about work and Janet's next photo-shoot. Cleo was laying on the floor, stretched out, his long ears draped over his face.

Megan said, "He is the oddest thing I've ever seen. Look at the way he sleeps."

"I know," Janet said.

"Hind legs turned one way. Front legs the other."

Janet grinned. "It took me by surprise the first time I saw it, too."

Nate came downstairs dressed in a pair of jeans and a polo shirt. "It's about time, sleepy head. Jess is waiting for you outside," Janet said.

"Yeah, I know." He grabbed his lunch for his outing on the water with Jess from the refrigerator and spied Janet's bagel, which had popped up in the toaster. "Is that for me?"

"Yeah, sure. You want some peanut butter on it?"

"No, I'll eat it plain. Gotta run. Bye Mom, Megan." He grabbed the bagel and ran out of the house.

"What time does their boat leave?" Megan said, cocking her brow.

"Seven-fifteen," Janet replied. She slipped another bagel into the toaster. "Want one?"

"No, I'm fine."

As Janet waited for her breakfast, the phone rang beside her. She picked it up. Her father was on the other end. He said, "Turn the TV on!"

Janet looked up and motioned Megan to go turn the set on in the other room. With the phone to her ear, she followed Megan. When she rounded the corner, the TV came on to show a large gray plume of smoke rising off the World Trade Center and stretching high into the open sky. She was speechless as she watched in horror.

"Is there coffee?" Neil said, entering the room.

Janet glanced at him then fixed her gaze back on the TV. She heard her father on the phone calling her name. When she found her voice, she said, "Yeah, we got it on. I can't believe it. What kind of plane was it?"

Neil stepped beside her, and his eyes bulged. "Oh, my God!" he muttered. He sat down on the couch and watched trance-like, his head wobbling. Megan nestled up beside him and put her hand over her mouth.

"Oh, shit, look at that! Another one!"

Out of the far left hand side of the screen another jet appeared and drove itself into the north tower, exploding in a huge fire-ball. Janet let out a shriek. Neil turned and pulled Megan toward him. He looked at Janet and then at the screen as it repeated the image over again.

"They say it happened an hour ago," William said on the other end. "And get this, the Pentagon was hit, too! They've grounded all the planes. What the hell's going on?"

Three days later –

Though Salem didn't have a large airport and didn't handle any of the major carriers, there was an eerie silence in the skies after the attacks. Janet strode out to the back yard, her eyes upward, and brought Neil a glass of ice water. He sat back on his heels from puttering around in the flowerbeds, took the glass from her and downed a swallow.

Neither of them had talked about the events on the eleventh, as if bringing the subject up would ignite the whole thing all over again. The horrors of watching the towers collapse killing thousands were still too close for her. She couldn't get the image out of her head of the couple holding hands as they jumped out of the 88th floor to their deaths. It would live with her forever.

She said, "It's coming along nice."

He appraised the rose bush, a Traditional Hybrid Tea he had planted. The bush would put out pink flowers the following year. "Let's hope I'm doing this right."

"Doing what right?" she said.

Neil wiped a bead of sweat off his forehead with the back of his gloved hand. "Planting this bush."

"Oh, I was talking about the garden in general."

He swept his eyes over the flowerbed. Mums and butterfly bushes, various ornamental grasses and ground coverings were in various stages of decline. "Ah, yes. It will look nice next spring, if I do say so myself." He gave her the glass, leaned over and pushed a banana peel into the fresh laid soil around the rose bush.

Janet cocked her brow. "What're you doing?"

He looked back over his shoulder. "Feeding it."

"Okay," she said.

He sat back on his heel. "Roses are potassium lovers. Bananas are rich in it, or so the book says. If you want healthy, vigorous roses, planting banana peels at the base of them is what you do."

"You're the expert."

"Far from it, my dear." He studied his efforts. "I heard Megan on the phone this morning with that husband of hers. Sounds like she's taking him back."

Janet sighed. "She loves him."

"Right." He took his gloves off, and she helped him get to his feet. "I hope she knows what she's doing."

Janet let the comment go unanswered. After a minute, she said, "I got a letter from Nadia."

"Did you? And how are she and Trev? I liked her. Real nice girl." He paused and looked off toward the distant fields beyond the stream. "So, what do you think?"

"About what?"

"The rose bush?"

Janet wrinkled her brow and forced a smile, ignoring the foreboding feeling forcing itself into her heart. More and more over the last few months, Neil forgot things he'd just said. "Yes, honey. It looks nice."

"They say if you put banana peels around the base of the bush it helps promote healthy roses."

"So, I've heard."

"Oh, so you've read the book?" he said, grinning.

"Glanced at it, yes." She patted him on the shoulder. "Say, you want some lunch? I was thinking of putting together a salad and some sandwiches."

"What kind?"

"Ham and cheese."

He smiled. "Sounds good. I'm in."

23

Three years later –

The attacks of 9/11 had a profound effect on Nate, and when Jessica announced two years ago that she was going to go to Ohio State instead of SFU, it was one more reason for Nate to enlist in the army. Janet tried to dissuade him, but there was no changing his mind, and it frightened her. Not because he impulsively enlisted, but because ever since Jessica left, he was a different person: distant and far away. She knew he brooded about Jessica's absence, but it was more than that. Had they fought? The last time she saw Jessica, things appeared okay between them, but who knew, and Nate wasn't saying anything.

He had now been in Iraq for the better part of six months. And the war, despite the President's declaring victory, was far from over. With each suicide bombing or I.E.D. going off, things just got worse.

Thanksgiving fast approached, but it didn't feel the same. There would be no plate set for Nate. Janet threw the last load of laundry into the washing machine and went to her studio to check e-mail. Nate usually sent one every week if he could get to a computer. Her inbox held nothing from him today, and hadn't for the last two weeks.

Neil shuffled in and sat beside her. He'd been outside winterizing the flowerbeds. His body moved erratically in the chair. "It's been two weeks and nothing," she complained.

Neil pressed his lips together and put his arm around her. "He's all right," he said gently. "He's probably busy, is all."

Janet shook her head. "It's not all right, Neil. It's Thanksgiving in three days, and he's over there with all those crazy nuts blowing themselves up. What's wrong with people?"

"I don't know. It's a different world over there." He touched her face with a trembling finger. "He's going to be all right. You have to believe that."

"I wish I could," she said, staring out the window at the hazelnut climbing the hill amongst the Douglas fir and hemlock. Her heart felt stripped, like the spiny branches poking through the shroud of evergreen.

They fell silent for some time, until Neil said, "Why don't we step out for awhile?"

Janet shrugged and turned around. "Like where?"

"I don't know, just take a ride?" he said. He stood and motioned her toward him. "Come on, it's too nice to stay inside."

She let herself be led out of the room, and an hour and a half later they were walking down a flower-lined street of one of the tiny hamlets peppering the Willamette valley.

Neil grabbed them a coffee and a bagel from a café, and they sat quietly looking out through the curtained window at the people passing by. "How about we pick up something for the house?" he said.

Janet sipped her coffee and set it down. "Such as?"

"Oh, I don't know. Maybe something to brighten the dining room or the mantle."

She nodded, but her thoughts were still on Nate. "We could do that."

"Are you feeling any better?"

"Some. Thanks for getting me out."

"You're welcome." He sipped his coffee. "I've been thinking and I've decided to turn in my license. I don't drive anymore, so I really don't see a need for it."

Where did that come from? Janet thought. She looked at him. "I see. This is sort of out of the blue."

"I know, but it's been on my mind awhile." He set his cup down carefully on the table. "'Sides, I haven't driven since the little trip I had up to the hospital, so I don't see what difference it makes."

"Are you all right?"

He eyed her and looked out the window. "Yeah. And you? I mean … you'll be my taxi from here on out."

She reached across the table and laid her hand over his wrist. "Of course I'll be okay with it."

They sat in their own thoughts a few more minutes until he said, "Let's go shopping."

They walked hand-in-hand down the street, peering in shop windows and occasionally going into them. Janet found a vase she liked and a trivet. On the way back to their car, she saw a dress shop, and in the shop window she spotted a blouse. "I think I'd like to go in and take a look. You mind?"

Neil shrugged and sat on one of the benches dotting the street's sidewalk. "Sure, I'm gonna stay here if you don't mind."

"Okay. I won't be long." She left him to enjoy the sunshine and stepped inside the store. As she walked past the racks, she smiled at the approaching clerk. "Just looking," she said. The blouse she was interested in hung near the rear of the store, and after a thorough search discovered it was out of stock in her size. After another fifteen minutes of looking for something else, she gave up and headed for the front door. When she opened it, she saw an empty bench. Knotting her brow, she looked up and down the street.

Where is he, she wondered? Maybe he went to find a bathroom or something. She sat, assuming he'd be along shortly. When ten minutes passed, the uneasy feeling turned into a bad one. Something definitely wasn't right. She got up and struck off toward the car, thinking maybe he'd decided to wait there. But the car was empty. Maybe he went down to the café where they'd shared coffee together earlier? He wasn't there, either. Her heart raced. *Don't panic,* she cautioned herself as she left the café. The village wasn't all that big. Surely, he couldn't have gone far. After another five minutes her heart thundered. *Where is he?*

She reached into her purse, her hand shaking, groping for her cell phone. She pulled it out and, just as she started to punch in 911, saw him walking across the street the next block up. She picked up her stride and broke into a trot. "Neil?" she called. "Neil!"

His head jerked in her direction, and he stopped. When she reached him, she saw an expression of fear and relief on his face. He shot her a smile. "There you are," he said. "I waited a while and I thought I'd missed you coming out of the store, so I thought maybe you went somewhere else."

Janet could tell he was making an excuse. She collected herself and took a deep breath. *Better call the doctor when I get home and make an appointment.*

Janet sat and watched as Dr. Childe ran through the checklist of cognitive abilities with Neil. With each answer Neil gave, the doctor acted fine until the memory test at the end. When Neil failed to repeat the words he had been asked to remember, Dr. Childe cocked his brow.

"Don't worry about it, Neil," the doctor said, patting him on the shoulder. "We forget little things all the time."

Neil frowned. "I can't believe I forgot 'em."

"It's nothing more than being put on the spot," Dr. Childe said, and his glance strayed to Janet. He scribbled out a couple of prescriptions and handed them to Neil. "I'm increasing your Madopar dosage, and while we're at it, let's help assist your memory a little. This is for Exelon, two milligrams, twice daily. I'd like to see you in two weeks."

As Dr. Childe excused himself from the room, Janet felt her heart sink and told Neil to get the appointment scheduled while she made a visit to the Ladies Room. When Neil was out of sight, she discreetly made her way back to the doctor's office and knocked on the open door.

Dr. Childe clicked his recorder off and looked up. "Yes, Janet?"

She came in and pulled the door shut behind her. "Can we talk?"

"Sure."

"I didn't want to say anything in front of Neil, but there's something you should know." She told him about the shopping incident, how Neil had disappeared and seemingly covered his actions up.

Dr. Childe paused, leaned back in his chair and steepled his fingers over his lips. After a moment of thought, he eyed her and said, "Neil's cognitive abilities are degrading, but it's hard to tell how far it will go. Let's see how he does with the Exelon, and if there's no improvement, I'll schedule more blood work and another CAT scan. In the meantime, watch him for the following things."

He leaned over and pulled out a sheet from his filing cabinet beside him. "Now, I want you to know it doesn't mean anything is actually wrong if he exhibits any of these behaviors, but it can be an indicator things aren't right. I'd also like you to start keeping a daily journal of his activities and any incidents."

Janet read the list; mentally checking off things that didn't apply, such as change in hygiene, and felt a little better seeing most didn't apply. She looked up and said, "If Neil is getting worse, is there anything that can be done?"

"There are various other medications that can help stem the progression of dementia, if that's what you're referring to. But I don't want to jump to conclusions just yet, and neither should you. He is seventy-five and it isn't uncommon for someone of his age to exhibit certain amounts of memory loss."

Janet nodded, and a question that had been in her mind since the shopping incident reared up, demanding an answer. She took a deep breath. "If he is heading for ... dementia," she said, forcing the word out, "does he have to know?"

Dr. Childe looked at her hard. "He has the legal right, Janet, and as his physician I'm bound by law to tell him."

"But if nobody can do anything about it," Janet said, "I just don't see how it does any good telling him. You know how he feels about what happened to his mother. It would be like a death sentence."

Dr. Childe eyed her then glanced to the picture of his family on the shelf beside him. Finally, he pressed his lips together. "I have to tell him if I diagnose it." And after he had said it, gave her a knowing glance, as if he'd just given her an option.

"I see," Janet replied, studying him. *What's he trying to tell me?* Suddenly, the answer clicked, and she said, "Forget the tests then."

"Okay, for the time being I can, but eventually Neil will start asking questions and when that happens, I'll have to diagnose him." He leaned back in his chair and held her with a consoling expression.

"How long?" Janet said.

"Depends," he said. He got up and came around his desk. "I'll do my best to spare him any anxiety. Go home. Enjoy your time with him, and I'll see you in two weeks."

Janet slipped out of bed, leaving Neil to his dreams, and showered. It was just after seven in the morning and she, Megan and Kyle's girlfriend, Debbie were going Christmas shopping in Salem. When she pulled back the shower door, she saw Neil leaning over the vanity running his hand over the side of his wobbling face.

"You're up early," he said.

"I'm sorry, did I wake you?" She pulled a towel off the bar and wrapped it around her hair, flipping it back into a turban.

He shot her a passing glance. "No, I was awake anyway. Coffee?"

"Yes, please."

He yawned and pulled his robe on. "So, what time do you need to be up to Megan's?"

"Around ten."

He nodded. "And will you be having breakfast with me?"

She wrapped a bath sheet around her and smiled. "Of course." She gave him a kiss on his cheek. "Be there as soon as I'm done."

After she got dressed, she scampered into her studio to check e-mail. When she woke her computer up, a message from Nate awaited her.

Hi Mom. All's well here and I have good news. I put in for leave and there's a chance I might be able to get home for x-mas. As soon as I know, I'll send a message along. Keep your fingers crossed. Hugs to you and Dad.

Janet's heart danced as she typed off a quick reply. Excited, she ran out to the kitchen to tell Neil, only to smell something burning. A moment later, the smoke detector went off. She rounded the corner to find Neil washing dishes, oblivious to the smoke pouring off the skillet.

"Neil!" she cried, running over to shut the burner off. Turning back to him, she said, "The bacon was burning. Didn't you smell it?"

Neil turned around surprised. "Oh, shit, I thought I'd shut that off." He opened a patio door and hurried over as she picked up the skillet billowing with smoke. Rushing out onto the patio, she set the pan down on the ground and doused it with their garden hose. When she came back in, he said. "I don't know what to say. I swear I turned it off."

Taking a deep breath, Janet struggled to remain calm.

Neil ran his hand erratically through his thinning hair and looked away. In a quavering voice, he said, "I'll clean it up. Why don't you check and see if the paper's here and I'll get us some coffee and toast."

But Janet shook her head. "No, that's all right, I'll grab a bite out." Suddenly, she felt very reluctant to leave him alone. She spied her cell phone on the island countertop and wondered if she should call Megan and cancel their shopping trip. She pulled a hunk of paper towels off the roll and started wiping the grease splatter off the stove. As she did so, a thought occurred. She turned around, and fixing him with a smile, hoped her growing panic wouldn't betray her. "Hey, I have an idea. Why don't I call my dad and see if he's around? If he is, I'll drop you off over to his place on my way into town and the two of can have breakfast out. You two can hang out all day. Sound like fun?"

He knotted his brow. "You don't trust me here alone, do you?"

"I didn't say that," she replied adamantly. "I just thought you might enjoy some company."

"I know what you said. I don't need a baby sitter. It was just an accident."

"I know," Janet said, scrambling for a convincing reason Neil would accept. Drawing breath, she said, "The truth is I'm worried about my dad. He's not himself these days."

"Really? First I've heard of it," Neil said, eyeing her dubiously. "He seemed all right on Thanksgiving."

"He puts up a good front," Janet lied, knowing the path this conversation was suddenly going down could easily turn into a slippery slope. She gathered her thoughts as her heart raced. "You know how I've been trying to convince him to come live with us lately? I think if he heard it from you, he might take it more seriously."

Neil looked back at her pointedly and was quiet a moment. Finally, he said, "Why do I feel like I'm being managed?"

"Neil," Janet said, fighting to keep her composure, "have I ever lied to you?"

He fixed her with a discerning gaze. "No."

"Well then," Janet said, "why would I start now?"

He shrugged. "You tell me. It just seems a little odd that I'm hearing about this now, especially right after what just happened."

"I know. And I've been meaning to tell you, but with everything going on, I keep forgetting."

"Hmmm ... Okay, but he knows about the room and that he's welcome here anytime. What makes you think he'd listen to me? Besides, what'd'ya expect me to say: 'Will, you're losing it. You better come live with us?' He'd throw me out of the house."

"Don't be silly. Just mention you could use some help around here. You know how he is. He likes to feel needed. Besides, you've told me yourself, you could use an extra pair of hands a lot of times."

Neil rubbed his chin. "Yeah, I have said that." He narrowed a hawk-like gaze on her. "Why do I still think I'm being managed though?"

Janet stared him down.

"Right. You're sure there's nothing more to this?"

"Yeah. Really that's all there is," Janet replied.

"Hmm." He shot her another dubious glance. "Very well, give him a call."

"Thanks. I really appreciate it." She resisted the urge to kiss him, lest he think otherwise and grabbed her cell phone. As she punched the numbers in, she drifted down the hall. As it rang on the other end she felt her stomach knot. She had to get Neil out of the house otherwise she'd have to call Megan and cancel.

That, in turn would lead to questions from his daughter that Janet wasn't ready to answer. Finally, her father picked up.

"Hi, Dad. How are ya?"

"I'm good. What's up?"

"I have a favor I need to ask. What're you doing today?"

"Planned on heading down to the local bookshop for coffee. Met a nice young lady there. Why?"

Janet edged toward the kitchen and peeked around the corner. Neil had gone back to washing dishes. In a low voice, she said, "I need someone to be with Neil today. He almost set the house on fire this morning."

"What?"

"He left a burner on and almost started a grease fire. I'm going to Salem for the day, and the thought of leaving him here alone scares the hell out of me."

"Umm … yeah, okay I guess. Is he all right?"

"Yeah." She steeled herself. "Look, I told him you were feeling a little down and could use some company."

There was a long pause.

"Dad?"

"Yeah, I'm here," he said. "Janet, I know you're worried, but–"

"But I don't have a choice, Dad," she interjected. "If I tell him the truth, he'll dig his heels in. I know you wanted to wait a while before moving in with us, but I need you here now. Please? I'm scared."

"Is he that bad?"

"No, but he's getting worse." She told him about Neil's disappearing act when they went shopping a few weeks ago and his increasing forgetfulness. "I'm so afraid I'm losing him, Dad," she said as her voice caught in her throat.

"Hey, hey there, Skeeter, don't worry. Look, if you need me there, I'm there. What time shall I expect you guys?"

She cleared her tightened throat. "I have to be in Salem by ten, so it'll be in the next forty-five minutes."

24

Janet saw Nate striding down the terminal of Portland's International airport with his duffle bag slung over his shoulder. He knifed his way through the crowded concourse to where she anxiously awaited behind the security checkpoint. When he crossed into the public waiting area, she ran up and threw her arms around him. *I can't believe you're home. Good Lord, look at you. You're a man. When did this happen?*

"Hey Mom," he said, dropping his bag and lifting her halfway off her feet.

She pulled back, looking at him. His face was the same, but the closer she looked, she saw a grim edge to his smile and a subtle dull sheen to what had once been shining eyes.

"It's so good to have you home," she said, touching his face, his hair, and his neck. She wanted to cradle his whole body in her arms.

"Where's Dad?"

She let go of him and cleared her throat. The thought of telling him the truth was tearing her heart out. "He decided to stay home. It's a long drive, and you know he's not much on being a passenger on long hauls."

Nate pressed his lips together. "Yeah, but it's only seventy miles. Everything all right, I mean, he hasn't been sick or had another you know...?"

"No, he's fine." Janet looked at him and gathered her courage. "He's just ... well, he's changed, Nate."

"How?"

She looked away, not wanting to have this conversation with her son, not now, not this way. "Your father's memory is fading. He forgets things easily."

Nate shook his head, and the rigid muscles in his neck tightened.

Janet gazed at her son, tracing the crease burrowing deep into his brow, kidnapping his beautiful smile. "We'll talk more later, okay?" She reached for his bag, grabbed the strap, felt its daunting weight.

"I got it," he said, picking it up with ease.

As they started for the exit, Janet cleared her throat. "By the way, I saw Jess the other day?"

"Did you?" he replied in a level tone. "How is she?"

"She asked about you," Janet said, carefully gauging his expression. She knew Nate better than anyone, but in the matter of Jessica, she had no clue. She went on. "I told her you were coming home for Christmas."

"That's nice." The automatic doors of the terminal slipped open and they walked through into the cold, crisp air. "So, is Jumpin' Jimmy's still open? I'm starved."

She smiled. At least that hadn't changed.

They stopped and grabbed a couple of burgers. As she pulled back onto the highway, Nate peppered her with questions about his father, and as she drove, she told him what the doctor had said.

"I decided not to have your father tested right away," she said. "If I do, and it's you know what, the doctor will have to tell him."

Nate pursed his lips and looked out his passenger side window. The only sound in the car for some time was the heater rustling the paper under his burger. Finally, he spoke up. "So you're gonna keep it a secret from him?"

She felt his eyes on her as the rolling, brown fields slipped past their windows. She knew he didn't know how she felt about secrets, but it didn't matter. She felt as if she'd been slapped across the face. "It's not a secret, Nate," she said more forcefully than she intended. "And we don't know for sure right now. No one does. And I don't see the point of putting him through it; believing he's going to end up like your grandma did."

Nate crumpled his burger wrapper and tossed it in the bag their food had come in. "It's okay, Mom, I understand. What's Megan think of it?"

"She doesn't know, and she doesn't need to know right now, okay?"

"Sure."

"Oh, guess what? You're grandfather's moving in with us."

"Really? When?" Nate said, brightening.

"Next week."

He sucked the last of his soda up through the straw. "Because of Dad?"

"Some, not all. You're grandfather isn't exactly a youngster anymore."

They were quiet a minute. He said, "It's hard to believe."

"What?"

"Dad. I just never thought..."

"I know. I've been praying it won't happen, but it appears it's going to, and there's nothing anyone can do about it." She paused. "I love your father more than anything in this world." Blinking, she rubbed the bridge of her nose. "I'm doing the best I can."

"I know, Mom." Out of the corner of her eye she saw him turn his lips into a crooked smile. "It's funny, most of my life, I thought Dad was this timeless wizard, scrutinizing everything. Sometimes it felt like no matter what I did it was never good enough. Then one day I realized, he wasn't criticizing me, he was teaching me to think things through. Because of him, I feel like I can handle anything now."

Janet swallowed and took a deep breath. *And you are both amazing.* "I love you."

He flashed a quick smile then sighed. "How bad is he?"

She patted his arm. "You'll see for yourself ... Nate?"

"Yeah."

"What happened between you and Jess? You don't have to tell me if you don't want, but I'd–"

"I know," he said, cutting her off. He stuffed his empty soda cup in the bag and shrugged. "I'll be okay."

Janet nodded, and forced herself to let go of trying to fix him.

Nate cleared his throat. "It's good to be home."

Janet finished setting the table for Christmas dinner when Megan and Brad arrived. It had been over a year since Megan took Brad back after catching him fooling around. He took his jacket off and handed it to Megan and sauntered into the room like he owned the place.

Janet suppressed the urge to let him know his kingdom was seventy miles north as she folded a napkin. *My, what style you have, you overgrown butterball. Those tight fitting Dockers and that plunging v-neck sweater must really get the gals all in a lather.*

Brad plopped down on the couch in front of the TV next to Nate. "Hey, kid, how's it going? Must be good being back home away from all those towel heads, eh?"

Janet saw Nate take a deep breath. "Things are fine."

"Right," Brad said. "So, Seahawks still ahead, or they blow another lead?"

"Still ahead," Nate said, getting to his feet. He strode over to Megan, hanging her jacket up in the closet, and put his arms around her. "Hey, sis. Merry Christmas.

"And a Merry Christmas, to you," she replied.

"And to you, too," Janet added, stepping beside Megan. She nodded toward Brad then shot a questioning gaze at Megan.

Megan shook her head. "So, where's Dad?"

"In the garage with my father. He bought him a new toy for the back yard." Janet said, smiling as she thought about the two of them trying to figure out how to install the garden accent lighting.

"I'm gonna go out to say hello," Megan said, and headed for the mudroom.

"So, Jan, how's tricks?" Brad said from the couch.

Janet frowned. *Tricks? Right. You're such a dick.* "I'm fine," she answered and called Cleo. "Come puppy, let's go for a bathroom break."

Ten minutes later, a crisp December breeze was nipping at Janet's face as Cleo wandered back and forth across the yard with his nose close to the ground. She zipped up her jacket, and as she walked with him, she tried to ignore the ominous knowledge that Neil was slowly moving away from her into a world in which she couldn't follow.

But it was Christmas so she had to suck it up and do her best to show nothing was wrong. Cleo trotted back on his leash line and looked up at her as if he knew she needed a friend. She bent down and ran her hand over the dog's head and over his long floppy ears.

"There you are," Megan said, coming up behind her.

"We needed a potty break," Janet answered. "So how are they doing in there?"

"Making a mess." She rubbed her hands together, cupped her fingers and blew hot breath into them. "Is Dad all right?"

"What do you mean?"

"He seems different. Quiet. And when I asked him how it was going, he looked at me as if he didn't know me for a second."

"Well, you know how he is when he gets involved in a project."

"Yeah, I suppose you're right." She shrugged.

"So, how bad are things with Brad?"

Megan shook her head. "I should've never gone back."

Janet let the remark hang between them. Finally, she said, "You could always leave, you know."

"Yeah, but I don't have a lot of options." She rubbed her thumb and finger together and pursed her lips.

Janet nodded. Her first impulse was to take the house her father had been renting off the market and give it to Megan but knew that wasn't the answer. Megan would never take charity. "Have you looked into getting an attorney? There is such a thing as support, you know."

Megan looked off. "Yeah, I know. I just hate the thought of going through all that shit." She took a couple of steps ahead, looked out over the fields running behind the house and turned around. "If you were me, what would you do?"

The sound of clacking tree branches filled the silence between them. Janet said, "Let's walk."

They skirted the flowerbeds, to the meandering stream running through the property. "I can't tell you what to do," Janet said as Cleo pulled at his leash, "but you have the right to be treated decently. You're not a maid."

Megan paused and knotted her brow. "Did you and Dad ever have real bad times where you thought maybe ... well you know."

"We had our moments," Janet admitted. "But your Dad always treated me like a person, and I always knew he loved me, even when we shouted at each other."

"Brad just walks out of the house and comes back when he's good and ready," Megan said. "Most of the time he's tanked up when he returns. He's not real nice then."

"He ever hit you?"

"No, but I know he wanted to sometimes," Megan said.

Janet glanced at her watch. "Well, whatever you do, you have a place to go if you need it. We better get in. I'm cold, and I imagine the turkey's about ready to come out of the oven."

"And Dad needs to get pried away from his new toy. Oh, your father mentioned he's moving in with you guys. Is he all right?"

"He's fine," Janet said as they headed back. "He just finally decided to take us up on our offer. Seems he got tired of being alone."

25

After Nate returned to Iraq, Janet settled in for the long winter months that spilled more rain than snow on the Willamette valley. The bleak gray days lumbered along at a dismal pace, as did her husband's steady descent into himself. At least she had her father with them now. Though he was older than Neil, he was spry and alert, and lately he had assumed many of the tasks Neil had once done around the house. Most importantly, he watched over her husband when she was away on shoots.

But William had his own problems. A loss of hearing in one ear frustrated him to no end. And then there had been the fight with prostate cancer at seventy, which he battled with radiation for three years only to end up having it removed anyway. A year later, he found out he was hyperglycemic. That led to a strict diet, which left him unhappy but determined.

Janet was astonished at her father's active lifestyle. He walked a mile each day, often in nasty weather after she got home from work, and attended a book club on Thursday afternoons, which raised her curiosity because he wasn't fond of fiction. After a little question and answer session, she ratted the reason out of him. A certain retired and very attractive professor of English Lit, named Lillian Maguire, attended it. Janet found the thought of her father and another woman holding hands quite endearing.

And, of course, there was golf, which happened to be in season now. He'd already been out four times, and during one of the rounds found out about a local gardening club from one of the members of the country club. The *Green Jeans Club*, which was run by a small group of retired men and women. It would be perfect for Neil to get him out and enjoy the sunshine, he had said.

Initially, Janet hedged at the idea. Though Neil's mind was still active and alert, he spoke less and less, and his Parkinson's kept him in a state of constant movement. She asked Dr. Childe what he thought, and he agreed with her father, saying it was an excellent idea.

So, on the strength of the doctor's recommendation and the idea that Neil would enjoy the outdoors, say nothing of being out of her hair on Saturday mornings while she took care of household chores, she decided to go along.

May 7, 2005 ᷉ –

Janet peeked out of Megan's dining room window at the gray canvas of clouds clinging to the summit of Mount Hood and let the curtain fall back. In the other room, her father, Brad and Kyle watched the Mariners play on TV while Neil sat in the recliner next to them with a lazy smile creasing his thin and bearded face.

Janet watched Megan eye her father as she spread the tablecloth over the dining room table and smoothed it out. Since business at the tiny gazette she worked for had been keeping her busy, she hadn't seen her father since March. When she met him at the door, her eyes widened. And over the last hour, her glance had fallen Janet's way more than once.

She caught Janet's attention and pointed deftly toward the deck. When they were outside, she said, "What's going on with him?"

Janet steeled herself. "Your father, he's umm … he's not the same man you saw at the St. Patty's day parade, Meg."

Megan blinked and looked off. "He hardly recognized me. I don't understand. How is this happening? Is it his Parkinson's?"

Janet swallowed hard. "No. There's something else."

"What?"

"The doctor believes it's Alzheimer's."

Megan's face blanched. "Alzheimer's?" she rasped. "Oh, my God."

Janet let her wrestle with that a moment, then said, "Yeah. It's hard to diagnose."

Megan pressed her lips together and glanced toward the sliding glass door. "Does he..."

"No," Janet said, meeting her gaze. "And I don't want him to know."

Megan nodded. "Right. So, what are you going to do?"

"What do you mean?"

"You know," she said, thin lipped. "Ship him off to some old folks home when he gets to be too much? I'm sorry, Jan, I don't mean to be unsympathetic, but it's usually how it goes. My grandmother died in one of those places. I don't remember much about her, but I remember going to see her. There were all these people just waiting around to die. In fact, they were dead. Their bodies just didn't know it. I never want my father to go through that."

"And neither do I," Janet said firmly. "Absolutely not. He will always have a place with me because he's always been there for me. I won't abandon him, I promise you."

"Thank you." Megan turned back to the railing. "When I was sixteen, just after Mom died, I was having this really bad day. It started with a dumb teacher getting in my face, and when I got home from school, my brother started dissing my father saying how he let my Mom die; saying if the same thing happened to us, he'd walk away, too."

Megan snuffed and threw her hair back over her shoulder. "I called him a liar. Dad would never do that. Anyway, when Dad got home after work, Trev got into it with him.

"I still remember Dad sitting on the porch after Trev stalked off. I had never seen my father cry before. He looked at me, and I wanted the world to go away. I wanted my mother back. I wanted things to be the way they were before the accident. Suddenly, every argument I ever had with my mom didn't mean a thing. I would've given anything to have her back, to have my dad happy again. I don't know how Trev could believe such stupid things. So, I guess you can see why I didn't exactly feel like opening my arms up to dear old brother when he came waltzing in."

"I'm sorry, I didn't know it would be so hard for you."

"You could've asked. But, I know you meant well, and my dad was really happy. So I sucked it up, just like everything else. Anyway," she said, "Dad was sitting there on the porch, and he just looked at me like I was his last friend in the world. Said, 'What about you, pumpkin, you think your dad wanted to let your mom die?'"

"I mean, what kind of question is that? I was only sixteen years old. I just looked at him, and my heart broke. Next thing I knew, he had his arms around me holding me tight. He said, 'I'll always be here for you, pumpkin. I'll never go away and leave you alone.'"

Her eyes watered. "But, now, he is going away, and even though I know he doesn't want to, it doesn't matter." She wiped her eyes with the palm of her hand. "You got to be careful with promises." She clenched her eyes tight. "Oh my God, I'm losing my dad."

Janet pulled Megan into her arms and held her. "Yes, we are." She looked up at the brooding clouds. *And it's not fair.*

239

"Happy Birthday to you. Happy Birthday to you. Happy Birthday dear Neil. Happy Birthday to you!" The family sang as Megan set the cake on the table in front of her father. He looked at the candle-lit cake with chocolate frosting with his name written across it in yellow icing and smiled.

"Make a wish, Neil," Janet encouraged.

He turned his gaze on her, studying her as if she were his newlywed bride. Janet felt her throat tighten and saw Megan fighting tears. It was moments like these that pierced her heart. She put her hand on his shoulder and squeezed gently, felt his hand reach up and touch her fingers. She leaned over and whispered in his ear, "I love you, and you are beautiful. I have a wish. Blow the candles out and make it come true."

He patted her hand, and as his body moved of its own accord, bent forward and blew out the candles. Everyone clapped and a moment later plates were being passed around with ice cream and cake. Janet set Neil's plate in front of him and took a seat by his side. Eating was an adventure for her husband now and though she didn't want to dote over him, she wanted to be nearby to help if he wanted it. He stabbed his cake with a fork, cut off a piece, and fought it to his mouth.

As he dabbed his mouth with a napkin, he said, "Very good, Megan."

"Thank-you, Dad. Are you having a good time?"

He nodded and focused on another piece. After several tries he got it to balance on his fork and into his mouth.

Megan watched him. She hadn't said anything during dinner while he struggled, Janet figured because her father was chatting her up. Now, Megan witnessed firsthand what her father went through every day. She moved to the other side of him and said, "You want help, Dad?"

He looked up at her, frowned and set his fork down. "I'm fine."

Janet sighed. She knew Megan wanted to help, but what Megan didn't know was her father's need to do things on his own: eating especially. He never said—but Janet knew—if he couldn't feed himself, it was over for him.

Megan looked as if she had just been slapped across the face and she gave Janet a 'what-did-I-say?' expression. Janet shook her head and mouthed the words, 'later.' She took a bite of cake and waited for the awkward moment to pass. Lately, when something happened that bothered Neil, he would forget about it after a few minutes and carry on with whatever he was doing before. Megan got up and left the table, and Janet saw the hurt look on her face.

When she felt Neil might be agreeable to a suggestion, she said, "Neil, honey, your ice cream's melting."

He turned his head toward her, and his smile reappeared. "Oh, yes."

She pulled the bowl forward and saw her father give her a look from across the room. He slipped into the kitchen. He had not been blind to what had just happened.

Neil picked up his spoon and dipped into his ice cream. "Chocolate." After he had taken a bite, he said, "Where's Megan?"

"She went to the kitchen to take care of dishes."

He gave her a puzzled look. "Why?"

Janet forced a smile. "You know Meg can't stand a cluttered countertop."

He nodded. "This is good," he said, dipping in for another bite. "Is that piece of cake mine, too?"

"Yes. It's your birthday cake. Megan made it for you." *God, this is getting hard and it's only going to get worse.* As Janet sat in her musing, the phone rang. Kyle picked it up. "Hey Nate! What's doing?"

Janet's ears pricked.

"Uh-huh, right," Kyle said. "Yeah, we heard about that … Keep your head low man … Yeah, we're doing cake and cream for him right now … What? Yeah, she's right here. Hey, great talking to ya. Aunt Janet, it's Nate."

Janet came beside him and took the phone.

"Nate, hi honey. How are you?"

"I'm good. I can't talk long. It's pretty late over here, but I just wanted say happy birthday to Dad."

"Well, he's right here," she said taking the phone over to the table. She put her hand over the receiver and said, "Neil, it's Nate. He's calling to wish you a happy birthday."

"Hello, Nate," Neil said. "Yes, I'm having a good time. Yes, having cake and cream. Where are you? Najaf, where's that? … uh-huh. What're you doing there? … Working with the locals. Sounds interesting. By the way, when are you coming home? Your mother misses you … Oh, okay. Well, you take care of yourself. Here's your mother."

Janet put the phone to her ear. "Nate, you still there?"

"Yes … Dad's getting a lot worse, isn't he?"

"Yes, honey," she said. The last thing Nate needed was to be worrying about his father, but there was nothing that could be done about it. "Are you eating okay?"

"I'm doing. It'll be okay, Mom. Look, there's guys piled up behind me waiting to get on the phone so I gotta go. I love you and tell Sis I said, hi."

"Okay. Be good. Love you." The line went dead and with it, Janet was reminded of the fleeting moments that were occurring less and less between Nate and Neil.

On the way home from Megan's, Janet thought about her future as she drove. Her husband, who sat beside her with eyes closed, was sinking into the oblivion of dementia and her father, though still energetic and sharp, was heading toward eighty. How much longer could she expect him to pick up the slack? Up until recently, she had pushed such thoughts away, but they were ganging up on her now. She turned off the interstate onto the arterial, heading west toward the Heights, and glanced in the rear view mirror at him gazing out the window.

"Thanks for talking with Megan," she said calling softly over her shoulder.

Her father stirred. "Don't mention it honey. Maybe we should've warned her a little more, don't you think?"

Janet nodded. "I guess it never occurred to me. When you live in the middle of it, you don't see the changes as clearly as someone outside of it does."

"I know," he answered back. "It hit her hard today. I have a feeling you're going see a lot more of her in the future."

They fell into their own thoughts a moment, until she said, "Do you ever resent me? I mean for begging you to move in with us?"

He wrinkled his brow. "No, why would you ask that?"

"I don't know. You were doing fine; going where you wanted, when you wanted, and now, you're sort of stuck watching Neil. I just wonder."

Her father leaned forward and put his hand on the back of her seat. "Skeeter, I don't do anything I don't want to. I came because you needed me. 'Nough said, okay?"

She reached back and put her hand over her father's bony fingers. "Right boss."

"'Sides," he added, "living alone isn't all what it's cracked up to be. Trust me on that one."

"It was good hearing from Nate and Trevor," she said.

"I didn't know Trevor called. When?"

"Shortly before we left. You were outside, I think."

"Oh, right. How is he?"

"He's good," she said. She remembered what Megan said to her out on the deck and pressed her lips together. She had never considered Megan's feelings about bringing Trevor back into their lives. But Neil was Janet's husband, and her priority. Bottom line: it made him happy, and hopefully at some point,

Megan would make peace with her brother. Or maybe even forgive him. That wasn't such a terrible thing, was it?

An hour later Janet turned into their long looping driveway. The sun had set over the western hills, and a multitude of glittering stars shone from a black sky. She rounded the tall privet, and as she pulled up to the front door, she saw a car she didn't recognize parked in the turn-around. It had California plates, and its front door opened as she threw her car in park and got out.

"Can I help you?" she said, clenching her fingers around her keys.

"As a matter of fact, you can," the man said.

"Mick? What are you doing here? I haven't seen you in ages," she said, letting out a breath she didn't know she was holding.

"I was in the neighborhood and thought I'd stop by."

"In the neighborhood?" she said. "Seattle isn't exactly a quick drive down the block from here."

"Actually, it's San Francisco now," he replied. He put out his hand to William. "Long time, no see. Sheeze, this is quite the spread. You win the lottery?"

"Not quite." *Although there had been a time when it felt like it.* "How's Sandra?"

"She's fine."

"And Vicky?" she said, going around to get Neil unbuckled.

Mick smiled. "Teaching Graphic Design at SFU. Sandy got her into the department four years ago. You look great!"

"Thanks. So what're doing here?" she said, bending down and gently nudging Neil. "Hey sleepy head, we have a visitor."

Neil opened his eyes and stared at her. "Home?"

"Yes." She helped him out and brought him around the front of the car. "You remember Mick, don't you dear?"

Neil swayed, his gaze wandering, and as it did, she saw Mick's smile leave his face. His glance darted back and forth between Neil and her. At last, he said, "Hey, Neil. How are ya?"

"I'm fine." He turned to Janet and said, "Can we go in?"

She led the way to the front door and opened it. Cleo waited on the other side, tail wagging and tongue lolling out of his mouth. She ordered the hound to the other room and said to Neil, "Why don't you head off to bed, and I'll be along after awhile?"

"Okay." He turned and left without another word.

She watched Neil as he jerked his way across the Great Room with her father tagging along. Although, she didn't share a bed with her husband anymore, she still made it a point to join him until he fell off to sleep.

"So, can I get you something to drink?" she said to Mick.

"Yeah sure. Whatever's available." He followed her out to the kitchen and said, "I'm sorry."

"For what?" she replied opening the refrigerator door.

When he didn't reply, she knew all that needed to be said had been said. She handed Mick his soda and poured a glass of milk. Neil liked warm milk and honey before bed. She put the glass in the microwave. "So, tell me. What brings you here, cause I know it's more than just a how-do-you-do?"

He took a gulp of his soda as Cleo wandered in. Bending down, he gave the dog a good scratch behind the ear. "Actually, it's you."

"Me?"

"Yeah. I work for a little magazine. Perhaps you've heard of it? The *Sierra*?"

"Yeah, just a little!"

"Well, they liked your last effort. You've won an Ansel Adams," he said with a broad grin. "Usually the winner's notified by mail, but I thought I'd come up and do it in person."

Janet couldn't believe it. She had been sending in submissions for the award for the last couple of years, mostly to pacify Neil. Finally, she found her voice. "You're kidding?"

"No, not this time," he said. "I always knew you were the best. Now, there's proof. There's going to be a press release soon." He stood up and turned his gaze toward the hallway Neil had gone down a moment ago. "Can you break free on a dime and get down for the awards ceremony?"

She took a deep breath, trying to keep her legs under her. "I think so."

Mick narrowed his dark gray eyes on her. "I need more than an I-think-so, Janet. Can you commit or not? We'll fly you down, but you gotta be ready when the time comes."

Janet bit her lip. Neil had always wanted this for her, but that was when he had his mind intact. He needed her now, or did he? To be honest, she couldn't say if she needed to feel needed or if she really was needed. She closed her eyes as the war of 'go' or 'not to go' waged inside her. Finally, she said, "Okay, I'm there."

"Great," he said. "Now that we've got that out of the way, tell me how you got all this, and don't leave out any details."

Janet grinned. "You'll never believe it, but first, I need to take care of something." She pulled the milk from the microwave and added a dollop of honey. "I'll be back in a bit. In the mean time, help yourself to whatever you want in the fridge."

After she settled Neil into bed, she joined Mick and Cleo on the deck and talked well into the night about life, work, and family. Eventually, the conversation drifted to Neil.

Mick took a swallow of soda and looked up into the night sky. "Are you okay?"

"I'm doing."

He nodded. "Good. I know how hard it can be. Sandra's father's the same way ... well, you know."

She eyed him. "I'm sorry."

"Sort of beats you up sometimes, doesn't it? Life, that is."

"Yeah, it does. But, you know what? I wouldn't trade a day of my life for some stupid dream if Neil weren't in it. He's my life. Everything I am is wound up inside him like a big knot. I couldn't untangle it even if I wanted to."

"Same way I feel about Sandra. So, what're ya going do, now that you're a big star? People'll be flocking to ya like locusts, ya know."

"Will you stop?" she said, swatting his arm. "But seriously, nothing. I'm gonna be who I am."

"Yeah, I figured. You never let things go to your head. Hey, it's getting late. I better get going."

"We have an extra room," Janet said, not wanting the night to end.

"I wouldn't want to impose."

Janet rolled her eyes. "Nonsense."

He wavered, seemingly debating the offer and said, "You sure?"

"Absolutely."

"Well, perhaps. You have anything stronger than soda?"

Janet grinned. "As a matter of fact, I do."

26

The press release for Janet's Ansel Adam's award happened yesterday morning with the ceremony later last night. Janet sat at a small, round table in her hotel room, nibbling on a Danish while perusing the paper. Turning the page, she glanced out the window at the heavy fog blanketing the bay bridge as the radio babbled on the nightstand next to her unmade bed. This weekend was the first time she had been away from Neil overnight in, well, she couldn't remember how long. It felt odd being alone–stranger yet, to be out of routine. She read an article, half paying attention to the words and folded the paper. Her flight wasn't until later that afternoon, and she felt restless.

She opened her travel bag, pulling out her itinerary. Maybe she'd go for a walk after she showered. Right now, she felt adrift in an uncertain future, and it frightened her. She eyed the complimentary blank pad and pencil on the table, pulled them in front of her and began to write.

You sleep five hundred miles away, yet I can almost feel you here beside me. I wonder if you know I'm gone or if you miss me? Sometimes I think you're evaporating right in front of my eyes.

I remember the night we met. You came along in that big old truck of yours and pulled me out of the snow bank. Who would've thought we'd ever meet again, let alone get married? We put up with a lot from each other didn't we husband?

Do you know I can still see you wading into the surf the day I first took you to my beach? It's like yesterday—you rolling up your pant legs and splashing in the water.

I'll always love you, and I'll keep telling you that so you won't forget. I'll tell you about our wedding on the beach and how you kissed me when you found out I was pregnant. You'll know how you looked at Nate when you held him right after he was born.

And I will tell you about the house you built for me, the excitement in your eyes as you planned every detail, right down to finding a place for Barney to rest.

These are the things I'll tell you every day so you won't forget. Ever!

She folded the page and sat thinking about what she had written. Until now, she avoided thinking about these things. They were just too painful as if doing so gave them life. But she couldn't keep her feelings away any longer or deny the steady gnawing pain. *Am I giving up?* She wrapped her arms around the tablet and held it to her chest tightly as she battled the dark thoughts threatening to overwhelm her.

I can't—I won't! He wouldn't give up on me—ever! I need to get out of here.

As Janet strode down the walk, the smells of coffee and pastries and flowering trees wafted around her. Above, birds darted back and forth from rooftops and ledges and swooped down to the walk to steal breadcrumbs or whatever else could be found. A street car motored along under the network of wires tying the city together as merchants opened their doors for another day of business.

She ducked into a coffee shop and grabbed a latte and continued her walk toward the wharves. As she joined in with the tide of people heading to unknown destinations, she pulled her cell phone from her purse and punched in her home number.

"Hello? Oh, Megan! I wasn't expecting you," Janet said.

"I spent the night," Megan answered. "Had to get out of the house. How'd the awards go?"

"Okay," Janet said, knowing Brad and her had probably had another fight. "Not what I expected."

"Oh?"

"Yeah, it was more like a who's who all trying to outdo each other," Janet said. "I left early."

"I'm sorry."

"Not a big deal," Janet said. "How's Neil? Is he up yet?"

"No, still asleep. Your father and I are having a cup of coffee. You want to talk to him?"

"Sure." When her father picked up, Janet said, "Hello? Dad?"

"Hey, Skeeter. How's my girl?"

"Ready to come home. How's Neil?"

"He's good," her father replied.

"Is he taking his meds without a hassle?"

"Not a problem," her father said.

"Liar," Janet quipped. "So, are you two going to the gardening club meeting this afternoon?"

"Thinking on it. I have a doctor's appointment this morning first. When's your flight due?"

"'Round eight-thirty tonight." She paused. "So, I see you have company."

"Yeah," Her father said in a playful tone. "We were just talking about you."

"I bet," Janet volleyed back. She paused and dropped into a serious tone. "She all right?"

She heard her father clear his throat on other end. "We'll talk later. So, what are you up to?"

"Shopping. Heading down to the wharf to get Neil a little something." She sipped her latte as she walked. "By the way, did he say anything about my not being there last night?"

"No, but I think he felt your absence," her father said. "He was restless. Look, I hate to cut this short, but I need to get myself around. Have to be downtown in an hour. You want to talk to Megan?"

"Sure. Hey, Dad?"

"Yeah?"

"I Love you."

"I Love you, too, Skeeter. Here's Megan."

"Hi Jan," Megan said, coming on the phone. "So, how's Mick?"

"Mick is Mick. His wife is a real looker, and boy does she keep him in line. But they are so in love. She's so good for Mick. They're good for each other."

"That's great?" Megan said, and fell silent.

Janet felt tears on the other end. "Hey Meg, you okay?"

"Yeah, I'm all right," Megan answered after a moment. She snuffed and continued, "He was just being an ass. Bitching about how I don't understand what he's going through at work and shit. That all I care about is my father. It's always about him, you know."

"I'm sorry."

"Don't worry about it. I'm where I wanna be." Megan cleared her throat. "Gonna do any shopping? I hear there are some fab boutiques in San Fran."

"No, just gonna pick up something for Neil. Give him a hug for me?"

"Absolutely. Speaking of my father, I better go check on him. Things are rather quiet in the other room. You have a safe trip and I'll see you soon."

"Okay. Keep him out of trouble," Janet replied, forcing a smile. If there were a way of getting home right now, she'd be on the next flight.

The days of summer slipped by, and with them, so did Neil's memory. Each night, Janet wrestled with a decision that was looming larger and larger in her mind. But always the answer remained: 'Not yet.' Added to her fears, was her father's failing appetite. Often, she'd seen him grimace when he thought no one was watching, and if someone did see, he passed it off as heartburn or indigestion. She tried to avoid thinking something was wrong, but something inside her warned her against it. Finally, the need to know won out after spying him nearly doubled over in pain the other night. She called Megan the next morning and asked her to come down and stay with Neil for the evening so she could take her father to dinner.

She sat with him at Jake's away from the crowded and noisy bar. Her father was in his favorite charcoal gray pullover sweater and tan Dockers. As he cut his steak, she watched him discreetly while nibbling her cob salad.

"Are you feeling alright?" she said, setting her fork down.

He stopped cutting and looked up. "Yeah, why?"

"You haven't acted like yourself lately," she said.

"And how exactly am I supposed to act?" he replied, giving her one of his patented raised brows.

She looked up. "You know what I mean."

"No, I don't," he said, returning to slicing his steak.

She frowned. "You haven't been eating very good and you've been sleeping late. It's not like you."

He stabbed a piece of meat, dragged it through a puddle of barbeque sauce, and put it in his mouth. He swallowed and said, "Don't worry, I'm fine."

"Hmm," she said.

He shot her a challenging glance. "I'm pushing eighty. I'm slowing down. I thought this was supposed to be a night out. Not an inquisition."

Janet bit back her growing frustration and forced a smile. "I'm just concerned. When did you last see your doctor?"

"A while back. I don't remember. There's nothing to be worried about. It's just old age." He wiped his mouth with a napkin and sat back. "So, what's up for the weekend? You never said this morning."

"Nothing."

"Good, I was thinking of going down to the bookstore tomorrow and having a cup of coffee with my lady friend and maybe lunch afterwards," he said.

Janet took her fork back up. "So how is she these days?"

"She's fine," he said. "And don't look at me like that."

"Like what?"

"Like I'm keeping something from you. I'm not," he said sitting back, knife and fork in hand. He stabbed a French fry, and as he put it to his mouth, stopped and winced.

Janet looked up. "What's wrong?"

"Indigestion. Been a pain in the ass lately." He took a deep breath and sipped a drink of water.

"That's more than heartburn, and you know it. You need see a doctor."

"I'll look into it?" he said, returning to his fries.

"Any other marching orders?"

The waiter came around and checked on them. After the man left, Janet said, "I'm not blind, you know."

He sighed and looked out through the window beside them. As he did so, Janet sensed a looming dread fall between them. She braced herself, reached over and tapped his arm. "Dad?"

"Yeah, I'm here," he muttered.

"Please tell me what's going on."

Clearing his throat, he held her in a tragic gaze. Her heart stopped as his eyes dampened. As he wiped them with his napkin, she saw him swallow hard. "I don't know how–"

"How–what?" she said.

He looked back out the window. "How to tell you."

"Tell me what?"

He sat with that for a minute. Finally, he said, "A year ago, I found blood in my stool so I went to have it checked out. Routine stuff." He stiffened his jaw and took a deep breath. "Well, as it turns out, it's not so routine. I found out four months ago I have colon cancer."

The words hung over Janet like a noose. He looked down at his plate and pressed his lips together. "I'm sorry," he said quietly. "I knew I had to tell you. I just couldn't figure out how to do it." He picked his water glass up, reached into his blazer pocket, and pulled out a small bottle of pills. He popped one in his mouth and downed it with a sip. When he noticed her looking at him, he said, "Something to ease the pain. Lately they're not doing jack shit, though."

"What are they doing about it?" she said, trying to wrap her mind around his confession.

"They are not going to do anything. I've decided to let things take their natural course. Chemo and radiation aren't anything I'm interested in."

Her mind cried out. *No, no, you can't do this to me. You can't leave me. Not now. I need you. Oh, please, please.* She drew breath, fighting for air. "So, you're just giving up?"

He reached across the table and took her hand. His fingers felt cold and scaled. "Skeeter, look at me. I don't want to go through that kind of hell. Not now. The thing that bothers me most, though, is leaving you." He winced, and his face hardened. "Yes, I'm scared, but I've had a good life. I've been given a second chance, and the thing is; I'm okay with it.

"You've been the one thing these past years that's brought happiness into my life. There's not a moment that goes by I don't think about how I almost blew it. You gave me peace. And now I'm going to give you something back."

Her eyes flooded and her throat felt as if it might close up at any minute as he sipped his water. "You probably don't remember, and maybe you do, but just before you two got married, I stopped over and took your husband golfing. Turned out he was awful at it, but it wasn't the reason I took him."

She wiped her face. "I remember." She closed her eyes fighting to control herself before she dissolved into a puddle of tears. "I was so scared that day. I thought we were done. He was so distant and unreachable, and it was all my fault."

The waiter came to their table, and her father shooed him off. "Yes, I know about your finding the letters. He was upset about it, but not so much at you, as himself. Everything was coming into question for him about the marriage. He still loved his departed wife and he was worried he wasn't doing the right thing by you."

Her father paused for another sip of water, set his glass down and continued, "But the thing that really concerned him were the years between you. He told me, 'someday, Will, I'm gonna be gone. What seems so far away right now to her is going to suddenly come, and then what? I worry about that. I don't want her to be all alone.' "

"That's when I knew he was the right one for you, and I told him so. That, that kind of love doesn't come along every day. Then I told him about you and how I almost lost you because of my foolish pride and hurt over being cheated on by your mother. Said to him; 'Don't throw away how you feel about her Neil 'cause of something you can't predict.' "

She bit her lip as her father's face blurred in front of her. Her lips trembled as she teetered on the brink of falling apart. Her father squeezed her hand and pulled her back.

"Janet, I want you to listen to me," he said. His voice strengthened. "I know this is hard, but Neil and I are getting up there, me especially." He paused as if collecting his thoughts and went on. "He's twenty years older than you and that's the chance you took when you married him. Now, unfortunately, you have to deal with it. But ask yourself this. Was it worth it? I think so.

"Now I have to say something I don't want to, but have to, because you need to hear it. Look at me." He waited for her attention. "I've been here with you and Neil long enough to know what's coming. You're a strong woman, Lord knows you are, but there's going to come a time very soon when I think you're going to have to make a decision, and you know what I'm talking about. He's a shell of who he once was right now, and it's only going to get worse."

He stopped speaking, but his words rang in her ears. She closed her eyes and steeled herself. "I know."

"Can you do it?"

She wiped her face again. "I don't know."

He looked down and let go of her hand. "It's okay." He got up, went around the table, and tapped her shoulder. She turned her face up at him, saw his kind and adoring smile and stood up and melted into his arms. The background music of Billy Joel continued to play. People continued their conversations around their dinner tables. Her world had just gotten smaller.

27

Ever since her father told her about his cancer, Janet lived in fear of the day that it would take him away from her. Her nights were restless, and she woke often before dawn to check on him and Neil. Her husband rarely spoke now, and his moods were in a constant state of flux between gentle peacefulness and sudden agitation. William handled Neil when he got excitable. For some reason, he was able to settle him down.

In the mean time, Brad and Megan's marriage continued to deteriorate. Megan's son, Kyle, and his girlfriend, Debbie, had gotten their own place, leaving Megan and Brad alone. The battles between Neil's daughter and son-in-law were getting ferocious. Many times Megan had come and stayed the weekend at the Heights. She said she wanted to be near her father. That was only part of it, though, and Janet knew it. She listened and offered support as much as she could, but she had her needs as well. For those, Janet turned to Neil's son, Trevor.

They spoke often by phone, and the friendship between them flourished. Trevor wanted to know everything about the lost years and of his sister's doings. She did her best to tell him all she knew except for Megan's wars with Brad. That territory was best left alone. Their last conversation, a week ago, ended with her fighting tears. Whether Trevor sensed them or not she didn't know, but it wasn't long after that, that he sent her an email telling her he was thinking of scheduling a trip to the states.

Her other main support came from her brother, Craig. Although, they didn't see each other often due to distance and busy schedules, he made a point of checking in with her every other day, and he, too, planned to come west for a visit. William was excited. He hadn't seen Craig in over a year and he seemed to grow more robust as his visit drew nearer. In fact, her father seemed stronger than ever. Maybe the doctors were wrong!

Janet finished the morning dishes, and after peeking in on Neil and her father, who were watching TV in the Great Room, she retreated to her studio to check email and to work on a submission for the Oregonian. Her Ansel award had brought a deluge of offers, most of which, she politely declined. She needed to be home. But the Oregonian project about people who populated the small havens and towns tracking along the interior corridor of the state was one she felt compelled to do.

She woke the computer and opened her email program. A message from Nate popped up. She opened it and read about his latest exploits. He had been transferred from Iraq to Germany, not all that far from his half-brother Trevor whom he went to see last week. Nate also said he had a new girlfriend—nothing serious yet. Her name was Tracy, and she was a supply sergeant on base.

Janet smiled. It was good to hear Nate was happy and doing well, and his being near Trevor made her feel good. She would not spoil his upbeat mood with the deteriorating events back home. She shot him off a quick note, telling him to send pictures so she could share with his father.

Janet minimized the screen page and brought her photo-editing program up. After she loaded a shot of Neil and her on the beach, she went to work. She had staged it on a blustery day when the surf was up. A thick, gray mat of fog climbed over the bluffs. As she zoomed in on a section of it, she heard a thud in the other room.

She bolted upright and ran out into the hall. When she came around the corner, her breath caught in her throat. Her father lay splayed across the floor as Cleo started barking. Neil sat watching TV, his gaze unwavering from the screen.

"Dad!" she cried. She dropped to her knees. Turned him over. His eyes were rolled back, his mouth agape. "Dad, please, no!" Suddenly, the world spun, and she sat in a confused daze. Then something clicked and she sprang to her feet. Ran for her purse. The cell phone wasn't there. *I left it where? The night table!* She ran to the bedroom, grabbed it and raced back to her father's side. Her hand shook as she punched in 911 and waited for an answer.

Cleo nuzzled her side. "No Cleo. Go!" She pointed toward the other side of the room as the operator came on. "2330 Orchard Heights Road ... My father collapsed. He's not breathing," she said. "No ... eighty ... Yes ... Yes ... No, I've never done it before ... Okay ... okay ... say that again."

She set the phone on the floor. Bent over and tilted back her father's head, pinched his nose, pressed her lips over his and blew. Over and over and over, she repeated it and with each attempt, the reality that he had slipped beyond her reach solidified in her brain. *No, no, it's too soon,* she pleaded with the universe and sat up, breathless. She beat on his chest. *Daddy, please, breathe, damn it!*

But he didn't breathe and she collapsed and cried out. Her father was gone. Neil still sat in his chair, watching TV, Cleo lay four feet away, his deep brown eyes staring at her. The TV spat out another question for the game show contestant. The 911 attendant's voice continued to mutter out from the cell phone.

Two weeks later, Janet sat on a wooden folding chair, staring at the long, mission oak table populated with pictures of her father and other memories. A small, gray pyramid urn made of polished marble sat center stage within the photos. The days that had passed since her father died had been a blur, and she felt more alone than she'd ever remembered feeling before. She folded her hands in her lap as the rail-thin funeral director read the liturgy in the stark funeral parlor room. The man's tenor voice fell as a whisper in her ear, and the small company of family and friends sitting around her were a nebulous shadow. Even Nate felt far away, though he sat beside her.

She closed her eyes, felt Neil's shifting body move back and forth, brushing her arm. Every inch of her body ached for his arms around her, and her heart cried for his comforting voice. *If only you could be present for me just this one day!* But she knew it wouldn't happen today, or the next. All she had of him now were fleeting glimpses of a smile–a sudden recognition for a moment then he'd be gone.

She existed off these moments day to day now. Her father's endearing and unflappable presence was gone. What was she going to do? All doors felt shut and locked, and the growing hole inside her threatened to consume her. Even tears would not come, and if they did, could she ever stop crying once they started?

That evening, Janet snuck out of the house with her father's urn. It sat in the car with her as she drove toward the coast. She eyed the stone container her father lived in now off and on as farms and wooded lands crept past the car. She made such trips in the past when life ganged up on her, but this time it felt different. There would be no answers waiting for her on the beach, only questions.

She merged onto the coastal highway, her thoughts focused on the task ahead. Whether her brother, Craig, would approve of what she was about to do, she didn't know, but it felt right. In a way, it seemed fitting that her father should be cast to the wind. He was never a man to sit idle, and the turbulent currents blowing off the north Pacific were seldom at leisure. Her eyes drifted toward the gray water peeking through the rangy cypress and Douglas fir. The trees had long laid claim to this mile of highway, and they stretched out to the tumbled rocks battling the ocean's relentless assault.

Suddenly, she found herself pulling over onto the shoulder of the road and sat there for some time with the urn in her lap, thinking about all that had happened between her and her father during her life.

I'm glad we ended this way, Dad. Most of our lives we were at odds with each other. I'm sorry you had to be saddled with the awful secret my mother put on you. Yet, if she hadn't of been unfaithful, I wouldn't be here.

I don't really know why I stopped here. I just felt like I had to talk to you one last time before I let you go. To let you know how happy I am we had these last years together.

I'll try to remember your advice. I know Neil's gone from me, but I also know somewhere deep inside, there's a part of him that loves me. And if I can't take care of him, then I'll have to break the promise I made. I just can't do it right now. I can't lose everything all at once.

She ran her fingers over the urn and set it beside her. She pulled the car back out onto the highway, and a half hour later, stood before her grotto with the urn in her hand. It was low tide, and the waves were swooshing in. A swirling wind whipped her hair about her face as she removed the urn's lid. At length, she turned her gaze up at the deep blue dome of sky. *I'm really an orphan now.*

"Time to run free, Dad," she whispered and tipped the urn slowly, allowing the ashes to slide out over the face of the rocky outcropping. When the last ash blew free, she took a deep breath, inhaling the brine of the ocean and went back home.

28

One year later –

Janet set Neil in his chair and turned the ball game on. It was one of the small things he still seemed to enjoy. Afterward, she went off to her office to go over her latest project and email. She opened Nate's note and felt her heart flip as she read about his heading back to the Middle East to help with the surge. Janet steeled herself and dashed a quick reply, letting him know to be careful on his second tour.

She hit the send button and peered out the window. The home care aide for Neil was due any time. The aide service recommended by Dr. Childe had turned out to be a tremendous relief. And when Janet had to leave for a shoot on a weekend, Megan was more than willing to abandon Brad and hop in her car and drive down to watch her father.

But an hour later, the aide still wasn't there. Janet had an appointment across town in forty-five minutes. She grabbed her cell phone, punched in the number to the service and inquired as to when the aide would be there. After a brief pause, the operator came back and said the aide had called in. There had been a family emergency the woman had to attend to. They'd send someone out as soon as they could. Janet sighed and after ending the call, contacted her appointment, letting them know she'd be there as soon as she could.

Frustrated, she got up and went to the Great Room where Neil sat watching TV. She found him with his shoes off and busy tearing pages out of one of her photo books. "What are you doing?" she said.

He looked up then continued tearing another page out. "Neil, stop that!" she said and marched over to take it from him.

When she reached for it, he eyed her indignantly and grabbed a hold of the binding. A tug of war ensued until she wrestled it away.

"Why don't we get you something to eat. Are you hungry?"

"Give," he commanded in a sharp, shrill voice, and swung his arm around, catching her square in the neck with a solid blow.

Surprised and frightened, Janet kneaded her neck and put some space between them. "Neil! That hurt. Do you understand? You hit me."

But he paid no attention to her and picked up a shoe and shot it at her, missing her by inches.

He yelled out again, "Give!"

Her heart raced. "No!"

Neil's face knotted, and a ferocious anger reared in his eyes. He bent towards the end table, picked up a glass candy dish and hurled it at her. The dish grazed her head and went crashing to the floor.

Janet froze as Neil glared back. Even though he weighed less than her now, he was still incredibly strong. At last, she gave up and threw the ruined book at his feet. "Fine, take it!"

He leaned over, and when he picked it up, his face melted back to the calm implacable expression. A minute later, he returned to stripping pages out until he had emptied the remaining sheets onto the floor.

Thirty minutes later, a knock came to her door.

"Hi, my name is Karen. I'm from the service," a tall, broad woman said after Janet opened the door. She let her in and showed her to the Great Room where Neil sat. Karen studied Neil's face and the strewn pages at his feet. "I take it, he just had a tantrum?"

"A little while ago," Janet said. "He threw a dish at me."

"I see. What's his name?"

"Neil."

Karen went and sat beside him. "Hi, Neil, you want to tell me what's going on with you?"

He turned a vacant gaze up at her and buried the page-less book cover under his arms.

"Is that what this is all about?" Karen said, pointing at the book. When he frowned, she went on, "Hmmm, well, no one's gonna take it away from you." To Janet, she said, "Has he ever struck out like this before?"

"He has his moods, but never physical. I'm a little unnerved."

Karen nodded. "Yeah, I can imagine. Dementia affects people in different ways. I'm guessing that book has some significance for him. He's on meds right?"

"Yeah, Aricept."

"Has he had it?"

"Yeah, right after breakfast."

"Well, why don't we let him hold onto his book for a while." She eyed the hallway and motioned Janet with a nod toward it. When they were out of Neil's earshot, Karen said, "I take it you live alone with him?"

"Yeah."

Karen pursed her lips. "I know you're upset, but don't be afraid. Just be calm, and when he gets agitated, give him room to calm down, unless he's in danger of hurting himself."

Janet shook her head. "Easier said than done."

"I know," Karen agreed. "I work with a couple of families with difficult loved ones. It's the hardest thing, watching someone you love fade away right in front of your eyes. Have you ever considered placing him?"

"I made him a promise I wouldn't, but I'm beginning to think–"

"A good idea and no one would blame you."

Megan's face flashed before her. *Oh, yes they could.* "It's just hard. He's always been there for me. I should be–"

Karen shook her head. "Your father would not blame you, I'm sure."

"He's not my father."

Karen's expression altered slightly as Janet saw her putting two and two together. Janet put her jacket on. "I'm sorry, I really have to be some place."

"You go on then. Neil and I will be just fine," Karen said as she walked Janet to the door.

When Janet got home, she had a long chat with Karen about Neil. In her heart, Janet knew what she had to do, but the thought of doing it was crushing her. She put her bags in the office after Karen left and noticed the cover of the stripped book on the dining room table. Next to it were the torn pages. She picked them up, set them on the counter and went to check on her husband who had fallen asleep in his recliner, head cocked to one side and snoring lightly. She pulled the knitted blanket draped over his lap up around his chest and tucked it in before heading out to the kitchen to cook herself dinner.

As she fried up a burger and fries her thoughts went to the dark decision she'd made while she was out, and also of the phone calls she had to make to Trevor and Megan. She ate quickly, put her dishes in the sink and pulled out a dish of macaroni and cheese for Neil. As she mashed it up and put it in the microwave, she gathered her courage.

"Neil, honey, time to eat," she said, waking him. He opened his eyes, studied her and smiled as he put out his arm to let her help him up. "You hungry?"

He gave her another smile as he trudged beside her out to the table and sat. Janet wrapped a bib around his wobbling neck and put his plate in front of him. Feeding her husband had become a humbling, yet endearing experience because it was one of the few times he now interacted with her.

She wiped his chin and ran her hand over his shoulder, which brought another smile, then cleared the table and walked him back to the TV where they watched the news. This was their routine over the last three months before putting him to bed. At ten o'clock, she helped him into his pajamas, pulled the sheets back and climbed in beside him. As she lay there in the dark with her arm wrapped around him, she rehearsed the upcoming phone call to Megan. *Keep it simple and don't go into to detail. And don't get drawn into telling her I've made any decisions. It's just a meeting to discuss where things are at with him, that's all!*

Once Neil was asleep, she crept out of bed and treaded down the hall to the kitchen. There, in the darkened room, she took a deep breath and began punching Megan's number in on her cell phone until the pages on her counter caught her eye. She flipped the cell phone shut and turned the light on.

The pages Neil had torn out of her book peered up at her and slowly she sifted through them, enjoying the memories each one brought. After the last one, she sighed and opened the empty book binding to put them in. Suddenly, her heart skipped as the picture of Neil and her, stared back. Their arms were around each other as they smiled out to the reader. As it reached out and seized her, stealing her breath, she realized he was holding on the memory of them as they once were. Her eyes blurred, and her throat tightened.

The family meeting took place in the Great Room. Janet set a platter of cookies on the coffee table along with a large carafe of coffee. Neil sat in his chair, his body wavering within the beam of sunlight streaming in through the front window. Megan bent over beside him, her hand stroking his arm. At last she kissed him on the forehead before retreating to the couch to join Brad. Nadia and Trevor sat in broad, wingback chairs next to Janet, their faces grave and watchful.

Nadia said, "The cookies are good."

"Yes, they are," Brad agreed, stirring sugar into his coffee.

Trevor turned a despairing eye toward Janet. "So, Janet, it's your meeting. Go ahead."

Janet took a deep breath; keenly aware of the gaze Megan was leveling at her. "Neil has become very difficult. I haven't told anybody because I've been trying to deal with it myself before I came to you." She paused. "I don't know how much more I can do. The doctor wants to place him."

"No!" Megan burst out. "I know where this is going, and it's not going to happen."

Brad let out a sigh. "Christ, Megan, give it a rest already, would ya?"

"No, Brad!" She turned to Janet, her face rigid. "You said absolutely, never. Remember?"

"I know what I said, Megan," Janet said. "But it's not that simple anymore. He's becoming dangerous to himself, and to me. Do you want something bad to happen to him?"

"Of course not! Look, if he's too much for you, we'll take him," Megan said.

"The hell we will," Brad snapped. "He belongs with Janet, and if she can't take care of him, then a nursing home."

"Shut up, Brad. This is my father, not one of your useless buds," Megan retorted, narrowing a withering gaze on him.

"Hey," Trevor said, his voice slicing through the air. "This isn't the time for this stuff. He's my father, too, and I don't want him in a home anymore than you Megan. But the fact is he's unmanageable."

"What would you know?" Megan sneered. "You were in Germany for twenty fucking years, nursing your childish anger over something our father had no control of. I find it odd that now you're willing to give up on him so easily after accusing him once of giving up on Mom!"

Trevor's face erupted in a deep red frown, and as he opened his mouth, Janet spoke up, "Stop it! All of you! Stop it." She panned the room, fixing her gaze on each of them, last of all, Megan. "You think I want to do this? Do you? Look at me, Megan! Do I look happy?" She paused to let her words hang in the air. "I love your father. He's my best friend, and the only man I've ever trusted." She swept her gaze around the room again, settling it on Neil who stared out the window at the budding hawthorn peeking over the sill. No one stirred. "And now it's time for him to trust me, because he can't make this decision on his own. I know very well how he felt about nursing homes," she said, well aware she had referred to him in the past tense, and went on, "And I made a promise never to put him in one. But there's no other way now."

Janet turned her gaze back onto Megan. "We both know, Meg, that were he able to speak with us right now, he'd want us to stop this bickering. I called this meeting because I need you guys. You're my family. You're all I have left except Nate. You think I want to be alone? You think I want to wake up in an empty house? If there was any way I could do this, I would. But I can't. I just can't. Hate me if you will, but this is my decision."

The room fell silent, each of them were withdrawn. Neil had closed his eyes, and had fallen into a gentle snore in his chair. At last, Trevor said, "I, for one, don't hate you Janet. You've been good to my father."

Megan shook her head. "Well, it seems I have no say in this, so I guess there's nothing more to talk about." She got up and marched out of the room.

Brad pressed his lips together and started to get up, but Janet shook her head and motioned for him to stay put. She went out to the kitchen and found Megan on the back patio, her back to the house and looking off over the flowerbeds. For a moment, she watched her then opened the patio door and went out. As she came beside her, Megan stiffened.

"What do you want from me?" Janet said.

"What'd you think? I want you to keep your fucking promise," she snapped.

"Even if it endangers your father? Is that what you want?"

"I don't see how it endangers him being here."

"No, I suppose you don't. Then again, and I don't mean this to be insensitive, you don't live with him."

"I offered."

"Yes, you did, but he's my husband."

"So, it's either your way or the highway?" Megan turned and faced Janet. "You could easily visit him in my house as opposed to a nursing home."

"And Brad?"

"Brad can take a fucking hike."

"Really? How long have I heard you say that, and you're still with him? Look, your father's an empty shell. He's not in there anymore, Meg. You know it, and so do I. He's gone!"

Megan's face shattered, and she shook her head. "He's not gone, not all the way. You're abandoning him. He'd never do it to you, and you know it! Please, Janet, don't do this. Don't put him in one of those fucking places."

"I have to. I can't take care of him any longer." She looked into Megan's glassy eyes. "How long have we known each other?"

"I don't know, thirty years. Why?"

"Have you ever known me to lie to you?"

"You're doing it right now."

"No, I'm not. I meant what I said when I told you, 'absolutely I'd never put him in one.' But I didn't know then what I know now. I love your father. You gotta believe that. And I love you, too. I've always considered you my best friend, even when you didn't know it. And I'll continue to believe that and love you whether you forgive me or not. Megan, I don't want to lose you over this, but it's out of my hands."

Megan wiped her eyes. "Not if you don't want it to be. But it is what it is. Do what you gotta do." She started back inside.

Janet called after her. "I'd like to involve you in picking out a place. He's your father, and you should have some say in it."

Megan looked back. At last, she said, "Fine. You win."

How can I get through to her? "I want to show you something. Stay here for just a minute please?" When Megan nodded, Janet went in and got the empty photo book Neil had torn the pages out of and brought it back out. She opened it and handed it to Megan. "When he went on his tirade and hit me, it was because I had taken this away from him. He was tearing all the pages out. I didn't know why until I saw the back cover." She pointed to the picture of her and Neil. "He was holding us like a baby in his arms. I didn't notice it until later that night. Do you have any idea how I feel about doing this, now?"

Megan looked at the picture and then out at the woods. At last, she said, "I'm sorry. I know you love him and this is hard for you, but I still feel betrayed."

29

Janet rolled Neil down Portland's crowded terminal in his wheelchair to the security checkpoint. Clustered around her, were Megan, Brad, Kyle and his girlfriend, Debbie. They found a spot near the long snaking lines waiting to be screened and looked for Nate. Janet's thoughts were on the day Neil would no longer be living with her. She longed for her father as she eyed Megan anxiously. The battle they'd had on the patio over Neil had echoed in her ears the last month. In the end, neither of them had won, but then, it wasn't about winning. It was about losing.

Losing Neil.

A crowd of travelers headed down the concourse toward them. Megan stood up on tiptoes and saw her brother. She waved and a moment later Nate appeared in his army fatigues and familiar duffle bag over his shoulder. When he saw them, he stepped up his pace and melted into the arms of his family. Janet held him a long time, let him go and watched as he bent over his father.

Strangers around them stopped to take in the happy reunion. Some of them clapped. One man yelled out, "Way to go soldier. We love you."

Neil looked up at his son and smiled. His head wobbled as Nate spoke softly to him. "Hey, Dad, how are you doing? I missed you."

There was no reply. Nate went on, "I brought something back for you to charm the nurses with at your new digs." He looked up at Janet as he said it and reached into his duffle bag. "It's called a *Thoub,* and it fits over your whole body like this," he said bringing out a long, white garment. He stood and held it up next himself to show his father. "They wear these a lot over there because it's so hot."

Neil reached out and ran his fingers down the cotton cloth shirt and pulled it to his cheek. His eyes lit as he rubbed it over his skin. Nate beamed. "I think he likes it. And it's comfortable as hell," he said to Janet. He turned to his sister. "Meg, maybe later we can talk?"

Megan nodded and shot Janet a wary glance.

Kyle said, "Hey, you got a tat."

"Oh that," Nate said, looking at his arm. He turned and gave his mother a sheepish grin, "You like it?"

"Yeah, dragons are cool," Kyle said.

Janet frowned and resisted the urge to ask if whoever had done it had used clean needles. "It's interesting. Come, let's get your father out of here and get something to eat."

That night, after Nate helped his father to bed, Janet invited him outside on the patio. She wanted to talk to him about his father's last day at home. She patted the patio chair next to her and waited for him to sit.

"It's so good having you home. I can't get over how much you've changed since I last saw you."

"I haven't changed that much, Mom," Nate replied, popping the cap off his beer. He took a gulp and stretched his legs out. Cleo got up and went over next to him.

"To me, you have," she said. She sipped her water and considered him adoringly. "So, how are you really?"

He nodded and carefully peeled back the label from the bottle. "I'm good. Geez, I can't believe how fast he's slipped away. He hardly remembers me."

"Me, either," Janet said. "Nate?"

"Yeah."

"I know we were both going to take your father to Hazelnut tomorrow, but would you mind spending the day up to your sister's instead?"

He fixed her with a penetrating gaze, his deep blue eyes burrowing under her walls and into her heart. "It's okay, Mom. I understand. We're all gonna be okay."

Janet rolled out of bed the next morning, dragged her robe over her shoulders and went to Neil's bedroom. Silently, she stood watching him in the dark as he slept. In a few short hours, she would put him in her car and take him to his new home in Hazelnut Manor. She sighed and left him, pulling the door shut behind her.

As she crept down the hall into the kitchen to put a pot of tea on, she fought to keep her emotions in check. Nate had left for Northgate late last night. She wondered if he was lying awake in bed right now thinking about his father and what she was about to do.

She sighed, went into her office and picked up the empty photo book Neil had put his indelible mark on. She closed her eyes and ran her fingers across the cover of the book. But crying would do her no good now. There would be plenty of time for that later. For now, she would make the best of her last day with Neil at home.

She forced her dark thoughts away as the teakettle whistled and pulled down a mug. As she spooned in honey and added a splash of cream, she realized how many habits she had adopted of Neil, but then, so had he from her. The public radio station murmuring at the end of the counter for one: the methodical way she read the paper for another.

No more.

She eyed the clock on the stove. It was pushing 7:30 AM. She went back down the hall and into his room, saw Neil lying on his side and climbed in beside him until the alarm in the other room went off.

Forty-five minutes later, she set dishes out for breakfast, and in the midst of buttering her toast, felt tears well in her eyes. She set the knife down, put her face in her hands and collected herself. *Not now!*

Drawing a deep breath, she walked into his bedroom. "Morning, Gorgeous, time for breakfast."

A smile blossomed on his lips, and his mottled hand stretched out and patted her soft brown cotton blouse. His vacant eyes swept over her face as she wrapped her fingers around his and got him up out of bed. "Come, up you go. Time to start our day."

As they sat at breakfast on the patio, Neil looked out over their backyard. His plate of scrambled eggs was half eaten and she was about to spoon another bite up for him but changed her mind. Let him enjoy his gardens one last time.

When the clock over the fireplace mantle struck ten o'clock, she steeled herself. The moment had finally come. Reluctantly, she picked up Neil's suitcase feeling like an executioner, and went to collect him from his chair. He looked up at her as she pulled him to his feet and shuffled toward the foyer. The walk to the car felt like forever and she opened the front door and set him inside, pulling the seat belt around his shoulder. He turned his face up toward her and frowned, but the furrowed brow faded when she kissed his cheek.

Traffic on the road heading into the city was heavy and in the distance, under a patchwork of tattered clouds, she spied the sprawling brick manor that looked more like a prison than a home for her husband. Then, all too soon, there it was.

She slowed down as Neil gazed out toward the manor. *I just can't do this! Not this way, not now.* She turned back onto the arterial that wove through the city and finally out into the hills toward the coast.

An hour later they arrived at Fogarty. She led Neil to the old bleached log they had sat on so long ago at the end of the footpath marching down to the sea. The damp gritty earth felt good under her feet as she unlaced his shoes and took his socks off. It was still three hours to high tide, but the gray ocean sent an army of waves at them nonetheless.

"Come, Neil," she said, getting up and extending her hand. As she pulled him to his feet, he burrowed his toes into the sand and followed her out onto the barren beach where they walked along the shoreline until they came to her grotto. She turned to him and put her arm around his waist, eyeing him with desperate hope.

"This is where we fell in love and where you married me. Do you know that? Right here in this exact spot. I can still see you in your suit. You were so handsome, and when you looked at me my heart broke. It was like I was the only woman alive. And you put this ring on my finger and you said those words: for better or worse, I will love you forever."

But his gaze veered off over the dunes. She caught the cry in her throat and put her hand to his chin, turning his face back to her. "I love you. I will always love you. If you're in there, please forgive me." She pulled his hood back and ran her trembling fingers through his windblown hair. "My beautiful husband. Please let me see you one last time."

But an empty, blank look was all she got. Threatening tears overcame her, and she peered up. The gray sky moved overhead, indifferent to her plea, and the air was wet with fine rain. A deep rumble rolled across the sky. The universe had answered. It had given him to her, and now it was taking him back. She clenched her eyes shut and grit her teeth. It was done. She had lost him and her body quaked in his limp and unresponsive arms. The gulls argued overhead as the waves slashed at the shore. In that moment, she would've given her very soul to feel his embrace around her and hear his comforting voice.

Then as she started to pull back, she felt his fingers clutch at her jacket, and little by little, felt his arms tighten around her. She opened her eyes to see him looking back with a bright, clear gaze. "Neil … is that you?" she said, daring to hope.

"Janet? Why are you crying?"

Her heart leapt and she pulled him into her arms and held him fiercely. "Oh Neil! There's so much I want to tell you." She pulled back and wiped her eyes. "Do you remember our first Christmas together? I ruined the turkey, and you laughed. I was so angry with you. But you gave me that boyish grin and how could I be mad? And then there was the time when Nate was so sick and I had pneumonia and you took care of him. You put him in his car seat and brought him in bed with you while I slept in the guest room. I remember getting up and looking in on you. He had his little hand wrapped around your fingers."

"He woke up every time my hand fell away," Neil said.

"Yes. Do you remember that? And when we first kissed? Do you remember standing on my porch? You were so nervous. I knew you wanted to kiss me, but you didn't how to begin so I kissed you instead. I can still see your surprise and delight. You were so sweet. And then there was the time I said you were beautiful, and your eyes watered and you told me that no one had ever said you were beautiful before. Do you remember that?" she said cupping his face in her hands and basking in his adoring smile. He nodded, and then, just like that … he was gone.

She had been granted five precious minutes, and though she knew she should be grateful, she wanted more. She wanted to walk with him until they ran out of beach and then back again. She wanted to tell him about how he took Nate fishing for the first time and that they brought home a stringer of sunfish. Nate was so excited and she spent a roll of film photographing him with his triumph. She wanted to kiss her husband again and be kissed back, wanted to feel his loving touch on her body, his fingers running through her hair, hear his gentle snoring when he slept. But he was beyond her now, and so she gathered her courage, pulled his hood up over his head and took his hand. It was time to begin a new life–a life without Neil at home.

30

Three months later –

The staff at Hazelnut Manor embraced them, and Janet spent as much time with Neil as she could and still take care of things at home. This week, she surprised herself by volunteering to run a craft program at the manor, and was pulling together an outline for this week's project in her office when she heard a car pull up in her driveway. She pulled the curtain back and peeked out the window. *Megan, I wonder what's up.* Her thoughts went immediately to Neil and her stomach knotted. She took a deep breath and tried to dismiss the multitude of crazy thoughts rushing at her as she headed for the hallway with Cleo traipsing behind.

"Hey. Can I come in?" Megan quietly said when Janet opened the front door.

"Of course," Janet said, stepping back and letting Megan slip past her into the foyer. It was quite apparent by Megan's wistful expression this had nothing to do with Neil, and Janet breathed a sigh of relief. But her guarded feeling remained. After she shut the door, she turned around and added, "Are you okay, Meg?"

Megan shrugged and glanced at Janet fleetingly. "Yeah. I umm … I've been doing a lot of thinking and … I was wondering if we could talk?"

"Sure, I'd like that," Janet replied, and felt her guard drop a bit more. Whatever was on Megan's mind, it wasn't an argument; that was clear. "Can I get you something to drink?"

"A cup of coffee would be nice, thank-you," Megan answered. "You hear from Nate?"

"Yep. He just put in for coming home next May. He wants to be here for your father's birthday," Janet said, ushering Cleo ahead of her as she led the way to the kitchen. She pulled a couple of mugs down and started a pot of coffee. "I heard Kyle's heading to college."

Megan sighed. "Yeah. OSU of all places."

"Really," Janet said, digging a couple of spoons out of the drawer. "Well, he'll be close by. That's something."

Megan drifted to the patio door and looked out over the backyard. "Yeah." She paused and Janet watched her pan the flowerbeds. At last, Megan said, "I walked out on Brad last month."

Janet looked up, surprised, not so much that Megan kept it to herself for so long, but that she had finally left Brad. "I see. Want to talk about it?"

"Not really. I should've never gone back to him to begin with."

"So, where're you staying?"

Megan turned around and slid a chair out from underneath the kitchen island. "Right now, with a gal at work, but I can't stay there long." She paused and sat. "Know of any reasonable apartments?"

"I might," Janet replied, and nodded toward a plate holding a coffee cake. "Can I twist your arm into sharing a piece of this? One of the neighbors down the road forced it on me, and I can't begin to eat it all."

Megan gave her a crooked grin. "Right ... Oh, what the hell. Sure. Slice up a piece."

"That's the spirit," Janet said. "So, have you seen Brad since..."

279

"No, thank God," Megan said. "He called my cell a couple of times and left me some email, but that's it. I think he knows we're toast, but he's just going through the motions. Besides, I don't expect I'll have Internet much longer anyway. Verizon likes to get paid ... regularly."

"Imagine that!" Janet said.

"Yes, imagine it," Megan quipped as she pulled the dish Janet put the coffee cake on toward her.

As Janet poured, she said, "But seriously, you're still working, right?"

Megan nodded. "Yep. Still there. Doesn't pay shit, but it's a job," Megan answered as she dug her fork into the slice of coffee cake.

"Hey, let's get outside." Janet said, picking up her plate.

They went out and sat in the bright sunshine talking about the weather, politics, local news until at last, Megan said, "Nate and I had a long talk when he was home. He told me when he was here on leave a couple years ago, he heard you crying late at night about Dad when you thought no one was around. He said you used to repeat things to him over and over again so he wouldn't forget. That after Dad got real forgetful, you'd write our names on little slips of paper along with our picture and put them in his pocket." She drew breath, pressed her lips together and went on. "That you put a heart around my name so he knew I loved him."

Janet sipped her coffee and thought back to that time. As difficult as it was, she wouldn't trade the memories for anything in the world. "I did everything I could to hold that monster back."

"I know that. And now there's something I want you to know."

Janet set her coffee down, searched Megan's face and as she did so, saw the harsh lines that had carried so much anger and hurt over the years, fade away. Megan leaned forward, took Janet's hand and said, "A few years back my father and I had a long conversation. He told me about the night on your beach.

It was right after my incident at the *Reporter.* He said it was a turning point for him. That you gave him reason to believe he could be happy again, and that you helped him see how much I needed him. That what happened to me wasn't his fault, and that what really mattered was me. That I needed him. He told me someday we'd need each other like that, too. He was right. I'm sorry I was such a bitch. You didn't deserve it. I just couldn't see straight. Anyway, can we start over again? I don't want to lose you."

Janet squeezed Megan's hand. There were no words that lived in this world to express how she felt. She sent a silent thank-you upward and said, "You won't" And maybe, just maybe, she wouldn't have to lose Neil completely. A part of him sat before her now. And another part of him lived through the eyes of her son. And still another part of him lived within her heart and soul. And for the first time in a long time, she had hope. She had Neil. For she suddenly realized a part of him would always be with her.

Resources

In the writing of this book, the author drew from his own experiences as a pastoral visitor at several local Nursing homes in upstate New York as well as serving for several years as a Hospice volunteer. What has been depicted in this fictional book is only an example of how Dementia may behave and therefore is not to be considered exhaustive. Below are some suggested texts and resources for further reading and research on Alzheimer's, Parkinson's Disease and Dementia.

Texts:
"Still Alice" by *Lisa Genova – PhD at Harvard University: Pocket Books, A division of Simon & Shuster.* Copyright © 2007, 2009 by Lisa Genova.
"The 36 Hour Day" by *Nancy L. Mace, Peter V. Rabins: Grand Central Publishing.* Copyright © 2012
"When Your Parent Becomes Your Child" by *Ken Abraham: Thomas Nelsen Incorporated.* Copyright © 2012

Websites:
Alzheimer's Foundation – alzfdn.org
Dementia Advocacy and Support Network International – www.dasninternational.org
National Parkinson Foundation – www.parkinson.org

The Michael J. Fox Foundation for Parkinson's research –
www.michaeljfox.org

About the Author

Ron is a practicing architect living in upstate New York. An avid hiker and photographer, he has traveled to Nepal, New Zealand and throughout the United States, Alaska and Hawaii collecting ideas for character driven stories of romance and adventure. Look for his upcoming novel, Beyond the Veil, situated in the dense rainforest of the South American Amazon Basin, which will be coming out soon to Amazon for Kindle, and to Barnes and Noble for Nook.

Connect with Ron via Facebook at R.J. Bagliere or on the World Wide Web at: www.rjbagliere.com